D1137623

Phillip Margolin was a practising criminal defence lawyer for twenty-five years, has tried many high-profile cases and has argued before the U.S. Supreme Court. His first book, *Heartstone*, was nominated for an Edgar, and he has also published short stories and contributed articles to law magazines, journals and books. He is married with two children.

Also by Phillip Margolin

THE LAST INNOCENT MAN

Phillip Margolin

SPHERE

First published in the United States 1981 by
Little, Brown and Company
Published by Bantam Books in 1995
Paperback published in 1997 by Warner Books
This reissue published in 2010 by Sphere

A CIP catalogue record for this book
is available from the British Library.

ISBN 978-0-7515-4560-9

Printed and bound in Great Britain by
Clays Ltd, St Ives plc

Papers used by Sphere are natural, renewable and
recyclable products sourced from well-managed forests and certified
in accordance with the rules of the Forest Stewardship Council.

Sphere
An imprint of
Little, Brown Book Group
100 Victoria Embankment
London EC4Y 0DY

An Hachette UK Company
www.hachette.co.uk

www.littlebrown.co.uk

*For Joseph and Eleonore Margolin,
great parents and good friends,
and Doreen, Daniel, and Amy,
the home team.*

ACKNOWLEDGMENTS

With special thanks to Don Nash for his support, Bill Phillips, Laura Evans, and Mike Mattil for their help, and Jed Mattes for finding this book a home.

And additional thanks to Irwyn Applebaum, Elisa Petrini, and everyone at Bantam for everything you have done for me.

And finally I want to express my gratitude to Jim Tower for taking the time to share his knowledge of Mercedes-Benz cars with me, and to Dan Bronson for his excellent screenplay and his advice on a knotty plotting problem.

THE LAST
INNOCENT MAN

PART I

TRIALS

1

David Nash could see the storm clouds closing in on Portland from his office on the thirty-second floor of the First National Bank Tower. The rain would be a welcome relief from the June heat. The first large drops started falling on the river. David watched for a while, then turned his back to the window. Across the room Thomas Gault shifted his position on the couch.

The newspapers called David 'The Ice Man' because of his unruffled appearance in court, but Gault deserved the title. It was almost eight o'clock. The jury had been deliberating for two days. But Gault dozed, oblivious to the fact that twelve people were deciding whether he should be convicted of murder.

The telephone rang and startled David. Gault opened his eyes. The phone rang again and David answered it. His heart was beating rapidly as he raised the receiver. His hand felt sweaty against the plastic.

'Mr. Nash,' Judge McIntyre's bailiff said, 'we have a verdict.'

David took a breath to calm himself. His mouth

was dry. It was always the same, no matter how many times he heard those words. They were so final, and despite his record of victories, they always left him with a feeling of despair.

'I'll be right over,' David said, replacing the receiver. Gault was sitting up and stretching.

'Moment of truth, old buddy?' he asked as he yawned. He seemed to be experiencing none of the tension that David felt.

'Moment of truth,' David repeated.

'Let's go get 'em, then. And don't forget how you're feeling. I want to interview you as soon as we hear the verdict. I talked to my editor this afternoon, and he's hot to get the book into print as fast as he can. Capitalize on the publicity.'

David shook his head in amazement.

'How can you even think about that book now, Tom?'

Gault laughed.

'With what you're charging me, I have to think about it. Besides, I want to make you famous.'

'Doesn't anything ever get to you?' David asked.

Gault studied David for a second, his grin momentarily gone, his eyes cold.

'Not a thing, old buddy. Not a thing.

'Besides,' he said, the grin back in place, 'I've been through a hell of a lot worse than this in Africa. Remember, those twelve peers of mine can't kill me. Worse comes to worst, I get a few years off to write at state expense. And the worst ain't gonna come, old buddy, because I have faith in you.'

Gault's smile was infectious, and despite his misgivings, David found he was smiling.

'Okay, Tom, then let's go get 'em.'

Outside, the rain and wind were twisting the large American flag that hung from the building across the street, winding it around itself and whipping it to and fro. One of America's symbols taking a beating, David mused. If he was the lawyer everyone said he was, the blind woman with the scales would also go down for the count when they arrived at the courthouse.

IF DAVID HAD not been famous already, the Gault case would have made him so. Reporters from Paris and Moscow had flown into Portland to cover the trial of the handsome defendant who looked like a movie star and wrote like Joseph Conrad.

At nineteen, Gault, a member of a violent L.A. gang, had been given a choice between jail or the Army. Gault loved the military and was a natural for Special Forces training.

At twenty-six, Gault turned mercenary, putting his skills to work in East and West Africa.

All during his years abroad, Gault had been indulging another passion, writing. Plotted and fleshed out during his African sojourn, and completed during six months of furious activity in a cheap apartment in Manhattan, *Plains of Anguish* made Gault rich and established him as a writer of note. The novels that followed increased his literary reputation. But they were not the only reason Gault's name was newsworthy.

Shortly after the movie version of his second novel was released, Gault married his leading lady. The gossip columns were suddenly full of stories about Gault's latest affair or drunken brawl. When Gault drove his Rolls-Royce through the bedroom wall of his wife's lover's beach house, the missus called it quits. Gault, fed up with Hollywood, headed for the quiet of the Pacific Northwest.

A year later Gault emerged from seclusion, carrying the manuscript for *A Ransom for the Dying*, which won the Pulitzer Prize. While working on the book, he had met Julie Webster, whom he was presently accused of beating to death.

Julie Webster Gault, the daughter of a former secretary of commerce, was beautiful, spoiled, and rich. To her parents' horror, she married Thomas Gault after a brief courtship that consisted of several violent couplings in various odd places and positions. The marriage was doomed from the beginning.

Julie Webster was incapable of loving anyone but herself, and Thomas Gault was similarly afflicted. By the time the novelty of working their way through the *Kama Sutra* wore off, the couple realized that they could not stand each other. Gault's drinking, which was excessive in the best of times, got worse. Julie started wearing high-neck sweaters and sunglasses to cover her bruises. Then, one evening, someone beat Julie Gault to death in her bedroom on the second floor of their lakeside mansion.

The police arrested Gault. He swore that he was innocent. He told them he had been sleeping off a drunk when screams from his wife's bedroom awakened him. He said he found Julie lying in a pool of blood and had knelt to take a pulse. A sudden movement behind him had made him turn, and he had seen an athletically built man of average height with curly blond hair standing above him. The intruder struck him on the head, Gault told the police, and he was unconscious for a few moments. When the police arrived, there was blood on Gault's hands and bathrobe and a bruise on the left side of his face.

Whether Thomas Gault or a mysterious stranger had taken Julie Webster Gault's life was the subject of a two-month trial. Famous writers and movie stars took the stand, either recounting the Gaults' marital battles or coming to the writer's defense. As the case neared its end, David was worried. Then Gault took the stand.

During the time that David represented him, Gault had not shown a single sign that his wife's death disturbed him. To the contrary, he seemed happy to be rid of her. But Gault was a great actor, and his performance as a witness had been superb. He emerged from two days of direct and cross-examination as a sympathetic figure. He had even broken into tears once while testifying. The jury had been sent from the room and never saw how quickly Gault recovered his composure.

Gault was like that. He had an innate ability to tune in on, and manipulate, the feelings of other people. David found him a fascinating yet frightening man. An original in whom he sensed a quality of evil. Everything he knew about Gault made him believe that the writer's detachment was genuine. Nothing appeared to touch him. Still, he wondered how Gault would react if the jury found him guilty.

FLASHBULBS EXPLODED, AND a thin, attractive woman from NBC just missed David's lower lip with a hand-held mike. David made a brief comment to the press as he elbowed his way through the crowd toward the courtroom. Gault followed, laughing and chatting with the reporters.

A local photographer asked Gault to pose for a picture, and Gault paused, sweeping his stylishly long brown hair backward to reveal his handsome profile. At a little under six feet, with a figure kept trim by constant exercise, Gault produced a good photograph.

Cameras clicked and the courtroom doors swept open. A stir of almost sexual excitement filled the courtroom when Gault entered. David watched the faces of the women. They wanted Gault. Wanted the thrill of lying next to him and wondering if his gift would be love or death.

Gault headed down the center aisle toward the low gate that separated the spectators from the bar of the court. A man dressed in jeans and a plaid shirt said something to Gault, which David missed. Gault laughed and raised his hand in a clenched fist salute.

David followed Gault to the counsel table. Norman Capers, the district attorney, was already in place. He looked tired. The bailiff was talking to a courtroom guard. David nodded to him as he sat down. The bailiff went into chambers to tell the judge that the parties were ready. A moment later he left to get the jury.

David felt dizzy. He turned toward Gault, curious to see if his client was showing any signs of tension. He was surprised to see the writer's eyes riveted on the door that led to the jury room. There was complete silence in the spectator section.

The door to the side corridor opened and David watched the jurors walk in. They moved silently, in single file, into the jury box. There were no smiles, and they scrupulously avoided looking at Gault or the lawyers.

David felt slightly nauseated. These were the worst moments. He scanned the box for the foreman. The folded white paper was in the left hand of juror number six, a middle-aged schoolteacher. He tried to remember back. How had she reacted to the testimony? Was it a good or bad sign that she had been chosen foreman?

9

The noise in the courtroom stopped. The bailiff pressed a button on the side of the bench that signaled the judge's chambers. Judge McIntyre entered from a door behind the dais.

'Be seated,' the judge said. His voice trembled slightly. He, like Capers and Nash, had been worn down by the grueling trial.

'Has the jury reached a verdict?' the judge asked.

'We have,' the foreman replied, handing the verdict form to the bailiff.

Gault leaned forward and followed the paper from the jury box to the judge's hand. Someone coughed in the back of the courtroom, and a chair moved, scraping along the floor.

Judge McIntyre opened the white paper slowly and read it carefully. Then, without looking at Gault, he read,

'Omitting the caption, the verdict reads as follows: "We the jury, being first duly impaneled and sworn, do find the defendant, Thomas Ira Gault, not guilty as charged in the indictment." . . .'

There was silence for a moment; then someone in the courtroom began to cry. David expelled a deep sigh and leaned back in his chair. Gault had not moved, as if he had not heard. There was pandemonium in the rear of the court as reporters pushed forward to reach the counsel table.

In the confusion the jurors were forgotten. David watched them file out. Not one of them looked at

10

the man they had just acquitted. Not one of them shared the joy the spectators were expressing. David knew why. In order to acquit, the jury did not have to believe Thomas Gault was innocent. The law required an acquittal if the jurors harbored a single reasonable doubt about a defendant's guilt. David was a master at creating reasonable doubt, and once again he had prevailed. But David knew what the verdict would have been under a less stringent standard. From the start Gault had proclaimed his innocence. Never once had he deviated from his original story. But David never believed that Gault was innocent. Not for a moment.

David stood up and moved away from the counsel table. Norman Capers had left the courtroom quickly. David wanted to shake his hand. He had tried a good case. Gault was being embraced by well-wishers as flashbulbs exploded around him. The solemnity of the courtroom had given way to a carnival atmosphere. The reporters were swarming around Gault now, but David knew he would be next.

David tried to feel something positive from his victory, but he was empty inside. There was no joy, no exaltation, at winning a case every other criminal lawyer in the country would have given his right arm to try.

He remembered how he had felt after his first murder case. It was funny. There had been no big fee involved. Hell, the case had been a court appointment. There had been no publicity. With the exception of a few old men who spent their retirement watching trials, no one bothered to come.

The defendant was a petty thief who had made the big time by shooting a shopkeeper during a liquor-store holdup. There had been nothing of worth in David's client and no question of his being anything but guilty, but that had not mattered to David, who had been overwhelmed by his trust. A man's life depended on the exercise of David's skills, and he had pushed himself to the point of exhaustion, knowing, all along, that he would fail. He had tried every legal motion, explored every avenue, but it had not been enough.

The guilty verdict had been returned quickly. Afterward David had talked with his client for an hour in the interview room of the county jail. The man did not seem to care. But David cared. That evening, alone in his office, David cried tears of frustration, then went home and got quietly drunk.

Those had been good days. There were no tears anymore. No emotional investments. All that was left was the winning and the money; recently, he was beginning to wonder if even that was important. David had reached goals that other lawyers only dreamed of achieving. He was a senior partner in a prestigious law firm, he was nationally known, and he was wealthy. All this had been accomplished at a whirlwind pace that left little time for reflection. Now that he had reached the top, he had time to catch his breath and look around. He wasn't sure he liked what he saw.

'How many does this make?' a reporter from the *Washington Post* asked.

'I'm sorry?' David said.

'How many murder cases in a row?'

David shifted away from his black thoughts and became 'The Ice Man.' If any of the reporters noticed his initial distraction, no one mentioned it.

'I'll be truthful with you,' he said with a confidential smile. 'I've lost track. Six seems right, though.'

'Why do you think the jury acquitted Gault?' a reporter with a foreign accent asked.

'Because he is innocent,' David answered without hesitation. 'If Tom hadn't been a celebrity, they wouldn't have prosecuted him. But I'm glad they did. Gave you fellows work and kept you off the street.'

'And made you a fat fee,' someone shouted.

The reporters laughed and David joined them, but he didn't feel like laughing. He was bone tired and he wanted to go home.

There was a stir to David's right, and he turned his head. Gault was moving toward him, his hand outstretched. The mass of reporters and well-wishers parted slowly, and David had time to study his client's face. For a brief second Gault winked; then their hands touched.

'I owe this man my life,' Gault roared. 'This

13

man is the king. And I am going to get him so drunk tonight he won't be able to defend anyone for a year. Now, any of you suckers who want to join us, form a line. I have enough booze back at my place to get even a reporter drunk. So let's get going.'

Gault grabbed David with one arm and draped the other over the shoulders of the thin, attractive woman from NBC. David knew it was useless to try to bow out. The crowd swept him along. On the courthouse steps David caught a glimpse of Norman Capers getting into a car parked a block away. David envied him his solitude and his clear conscience.

2

It was an old wooden door.

The type you expected to find in a high-school classroom. Long ago someone had painted the windowpane in the upper half a light green to give the occupants of the room more privacy. The lock still worked, but the mechanism was slightly out of line. The door opened with a metallic click, and David looked up from his file. A teenage girl dressed in a dirty white T-shirt and ill-fitting jeans hesitated in the doorway. Monica Powers, the deputy district attorney, stood protectively behind her.

'This is Mr. Nash, Jessie,' Monica said. David stood. Detective Stahlheimer continued to work on the tape recorder at the far end of the wooden table. It was hot and humid outside, but it was cool in the room. The wire mesh in the room's only window threw crisscross shadow patterns across the detective's broad back.

'Mr. Nash represents Tony Seals,' Monica continued. The girl looked puzzled.

'T.S.,' Monica said, and Jessie nodded. David watched her carefully. She was nervous, but not afraid. He imagined that she would never be afraid again, after what she had been through.

The girl interested him. Nothing about her suggested that she was a survivor. Her body was loose and sloppy. She wasn't ugly. 'Plain' was a better word. Unkempt strands of brown hair straggled down past her shoulders. The shoulders were rounded and the arms heavy. David would have picked her to fail, to fold under pressure. She hadn't. There was steel there, someplace. A fact worth noting when he began to prepare his cross-examination.

'Mr. Nash wants you to tell him what happened on the mountain. He'll probably ask you some questions, too.'

'Do I have to?' the girl asked. She looked tired. 'I've said it so many times.'

'But not to me, Jessie,' David said in a firm, quiet tone.

'And why should I tell you . . . help you, after what they done to me?' she challenged. There was no whine in her voice. No adolescent stubbornness. Monica had told him she was sixteen. It was an old sixteen. A runaway for the past year and a half. Then, this. Life had leapfrogged her over adolescence.

'So I can find out what happened.'

'So you can get him off.'

'If there's a way to do it. That's my job, Jessie, and I'd be lying if I said otherwise. But lawyers usually don't get guilty people off, and I want to find out what happened so I can decide whether to tell T.S. to go to trial or plead guilty or what. Only I won't be able to tell him one way or the other if I don't hear your version of what happened.'

Jessie looked down at her sneakers, thinking. It was working, David thought. His power over people. The ability to persuade. The trick he had used so many times was now as natural a part of him as his arm.

At thirty-five, David still looked open and honest, like a little boy at an American Legion oratorical contest. Jurors trusted him. When he looked them in the eye and told them that his client was innocent, they believed him. When he told a witness, like Jessie Garza, that he was interested only in finding out the truth, they spoke to him. More than once David had seen the shock on the face of a witness as something innocently revealed during an interview was used to destroy the prosecutor's case.

Jessie shrugged and walked over to a chair near Detective Stahlheimer, turning her back to David.

'I don't care,' she said. She didn't say anything else, David noted. She knew the routine.

'I think it's ready,' Stahlheimer said. Monica sat down across from David and beside the girl. She was immaculately dressed, in a double-breasted charcoal-pinstripe cutaway jacket, a matching skirt, and a cream-colored, ruffle-front blouse. Monica looked more beautiful now than she had when they were married. Their eyes met for a moment; then David looked away. He always felt a bit uncomfortable

17

when he had a case with Monica. Their divorce had been relatively amicable, but being in her presence stirred up feelings of guilt best left buried.

'This is Detective Leon Stahlheimer,' the detective said into the mike. 'It's Thursday, June sixteenth. The time is ten-oh-seven A.M. I am present in a conference room at the Juvenile Detention Center for the purpose of an interview with the victim in an attempt murder. Present are Jessie May Garza, Deputy District Attorney Monica Powers, and David Nash, the attorney for Anthony Seals.'

Stahlheimer stopped the tape and played it back. David took a pad out of his attaché case and wrote the date, the time, and 'Jessie May Garza' at the top. Monica leaned over and said something to the girl which he did not catch. Jessie crossed her fat forearms on the table and rested her head on them. She looked bored.

'Okay,' Stahlheimer said.

'Jessie,' David started, 'I represent Tony Seals, one of three boys who you claim tried to kill you several weeks ago. The purpose of this interview is for me to find out what happened and, more specifically, what part Tony . . . You know him as T.S., don't you?'

She nodded.

'You'll have to talk, Jessie, so it goes on the tape,' Monica said.

'Yes. T.S. It meant "Tough Shit," he said. I never even knowed it meant Tony.'

'Okay. I'll say "T.S.," then.'

'It don't make no difference to me.'

'Now, Jessie, I don't know what impression you have of lawyers from TV or the movies, but I'm no Perry Mason and I'm not trying to trick you here. The purpose of this talk is to find out what happened, and if I ask a question you don't understand or if you say something you want to change, ask me to explain the question or just say you want to change what you said. Okay?'

The girl said nothing.

'Why don't you just start at the beginning.'

Jessie sat up, then slouched back in the chair.

'Like, when?' she asked.

'Well, when did you first meet T.S., Sticks, and Zachariah?'

'I don't know. It was at Granny's. Whenever I started living there. Because Zack was there already, you know, and then T.S. and Sticks moved in about a week after I got there.'

'Who is Granny?'

'I don't know her last name. I heard someone call her Terry once.'

'What does Granny have going on over at her place?'

'Well, it's where a bunch of people used to crash. There was always guys who worked the carnivals when they came through. Then she used to let people fix up speed, and she used to do acid and everything, and then everything changed because Zack and Sticks

19

OD'd. All of them came damn close to OD'ing on pure heroin and, let's see, and so like, so like her old man's in the Navy or used to be, and she changed old mans. This guy Norman is now her new old man.'

'Is he young?'

'Oh, he's about twenty-three.'

'But she's quite a bit older, isn't she?'

Jessie laughed sarcastically.

'Like a hundred.'

'She liked having young boys like T.S. and Sticks around?'

'Yeah. She dug it.'

'Did she go with Zack for a while?'

'No. She brought Zack into the house to bring him off the needle from speed 'cause he was gettin' to the point where he needed speed all the time.'

'Were you guys speeding quite a bit the night it happened?'

'I hadn't took speed for almost two weeks 'cause the last time I did, I overacted on it.'

'What about Sticks and Zack?'

'No. Like I said, they quit speed and chemicals altogether 'cause they almost OD'd.'

'And T.S.?'

'Man, like he was constantly fucked up. Yeah, he was doin' speed and acid. But I don't know what he was into that night specifically, except for pot, 'cause we was all smoking that.'

'Well, did he seem awake and aware that night or what? How did he look?'

'I guess he was stoned. We all were, a little.'

'When you say "stoned," what do you mean? Can you describe how T.S. looked?'

'Well, he was talking slow and his pupils were big and he was dreamy. I don't really remember that much. I remember in the car, going up to the park, I was in the backseat with T.S. and he was tripping out, you know, like gazing off in his own little world. My problem remembering is I took some downers before we left and I slept through most of the ride.'

'Why did you go out there?'

'Around two that afternoon Zack tells me how there are pounds buried out by the park in a place he knows and how they're gonna get it that night. So I asked if I could go.'

'Were Sticks and T.S. around when he said this?'

'Oh, yeah. Sticks was teasin' and sayin' how they shouldn't take me, but Zack said I could come.'

'And T.S.?'

'He didn't say nothin' I can remember.'

'Okay, what happened when you got to the park?'

'Well, it took a while. I remember Sticks was driving, but Zack had to take over because Sticks was tired and got lost. Then, when we got to the place where Zack said it was, we didn't find it right away.

'We parked the car and Sticks crawled into the backseat to sleep. Then me and Zack and T.S.

went into the woods a ways until we came to the railroad tracks. There was one shovel, which Zack carried, and T.S. had a flashlight. I remember about four trains goin' by, because Zack would say to turn off the flashlight when they came, so no one would see us.

'Anyway, we walked up and down the tracks and every so often Zack would say he thought this was it. Then he'd change his mind. Finally he said this was it at a spot about twenty feet from the tracks, and we started digging.'

'Did you dig, too?'

The girl looked directly at David and smiled, as if amused by some private joke.

'Yeah, I dug. I dug almost the whole goddamn hole. Zack did almost nothin' and T.S. dug a little, but mostly he held the flashlight. And when I'd get tired, Zack would say to keep diggin' or I wouldn't get any of the weed.'

'Did you get sore?'

'Sure, but I wanted the pot.'

'Do you think there really was marijuana out there?'

'I really kind of doubt it in my mind now, because . . . well, at first, I thought . . . yeah, really, I thought there was some out there, because Zack kept sayin' dig, dig, dig, like he was determined to get it. But, now, well, when I got shot, I was in the hole and I've been thinking about it a lot. Now I think they was having me dig my own grave.'

22

David felt a chill. Just a moment, then it was gone. He saw the acne-marked, hollow-cheeked face of Tony Seals during their interview at the county jail. The eyes dull, the dirty, uncombed hair thick with grease. He was suddenly sick with himself.

'How did it happen?' David asked. 'The shooting, I mean.'

'Like I said, the tracks was behind us and I had been digging for a long time and I was tired. T.S. was standing above me and behind me to my right with the flashlight. I couldn't see Zack, but I think he was to my left, because when the train came, he was the one that said to put out the light, and I'm pretty sure the voice came from there.

'Every time a train would come the light would go out. This time the light went out and Zack said, "Keep digging." I said okay, then I heard the shot out of my left ear.'

'What happened then?'

'I was in the hole and I froze. I didn't feel no pain right then, but I was scared. I called for T.S. and Zack, but they didn't say nothing. It was dark and cold, and when the light didn't go back on, I called again. I was feeling weak and I slumped down in the hole and I was leaning against the side of the hole on my stomach with my head and arms just over the rim.

'I called again and this time I seen their shadow. They was about forty-five feet away near some trees and I yelled, "I've been shot," and they walked back.

23

Zack said, "Let's see," and he squatted on the edge of the hole and said he didn't see nothin', just a clot of dirt on my shirt. Then T.S. and Zack looked under the shirt with the flashlight, and they said they still didn't see nothin'.

'I told 'em again I was shot and I was getting more tired. They said they'd go for help and walked off. I said, "No," I was comin' with them, but they just walked off and I crawled out of the hole by myself.'

The look of boredom had disappeared from Jessie's eyes, and David could see that she was reliving the incident. She had a faraway look, and there was a rigidity in her body that had not been there before. Monica gave Jessie a glass of water, then looked across at David. He could read her unspoken criticism of him for representing Tony Seals.

'The car wasn't far from where we was digging, but it was hard getting back. I was feeling weak and I couldn't breathe. By the time I got there, all three of 'em was by the back of the car talkin'. I asked 'em to help me, but they acted scared and stood away, like they didn't want to be near me. The back door was open where Sticks had got out, so I laid down in the backseat. The pain started gettin' real bad then and I was cryin' and blood started coming out of my mouth and nose and I got so dizzy I shut my eyes and just laid there. I could taste the blood and that was scaring me worse than the pain. Someone started the car and I thought we were going to the hospital, 'cause that's what I asked them and they said they would.'

'Do you remember the car stopping?'

'When they dumped me out?' Jessie asked bitterly. 'Yeah, I remember that. I was lying with my head on the driver's side, but facing the back of the car and the car had been bouncing a lot like we was on a dirt road and then they stopped and the passenger door opened. Sticks or Zack, I don't know who, said to get out. That there was a kind of a plant that would stop the bleeding. I knew what they were up to, so I said I couldn't move, I was in pain. Then T.S. and Sticks grabbed my legs and pulled and Zack was on the other side pushing me out. I tried to go into the front seat and I was hanging on underneath the seat and they was pulling me out by the feet. I was really scared then, 'cause it was so dark and I didn't want to be alone. Then Zack said again how I should let go because there was a plant that stopped bleeding and I said, 'Bullshit, there's no plant that stops bleeding. Take me to the hospital.' And that's when Zack hit my fingers with the gun and I let go and they dragged me onto the ground a ways from the car.

'I lay there. I think I was cryin' 'cause they were gonna leave me alone in the dark and the pain was gettin' worse. I heard the car door slam and I yelled to them to take me with them. I even said I wouldn't take none of the pot. Then I heard two shots and I just shut up. I laid there not moving until the car drove off. I didn't move then, either.

I thought maybe one of them was waiting for me to move.

'About two minutes later they turned around and fired the rest of the shots in the gun off at me.'

It was very quiet in the room. David was having trouble taking this in, which was unusual for him. He was an old pro at this sort of thing. How many mutilated bodies had he seen in photographs or in person? How many human tragedies had he been involved in? What was this girl to him?

'How close did the shots come to you?' David asked.

'One bullet spit up dirt right near my head. So did another.'

'Did you hear any of them say anything when they left?'

'Yeah, someone said, "I think we got her," but I don't know who.'

'Do you know who shot at you from the car?'

She shook her head and put it down on her crossed arms again. She looked very tired.

'How did you get down to the bottom of the mountain? It's several miles from where the shots were fired.'

'I crawled.'

'Crawled?'

'I got scared lying there. I stayed curled up for a while, but the pain wouldn't stop and there was no sound up there. Just the wind and animals in the woods. I didn't want to stay put,

so I crawled. And it took hours and it hurt so
much.'

There were tears in her eyes and David felt
dead inside.

'But I wasn't gonna let them do this to me. So I
crawled and sometimes I walked a ways and I got to
the bottom and just fell in that ditch, and anytime a
car come by or a truck I'd pull myself up. That was
the worst. Even worst than the shooting and being
alone. No one would stop for me or help me.'

The tape recorder spun on. The rays of the sun
created splotches of light on the tabletop. Monica
placed her arm around Jessie's heaving shoulders
and spoke soothingly. David stared at the wall. It
took every ounce of control he had learned in the
courtroom to keep his features from showing any
emotion. Sometimes he wondered if that wasn't one
trick he could do now without trying.

MONICA AND DAVID agreed to meet by the reception desk, and Monica took Jessie back to the
girls' detention area. It was a little past noon
and the reception room was empty. David sat
down on a couch in the corner. The interview
had shaken him, and he wanted some time to
calm down.

A teenage boy walked up to the reception desk
and David thought about the man-boy, Tony Seals,
whom he was being paid so much money to represent. Eighteen years old, his brains burned out by

controlled substances, not caring about anything or anyone, not even himself.

And the boy's parents. David would never have come into the office the day after the Gault verdict if Anton and Emily Seals had not been old and valued clients of his firm, and close personal friends of Gregory Banks, one of the senior partners and David's closest friend.

During the meeting Anton Seals had sat straight-backed and expressionless, wearing his conservative pinstriped suit like a uniform. His only show of emotion had been the constant stroking of his wife's hand. Emily Seals had also kept her composure, but David could see that her eyes were red-rimmed from crying. The Sealses represented old money. They were elegant people. Neither of them fully understood what their son had done to Jessie Garza, himself, or their lives.

'Why did you shoot Jessie Garza?' David had asked Tony Seals yesterday at the county jail. Even now David did not know why he had asked the question. You didn't have to know why a person violated the law to get him off.

'She was a pain in the ass.'

'You shot her because . . .'

'Well, you know, she knew how to get drugs, so we used her like that for a while, but she was a pain in the ass. Then she tore up some marijuana plants that Sticks had growing. So we were talking about what a pain in the ass she was and how no one liked her because she's got such a big mouth and Zack says he'll bump her off.'

'Just like that?' David had asked. 'Just because of the plants?'

'I guess so. Zack was always talking like that. About how he was a hit man. He said he'd killed guys before, but Sticks and me didn't believe him even though he was always flashing this gun around. We didn't think he'd use it.'

'Why didn't you try to get Zack to take her to the hospital after she was shot?'

'I did say we should back at the hole, but Zack said, "Don't worry about her, she's just gonna die," so I forgot about it. Besides, I was real tired and I didn't want trouble with the cops.'

David saw Monica walking toward him and he stood up.

'Is she okay?' David asked when they were outside.

'It depends on what you mean by "okay." Physically, she's doing fine. Psychologically . . .' Monica shook her head. 'She's one tough cookie, Dave, but I don't know. And her ordeal on the mountain isn't the worst part. We're holding her until the trials are over; then we want to send her back to her parents in Montana. Only they're not sure they want her.'

'Shit,' David said.

'Yeah,' Monica answered bitterly, 'but that's life, right? Why the interest?'

David shrugged.

29

'She got to you, right? You better watch that, Dave. It's bad for the old "Ice Man" image.'

'Give me a break, Monica,' David said without anger. 'I'm not in the mood.'

Monica sensed his exhaustion and backed off.

'Say, I haven't congratulated you yet on the Gault verdict.'

The way she said it, David wasn't certain it was a compliment, so he said nothing.

'Norm says you tried a good case.'

'We both did.'

'Who's going to play you in the movie?' Monica asked with a mischievous grin. David laughed.

'You angling for a part?' he asked.

'Oh, I don't know. Maybe if Tom Cruise gets the lead.' She struck a pose. 'Whadda ya think? Do I still have what it takes?'

'Yes, Monica, you still do.'

And they were suddenly too close to personal problems for comfort.

'Look,' David said to change the subject, 'is there any possibility we can deal on this one?'

'Not a chance, Dave,' Monica answered.

'Not even if I threw in Tom Cruise?' David asked with a smile.

'Not even for Tom Cruise.'

'That's what I thought, but I had to try.'

'You always do.'

They stood together for a moment, until they both realized they had run out of conversation.

'Take care of yourself,' Monica said. David knew she meant it. She was the one who had been hurt most by their divorce, and that fact always made him feel bad.

'You, too,' he told her. They walked out to their cars, and David watched Monica drive off; then he shut his eyes and sat in the hot car for a moment while the air-conditioning came on. He didn't need a case like this so soon after Gault. He needed a vacation. But, then, he always did. He couldn't remember the last time he had not been under pressure. The difference was he had never thought about it before.

3

Darlene Hersch was out of breath by the time she reached the squad room. The clock over the water fountain told her the bad news. She had sprinted from the car and she was still late. There was nothing she could do about it now. Only she hated to make a bad impression. All the other officers in the special vice unit had been on the police force for several years. She was new, and it looked bad to be the only late arrival.

The squad room was small. The dull-green paint on the walls was peeling, and the linoleum-tile flooring buckled in places. Rows of clipboards hung from two of the walls. A bulletin board occupied the third. All the space in between was covered by cartoons about police work, bulletins about office procedure, and a large poster that gave instructions about what to do in the event of a fire.

A sink and a countertop ran along the outer wall. The countertop was littered with paper cups, and two pots of coffee steamed next to the room's only window. The center of the room had been taken over by two long Formica-topped tables. Sandra Tallant and Louise Guest, the other policewomen on the squad, sat at the end of the table near the door. Darlene slid onto a metal bridge chair and hoped Sergeant Ryder would not notice that she was late.

'Have another rough night, Darlene?' Ortiz asked in a loud voice. Darlene flushed. Neale grinned and Coffin snickered. Sergeant Ryder looked up from the desk at the front of the room, and Darlene turned her head and glared at Ortiz. Ortiz winked. The bastard.

Ortiz perched on the countertop near the coffee-pots. He was handsome, and he knew it. With his dark complexion, shaggy mustache, and thick black hair, curled and cared for like D'Artagnan's, he played the lady's man. Darlene thought he was an asshole.

Sergeant Ryder stood up and checked his notes on the clipboard he always carried. A big, insecure man, he was always rechecking his facts, as if he feared that they would change if he did not keep constant track of them.

'Are we all here?' he asked rhetorically. He had known the precise number of people in the room every minute since he had arrived.

'Okay, for those of you who have not been keeping up with the captain's weekly bulletin on develop-ments in the law, last week the public defender filed a motion claiming that the equal-protection rights of Vonetta Renae King were being violated. . . .'

'They got us there,' Ortiz called out. 'Vonetta's been violated more than any whore I know.'

Coffin giggled and Ryder stared at him. Coffin covered his mouth and coughed.

'Is it all right if I continue, Bert?' Ryder asked in a tired voice. He knew there was no way to keep Ortiz from acting the clown. He also knew that Ortiz was one of his best vice cops. It all balanced out.

'As I was saying, the public defender is claiming that the prostitution laws are being unfairly enforced, because only the . . . er . . . females are being arrested. Since the statute makes anyone guilty who offers or agrees to have sex for a fee, the PD is saying that that includes the trick too.

'Chief Galton agrees. You ladies will work with a male cover. You are to stay within eye contact at all times.'

'Sergeant?' Darlene asked.

'Yes.'

'I've been thinking about this. We'll be dressing up like prostitutes, right?'

'Yes.'

'Well, what about entrapment? I mean, isn't that planting the idea in the john's head?'

'The legal adviser said it's not, but it's best to let him bring up the subject of sex and the price.'

'How far are we going to have to go to make a bust?' Louise asked.

'Yours is made pretty well already,' Ortiz said. Coffin laughed, then looked embarrassed and stopped.

'Come on, Bert, for chrissakes. This is important,' Ryder said.

And it was important, Darlene thought. And goddamn Ortiz and Coffin and Neale. Why wouldn't they take the women seriously instead of treating them like secretaries in uniform?

'That's a good question. The way the law reads, you don't have to . . . er . . . uh, have sexual relations with the trick to make a case. The law is broken if the male offers or agrees to have sexual intercourse, which you ladies know what that is, or deviate sexual intercourse, which is, uh, as the statute says, contact between the, er, genitals of one person and the, er, mouth or, er, anus of another.'

Ryder blushed. Actually blushed! Darlene wanted to laugh, but it was too sad a state of affairs. Why wouldn't he say 'blow job' or 'asshole' or any of the other words he used when women weren't around?

'So if you get such an offer for money, you can make the arrest.'

'How are we going to work this?' Ortiz asked.

'I don't want any arrests made alone on the street. We don't want anyone freaking out on us. Bring the trick to your male cover. There's less likelihood of trouble with a man there.'

'What if the trick wants you to get in his car?'

'Absolutely not. We don't get into cars. I don't want you ladies isolated from your cover. If a trick asks you to get in his car, tell him there are cops around, and they'll make a pinch if they see you get in the car. Suggest a meet where your male cover is waiting. If the trick insists, brush him off.

'Okay, any more questions? No? Good. Now, I want good collars. There are certain judges, and you know who I'm talking about, who are going to jump at a chance to throw out these cases. You just wait until we bag a doctor or some big-shot attorney. So don't give them the chance.

'All right, I want Tallant and Coffin to work the area around Ninth and Burnside. Louise, you and Neale take the area by the Hilton. And Darlene and Bert, you take the park blocks.'

DARLENE STRAIGHTENED HER tight black miniskirt and dipped her knees so she could adjust her blond Afro wig in the sideview mirror of the unmarked police car. The California-surfer-girl effect produced by her straight blond hair, large blue eyes, and deep tan had been destroyed by false eyelashes, tons of pancake makeup, and gobs of red lipstick. Grotesque, she thought, as she put the finishing touches on the wig.

'Not bad, Darlene,' Ortiz chuckled. 'You may be in the wrong line of work.'

'Stuff it, Bert,' she snapped, still angry at him for the incident in the squad room.

'You know, Darlene, your trouble is you never took the time to get to know me. Now, if we had a drink after the shift, you'd get to see the real me.'

'Look,' she said, straightening and looking him in the eye, 'I don't have time for any of your macho shit tonight. Hand me my coat, please.'

There was heavy emphasis on the 'please.' Ortiz laughed and pulled a cheap rabbit coat out of the trunk. Darlene was wearing a fire-engine-red sweater that left her little room to breathe. She kept the coat open so the sweater showed. Black panty hose and high black boots completed her official whore uniform. She checked her purse to make sure she had not forgotten her service revolver.

Ortiz had picked a darkened parking lot for his surveillance post. An office building occupied the other half of the block on the same side of the street. There was a jewelry store, a shoe-repair shop, a beauty salon, and an all-night café across the way. The only illumination came from a series of evenly spaced streetlights.

'What's the plan?' Ortiz asked, suddenly all business.

Darlene looked up and down the street. It was a one-way street going south.

'I'll walk down the block to the corner, across from the café. That way I can get the traffic on both streets. Will you be able to see me from here?'

'Yeah. Just stay under the streetlight on the corner. This building blocks a little of my view.'

'If I get a proposition that's good enough for an arrest, I'll pat my wig. Then I'll have the trick come to the lot.'

'How are you going to do that?'

Darlene hadn't thought about the story she would use to lure the trick to Ortiz. Ortiz leaned against the side of the car watching her.

'I'll tell him I have a car in the lot and the keys to my room are in it. How's that?'

Ortiz stood up and stretched.

'Good. There's enough shadow here to keep me hidden until you're almost to the car.'

'Okay,' Darlene said. She turned her back to Ortiz and started across the parking lot. There were butterflies in her stomach, and she had a sudden urge to go to the bathroom. She always did when she was nervous, and she was suddenly nervous and a little scared.

'Darlene,' Ortiz called after her, 'don't take any chances.'

DARLENE HAD BEEN standing near the corner for fifteen minutes when the beige Mercedes drove by the first time. She got a fast look at the driver as he went by. Blond, good-looking. He had smiled at her. Darlene had smiled back, hoping he would stop, but he hadn't. Darlene had no idea why she had brought the rabbit coat along. It was way too hot for it. If she didn't get a nibble soon, she was determined to take it back to the lot. She glanced back toward Ortiz but couldn't spot him in the shadows.

The Mercedes drove by again and pulled to the curb across the street. The man signaled to her and she walked toward him, remembering to swing her hips as she went. She had to concentrate to keep from stumbling in her high-heel boots.

'Nice night,' the man said. He was a little nervous, but trying to be cool, Darlene thought.

'Nice enough,' she said. 'What are you doin' drivin' around in this big old car all by your lonesome?'

The man smiled. Probably married, Darlene thought. Where was the little woman while Papa was out cavorting? Bridge club? Maybe home watching TV while hubby is at a 'business' meeting. She could imagine how that pretty face was going to look when Papa had to explain to Mama that he had been arrested for prostitution.

'I'm just driving around, looking for a little fun. How about yourself?'

'I'm just hangin' around, sugar. Lookin' for a little fun myself.'

'I know a place where we can have a lot of fun. You want to come along?'

Darlene leaned over and rested her elbows on the window of the car. The top buttons of her sweater were open, and the blond man couldn't keep his eyes off her cleavage. This close, she could smell the liquor on his breath. He had been doing some heavy drinking, but he appeared to be able to hold it.

'I'd love to have some fun, sugar. What kind of fun did you have in mind?'

'Fun. You know,' he said evasively.

39

The trick was getting more agitated. Maybe he was new at the game. Darlene was beginning to get impatient. She wanted him to say the magic words so she could make her first arrest.

'Are you thinkin' of the kind of fun I'm thinkin' about?' she asked with a smile that she hoped looked lascivious.

The trick looked up and down the street.

'Look,' he said, 'why don't you get in and we can talk about it?'

'You have any money, sugar?' Darlene asked, trying to speed things up. The blond looked startled.

'Why?'

'The type of fun I'm thinking about could get expensive.'

The trick seemed very agitated. His eyes were darting back and forth rapidly.

'Look,' he said, 'I don't want to stand around here. There are cops all over. If you want to get in, get in.'

Darlene patted the wig with her right hand.

'Why are you worried about cops? I don't see any cops.'

'I can't wait anymore. Do you want to do business or not?'

Darlene felt her stomach churning. So close. She didn't want this one to get away. If she could just make him wait a minute. She was almost there.

ORTIZ SAT UP when the Mercedes slowed down.

He slouched back down in the front seat of the unmarked car when it sped up and drove on. This whole assignment was a waste of time, he thought. Busting some poor slob who wanted a little pussy and had to pay for it. That wasn't why he'd joined the force. Why did they have to take him out of narcotics just as he was beginning to get some heavy action? And working with Darlene Hersch ... Jesus H. Christ, if that wasn't the luck of the draw. Miss Tight Ass herself. Then again, maybe she wasn't such a tight ass. Sometimes it was the ones who gave you the hardest time that wanted it the most and just wouldn't admit it to themselves. He wondered what she'd be like in bed. Good old Darlene. He chuckled to himself. Probably want to be on top. She sure acted like it most of the time.

There was that Mercedes again. And it was stopping. Ortiz sat up. Darlene was wiggling over and talking to the driver. He couldn't see much of the guy from this distance.

She was leaning over now and resting on the ledge of the driver's window. Must be a live one. Yup, she was patting her wig. Now all she had to do was get him to drive into the lot.

Ortiz was wearing a light jacket. His revolver was in a holster on his belt. He checked it. Someone who drove a Mercedes was probably going to be no trouble, but no use taking chances. Darlene was still leaning on the window. Nice ass. Even from this distance. Ortiz wondered what was taking so long.

41

Christ, he was tired. He had a thing going with a cocktail waitress at the Golden Horse, and they had been at it all night. He yawned and shook his head. He should cut down. Too many women could kill you. Just like cigarettes. Still, he ... What the—

Darlene was walking around to the passenger door and getting in. The car was driving off. Ortiz jammed his key into the ignition. The engine turned over and he started out of the lot. Shit! He remembered. The street was one-way, the wrong way. That dumb cunt. If he went around the block, he'd lose them for sure. It was late and the street was deserted. He made up his mind and wheeled right. His tires squealed when he made the turn. That stupid bitch. When he made his report she would be ... Of all the dumb things to do. He picked up the radio mike. He might need assistance on this one if the Mercedes got too big a lead. He was about to make the call when he changed his mind. If he reported what was happening, it would be real trouble for Darlene. He didn't want that. Besides, everything would be okay if he could keep the car in view.

He made the turn onto Morrison, and there it was. Two lights away, but there wasn't much traffic. He relaxed and slowed down. He didn't want the driver to spot him. Why did Darlene have to prove how hard she was? She wouldn't be half-bad if she could get the chip off her shoulder. He'd bawl her out for sure once they made the bust. No, he'd have

Sandra or Louise talk to her. She'd never listen to a man.

'WHAT'S YOUR NAME, sugar?' Darlene asked as they turned onto the freeway. The man turned his head and smiled. He had nice teeth. Straight and gleaming white, like a movie actor. A good-looking guy. She couldn't figure out why someone that good-looking would have to pay for it.

'What's your name?' the blond countered cautiously.

'Darlene.'

'A nice name. You shouldn't wear so much makeup, Darlene. A pretty girl like you doesn't need it.'

'Well, thanks,' she said, patting her hair as she looked in the rearview mirror. Ortiz was still there. Good. She had counted on Ortiz's following her. She had been nervous until she spotted him when they turned off Morrison. He would be fuming by now, she thought with satisfaction. Well, fuck him. This was going to be an A-one bust.

'You look like you have nice breasts, Darlene,' the trick said without taking his eyes off the road. There was a hard edge to his voice when he said it, and Darlene felt uneasy for a moment.

'Thank you,' she said. 'Do you have some special plans for them?'

The trick laughed but didn't say anything. Ortiz was several car lengths back. A moving van changed lanes, and its width blocked the police car from view.

'Wife doesn't treat you right, huh?' Darlene asked. The trick still didn't answer, but he did turn and look at her. He was smiling, but there was no laughter in his eyes. They made her nervous and she felt a fleeting sense of desperation.

'Well, Darlene will treat you right. Now, just what do you want Darlene to do for you?' she said, making her voice low and sexy.

THE TRUCK WAS still blocking Ortiz's view when the Mercedes turned onto the exit ramp. Ortiz swore and almost missed the turn. He still hadn't got close enough to get the license plate, and he couldn't afford to lose them. Traffic was heavy when he got to the end of the ramp, and the Mercedes's lead was increasing. He finally pulled into the traffic and the Mercedes disappeared. He slammed his fist on the dashboard but continued to scan the neon-lit restaurants and motel parking lots on both sides of the street. Nothing. Nothing. Come on. Where are you?

Then he saw it. The Mercedes was just stopping in front of the office of the Raleigh Motel. Ortiz tried to read the license as he passed the motel, but the angle was bad and he was going too fast. Through the rearview mirror he saw Darlene getting out of the car. He pulled quickly into the McDonald's next door to the motel.

*

'I DON'T WANT to discuss business here, Darlene, but I can assure you that you will be paid well.'

They were off the freeway, and she couldn't be sure that Ortiz had seen them exit. Damn that truck. There was something about this guy that was starting to bother her. He would not commit himself, and she was beginning to think that she had acted too hastily.

The trick turned the car into the parking lot of the Raleigh Motel. Darlene pressed the side of her purse and was comforted by the feel of the gun's outline. Ortiz wouldn't be frightened in a situation like this if he was busting a female prostitute. She looked out the back window. Where was he? She couldn't see the police car anywhere.

'I want you to register for the room,' the trick was saying. 'I'll pull around and park.'

'I don't . . .'

'There's nothing to it,' he said, smiling and handing her a roll of bills.

Darlene took the money and slid out of the front seat. The trick drove toward the rear parking lot, away from the motel office. An old man in a plaid shirt was squinting at a used paperback through a pair of thick-lensed, wire-rim glasses. He looked up when Darlene entered.

'I'd like a room,' she said.

The old man slid a registration card across the desk without comment. She took a pen from a plastic holder on the desk and filled in the squares for name and address using her own name and the address of the North Precinct. It would be good evidence when the case came to court.

'Thirty-five bucks in advance,' the clerk said. He was looking at her breasts without the slightest attempt at concealment.

'How come you didn't ask me how long I'm staying?' Darlene said as she laid down the money. The old man cocked an eyebrow at her, shook his head slowly, and took the money without answering.

'Second floor on the street side,' he said, handing her the key. The old man was reading again by the time the office door swung closed.

The office was separate from the motel rooms. Darlene crossed the parking lot and walked up the stairs past an ice machine. Her heels clanged on each metal stair and stopped when she reached the concrete landing that ran the length of the second floor on the outside of the building. Her trick was nowhere in sight. She paused outside the door of the motel room and looked down the length of the landing. She thought she saw someone standing in the shadows at the other end, but she wasn't sure. She was starting to feel nervous again. This guy could be a freak. She decided to keep her hand on her gun. She could do it by simply putting her hand in her purse. She'd have to keep some distance between them.

She opened the door and flipped on the light. The combined odor of cleaning fluids and stale air assailed her. Where was the air-conditioning unit? Motel rooms always depressed her. They were so sterile and so impersonal. She often thought that hell must be a series of motel rooms where people sat, alone and unconnected.

There was a queen-size bed covered by a faded yellow bedspread. Two pillows were tucked under the spread and two cheap, natural-wood-colored end tables with matching lamps flanked the bed. A dresser with a large mirror faced the bed. A color TV perched on one corner of the dresser; a phone, with instructions for dialing out-of-town and local calls, sat on the other. Two sagging Scandinavian chairs were the only other furniture. Darlene sat in the one facing the door and put her hand in her purse. The door opened.

'Hi, Darlene,' the trick said. He was of average height, maybe a little under six feet. His slacks were light brown. The flowered shirt looked expensive. So did his polished shoes. She noticed that he locked the door when he closed it, and she tightened her grip on the revolver.

'Why did you do that?' Darlene asked nervously. The trick grinned.

'I thought we could use a little privacy,' he said. He had been moving toward her, but he stopped when he reached the bed.

'Why don't you take your clothes off?' he asked quietly. 'I want to see those breasts we were talking about.'

Darlene decided everything had gone too far. She had made a mistake and she wanted to get out. Maybe the guy was a freak. Maybe he just wanted her to get nude, then he'd beat off. There'd be no violation of law. Just some sick bastard whose wife didn't satisfy him. She'd be a laughing-stock. She felt ill. Why hadn't she followed instructions?

'Look,' she said, 'this isn't a peep show. If you want to have sex, say so, or I'm leaving.'

'Don't go, Darlene,' he said, 'I'll make it worth your while.'

His voice was husky now. She could almost feel his sexual desire. He was moving again. Almost to her. Darlene made her decision. She was going to end this right now. She would say he propositioned her. She had to. She'd make up a story. The trick would cop a plea anyway. He'd be too embarrassed to go into court for a full-blown trial.

'Forget the money, mister,' she said, standing. 'You'll need it for a lawyer.'

The trick froze.

'What?' he said.

'You heard me. I'm a cop and you're under arrest.'

FROM THE CORNER of the McDonald's lot Ortiz watched Darlene climb the stairs. She walked to the door near the far end of the landing and looked around before entering one of the rooms. A few seconds later a blond man walked out of the

48

shadows at the other end of the landing and walked quickly to the door. It was too far to get a good look, but the man was slim and athletic looking. He could see the flowered shirt and tan slacks pretty clearly.

When the door to the motel room closed, Ortiz started to worry. He should be up there, but he didn't want to ruin her bust. He tried to decide what to do. Ryder had paired them because of his experience. If anything happened to Darlene, it would be his fault. Ortiz made up his mind. He sprinted across to the motel.

Ortiz heard the scream as he reached the stairs to the second floor. He froze and there was a crash and a second scream. The lights were on and he could see the man's blurred silhouette through the flimsy motel curtains. It was all happening very fast. He realized that he was not moving.

The lights went out and he took the stairs two at a time. Someone was moaning in the room. Someone was breathing hard. He crashed the heel of his shoe into the door just above the lock. There was a splintering sound, but the door held. He swung his foot again and the door crashed inward. The globe lamp that hung outside the door turned the room a pale yellow. Darlene was sprawled like a rag doll against the side of a chair in the far corner of the room. Her head hung limply to one side, and blood trickled from the corner of her mouth. There was a jagged red slash across her neck, and the floor around her was covered with blood.

Something exploded across Ortiz's eyes and he dropped his gun. He was propelled into the room and he felt a burst of pain in his neck and upper back. His head crashed into the metal edge of the bed as he twisted and fell. He slumped against the bed. There was a man standing in the doorway, in the light of the globe lamp. Standing for a moment, then bolting like a startled deer. Ortiz felt consciousness slipping away. He tried to concentrate on the face. The blond, curly hair. He would never forget that face. Never.

4

'David, come over here. There's someone who wants to meet you.'

David looked around and saw Gregory Banks standing near the fireplace with several other people. Gregory was a political ally of Senator Martin Bauer, and he had organized this cocktail party at his spacious riverfront home to help raise funds for the senator's reelection.

Gregory was a large man. An ex-boxer and ex-Marine, he had started his adult life as a longshoreman and union organizer, then gone to night law school. Gregory worked as a lawyer for the unions, and the unions had made him a wealthy man.

The summer before his last year in law school, David had driven cross-country and fallen in love with Portland. One week after graduation, David said goodbye to his family and flew west from New York to take the Oregon bar examination. He had never regretted the move. East Coast law schools tended to push their graduates into corporate practice and left them with a feeling that there was something grubby and demeaning about opening a solo practice and actually going into a courtroom. In

Portland the feeling was different. There still existed a spirit of individualism that encouraged a person to try to make it on his own. Within a week of passing the bar, David hung out his shingle on the fourth floor of the American Bank Building.

David was good and soon developed a reputation as the man to see if you were charged with a serious crime. He also volunteered to take ACLU cases, pro bono. While working on a prison-rights appeal, David met Gregory Banks, another volunteer. Despite the difference in their ages, they hit it off immediately. One evening, Banks invited David home for dinner and broached the possibility of David's joining his firm. David took a week to decide. He disliked the idea of giving up a measure of his independence, but he liked the idea of being associated with Gregory Banks. He accepted, and by the time the firm moved its offices to the First National Bank Tower, he was a name partner.

'David, this is Leo Betts, a professor at the law school,' Gregory said, introducing a tall, hawk-nosed man with greasy, shoulder-length hair. Professor Betts was standing next to a mousy woman in her early thirties.

'And Doris, his wife,' Gregory added. David shook hands with the professor.

'Leo read your brief in the Ashmore case.'

'An excellent job. I'm having my first-year criminal-law class read it as an example of first-class appellate argument.'

'I'd look on it as a punishment assignment,' David said. 'It was over a hundred pages.'

Everyone in the group laughed, and Gregory indicated another couple, a short, balding man and his tall, elegantly dressed wife.

'John and Priscilla Moultrie. John's with Banker's Trust and Priscilla teaches at Fairmount Elementary School.'

Gregory had an annoying habit of introducing a person by telling his line of work. David nodded at the couple, but his attention was on an attractive young woman who had wandered over and was standing on the fringes of the group.

'What is the Ashmore case, Gregory?' Mrs. Moultrie asked. The young woman was watching him and their eyes met momentarily.

'Isn't Ashmore that fellow who raped and murdered those schoolchildren?' her husband asked.

'Yes,' Professor Betts answered with a smile. 'David was able to get the conviction reversed by the state supreme court two weeks ago. A monumental job. He convinced the court to overrule a line of cases going back to eighteen ninety-three.'

The young woman smiled tentatively, and David nodded. He would make a point, he decided, to talk to her as soon as he could break away from the conversation. The Ashmore case was not one of his favorite subjects.

'Does that mean he'll go free?' Mrs. Moultrie asked.

'No,' David sighed. 'It just means that I have to try the whole mess over again. It took a month the last time.'

'You defended that man?' Mrs. Moultrie asked in a tone that combined amazement and disgust.

'David is a criminal lawyer,' Gregory said, as if that were an adequate explanation.

'Maybe I'll never understand, Mr. Nash' – she seemed to have used his last name intentionally – 'but I knew one of those children, and I don't see how you could have represented someone who did what that man did.'

'Someone had to represent Ashmore, Priscilla,' Gregory said.

'I heard he tortured those children before he killed them,' Mrs. Moultrie said.

David almost instinctively said, 'That was never proved,' but he realized in time that, for Mrs. Moultrie, that was not the issue.

'A lawyer can't refuse to represent someone because of the nature of his crime,' Professor Betts said.

'Would you have represented Adolf Hitler, Professor?' Mrs. Moultrie asked without humor.

There was a moment of uncomfortable silence. Then Professor Betts answered, 'Yes. Our judicial system is based on the premise that an individual charged with a crime is innocent until proven guilty.'

'But what if you know your client is guilty,

Mr. Nash? Know for a fact that he held three schoolchildren captive for several days, raped them, then murdered them?'

'Oh, now, Priscilla. That's unfair,' her husband said. His face was red, and it was clear that he disapproved of the course the conversation had taken.

David felt uncomfortable. Professor Betts had been defending him, but why did he need a defense for doing something that he was ethically obliged to do? Why should this woman he had never met before feel such obvious hostility toward him?

'I'm afraid I can't discuss the facts of the case, Mrs. Moultrie. I'd be violating my client's confidence if I discussed his guilt or innocence with you.'

'Hypothetically, then. I really want to know.'

'You represent a guilty man as hard as you do an innocent man, Mrs. Moultrie, because the system is more important than any individual case. If you start making exceptions with the guilty, sooner or later you'll make exceptions with the innocent.'

'So you represent people that you know are guilty?'

'Most of my clients are guilty.'

'And you . . . get them off . . . win their trials?'

'Sometimes.'

'Doesn't it ever bother you?'

DAVID WATCHED THE scattered lights on the houseboats moored across the river. The sun was down and a cool breeze drifted inland, gently rearranging the lock of thick brown hair that fell across his forehead. It was pleasant standing on the terrace. The shadows and stillness soothed him.

Somewhere upriver the shrill blast of a tanker's horn punctuated the darkness. The sound died and the river was at peace again. David wished that he could restore his inner peace as easily. The discussion about the Ashmore case had upset him. It had stirred something inside that had been lurking for too long. Something ugly that was starting to crawl into the light.

This morning at the juvenile home, interviewing that young girl. What happened? When she was describing her ordeal, he had felt shame and pity for her. He had become emotionally involved. That should never have happened. He was a professional. One of the best. He was not supposed to feel pity for the victim or revulsion for his client.

Something was definitely wrong. He was getting depressed too much lately, and the feeling was lasting too long. There had been times in recent weeks when his mood would plunge rapidly from a high, floating sensation into deep melancholy for no apparent reason. And that feeling. To live with it too long was to experience a kind of death. It was as if his spirit evaporated, leaving his body a hollow shell. He would feel empty and disoriented. Movement was impossible. Sometimes he would sit immobile, on the verge of tears, and his mind would scream, 'Why?' He was in excellent health. At thirty-five, he was at the top of his profession, making more money than he ever had. Everything should have been going so well, but it wasn't.

There had been a time when losing any case had been a deep, personal defeat, and winning, a magnificent triumph. David had lost those extreme feelings of involvement somewhere along the way. One day he had won a very difficult case, and it just did not matter. Another time a client received a long prison term, and he felt nothing. His world had shifted from dark black and bright gold to shades of gray.

If his professional life was empty, his personal life was even more so. He had heard more than once that he was envied by other men for the steady parade of beautiful women he escorted. Few people knew that the routine had grown old a long time ago.

His one attempt at marriage had been a disaster that lasted officially for two years, but which ended emotionally after eight months. Monica resented the long hours he worked, and in truth, he was rarely home. There had been so many big cases. He was just starting to reach the top then. Everyone wanted David Nash, and there didn't seem to be enough time for his own wife.

There had been violent arguments and too many stony silences. Monica had accused him of infidelity. He denied her accusations, but they were true. He was trying cases in other states now, and if some Texas filly wanted to warm his bed . . . well, he was a star, wasn't he? In the end the constant bickering exhausted them both, and whatever had motivated them to marry was not strong enough to keep their marriage together.

Monica had gone to law school after the divorce. David thought she had done it to compete with him. It was certainly not coincidence that led her into criminal prosecution. The tension was there whenever they tried a case against each other. David sensed that their legal battles were, for Monica, only an excuse for carrying on a personal battle of which he had never been a part. That, of course, was the problem with their marriage. If David had cared about Monica, it would never have broken up. But he had ignored her, and he felt guilty that she still felt a need to prove something to him.

David had seen little of Monica between the divorce and her graduation from law school. After she joined the district attorney's office, their friendship had renewed. They were much better friends than spouses. Sometimes David wondered if he hadn't made a mistake with Monica, but he knew that if he had, it was too late to rectify it. Their problem was that they had met at the wrong time.

David took a sip from his glass. The gin tasted too sweet. He carried the drink to a corner of the terrace that was not illuminated by the lights from the house and sat down on a lawn chair. He closed his eyes and tilted his head back, letting the chair's metal rim press into the back of his neck.

Monica was an attractive woman, and she was a different, stronger person than she had been when they'd met. David was different, too. He had toyed once with the idea of trying to reestablish their relationship, but had given up on the idea. He wondered what she would say if he tried.

The terrace door opened and a splash of sound interrupted David's thoughts. He opened his eyes. A woman was standing with her back to him, staring across the river as he had moments before. She was tall and slender, and her long, silken hair looked like pale gold.

She turned and walked along the terrace with a dancer's grace. The woman did not see him until she was almost at his chair. He was hidden by the shadows. She stopped, startled. In that frozen moment David saw her set in time, like a statue. Blue eyes wide with surprise. A high, smooth forehead and high cheekbones. It was the woman he had seen earlier on the fringes of the group that had been discussing the Ashmore case.

The moment ended and the woman's hand flew to her mouth. She gasped. David stood up, placing his drink on the terrace.

'I'm sorry if I frightened you,' he said.

'It's not your fault,' the woman answered, waving her hand nervously. 'I was thinking and I . . .' She let the sentence trail off.

'Okay,' David said, 'you've convinced me. We're both at fault. How about calling it a draw?'

The woman looked confused; then she laughed, grateful that the awkward moment was over.

'My name is David Nash.'

'I know,' the woman said after a moment's hesitation.

'You do?'

'I . . . I was listening when you were talking to that woman about the murder case.'

'You mean that Ashmore business?'

'She upset you, didn't she?'

Now it was David's turn to hesitate.

'It wasn't pleasant for me to try that case, and it won't be pleasant to retry it. I don't like to think about it if I don't have to.'

'I'm sorry,' the woman said self-consciously. David immediately regretted his tone of voice.

'You don't have to be. I didn't mean to be so solemn.'

They stood without talking for a moment. The woman looked uneasy, and David had the feeling that she might fly off like a frightened bird.

'Are you a friend of Gregory's?' he asked to keep the conversation going.

'Gregory?'

'Gregory Banks. This is his house. I thought you were with that group that was talking about the case. Most of them are Gregory's friends.'

'No. I really don't know anyone here. I don't even know why I came.'

She looked down, and David sensed that she

was trapped and vulnerable, fighting something inside her.

'You haven't told me your name yet,' David said. The woman looked up, startled. He held her gaze for a moment and saw fear and uncertainty in her eyes.

'I'm afraid I have to go,' she answered anxiously, avoiding his question.

'But that's not fair,' David said, trying to keep his tone light. 'You know my name. You can't run off without telling me yours.'

She paused, and their eyes met again. He knew that she was debating whether to answer him and that her answer would determine the course of the evening.

'Valerie,' she said finally. 'Valerie Dodge.' And David could tell by the firmness in her voice that Valerie had resolved her doubts in his favor, at least for the moment.

David had a lot of experience with women, and there was something about this one that he found intriguing. Common sense told him to go slowly, but he noticed a change in her mood. When she told him her name, she had committed herself, and his instincts told him to take a chance.

'You're not enjoying yourself here, are you?' he asked gently.

'No,' she answered.

'I wasn't either. I guess that woman upset me more than I'd like to admit. Look, I'd like to make a suggestion. I know a nice place in town where we can grab a late supper. Are you interested?'

'No,' she said, momentarily dashing his hopes. 'I'd rather you just take me to your house.'

DAVID'S CANTILEVERED HOUSE strained against the thick wooden beams that secured it to the hillside. In the daytime you could stand on one of several cedar decks and look across Portland toward the snow-capped mountains of the Cascade Range. In the evening you could stand in the same place and see the Christmas-light grid of the city spreading out from the base of the hill.

The house was modern, constructed of dark woods that blended into the greenery of the West Hills. It had three stories, but only one story showed above the level of the road, the other two being hidden by the hillside. The house had been custom-built to David's specifications, and the east wall was made almost entirely of glass.

David helped Valerie out of the sports car and led her down a flight of steps to the front door. The door opened onto an elevated landing. The landing looked down on a spacious, uncluttered living room, dominated by a huge sculptural fireplace that resembled a knight's helmet with the visor thrown back. The fireplace was pure white and the carpeting a subdued red. There were no chairs or sofas in the room, but a seating platform piled high with pillows of various colors was incorporated into the sweep of the rounded, rough-plastered walls. The only other furnishings in the room were a low, circular light wood table and several large pillows.

A spiral staircase on the left side of the room led upward to the bedroom and down to the kitchen area. A balcony that ran half the length of the third floor overlooked the living room.

'This is magnificent,' Valerie said, taking off her shoes and walking barefoot across the carpet to look at a large abstract painting that hung to the left of the fireplace.

'I'm glad you like it. Do you want the grand tour?'

She nodded, and he led her downstairs into the kitchen and dining room, then back to the second level. The den was located on the south side of the house, and it looked out onto the hillside. It was small and cluttered with briefs, legal periodicals, books, sheets of paper, and pens and paper clips. A bookcase was built into one wall, and a filing cabinet stood in one corner. The walls were decorated with framed clippings from some of David's best-known cases. Valerie skimmed the texts of a few of them.

'Did you win all these cases?'

'Those and a few more,' he answered, pleased that she had noticed them.

'Are you famous?'

David laughed.

'Only in circles that you're not likely to travel in.'

'Oh, for instance?'

'Murderers, dope fiends, pimps, and rapists.'

'How do you know I'm not a rapist?' she asked. She had attempted to ask the question coolly and casually, but a tremor in her voice betrayed her nervousness. She heard the tremor and looked away, embarrassed, when he looked at her.

'I still haven't shown you the top floor,' David said evenly. He led her up the spiral staircase to his bedroom. The lights were off and the bedroom curtains had not been drawn shut. They could see the moon floating above the pine shadows.

Valerie walked across the room and pressed her forehead against the cool glass of the picture window, watching the lights of the city. David stood beside her and gently touched the smooth skin of her shoulder. She turned to face him and he took her in his arms. His lips pressed softly against hers. She hesitated for a moment, and her body tensed under his touch. Then she flung her arms around him, pulling him into her, returning his kiss with great passion.

David stepped back, surprised at the ferocity of her reaction. Valerie looked into his eyes and unfastened the straps of her summer dress. It floated down the long lines of her body in slow motion. She stood in the moonlight, her face in shadows.

David took off his clothes, his eyes never leaving her. Her body was magnificent. An athletic figure with breasts that were small and perfectly formed. He watched the gentle rhythm of her breathing and the rise and fall of her rib cage under her smooth, tanned skin.

They touched and she melted into him. They stroked each other, and he forgot where he was and who he was. There was desperation and abandon in her lovemaking, and she moved under him with violence and passion until her body suddenly arched and her eyes closed tight. He could feel her fingers digging into his back and he heard her gasp, then moan.

They held each other for a while; then David rolled slowly to his back. She pressed her head to his chest and sighed. He wound his fingers through her long blond hair. His fingers strayed to her cheek. It was damp with tears.

'Don't cry,' he whispered.

'I'm always sad after I make love. Really make love. I feel ... I don't know ... as if I'd lost something.'

He sat up and gently pushed her back. Moonlight illuminated her hair and made it look like strands of gold against the pale blue of the pillow cover.

'You're very beautiful,' David said. She turned her head away from him.

'Have I said something wrong?' he asked.

'No ... I ... it's just that ...'

He placed a finger over her lips, then kissed them. The longing he felt for her welled up in him. She drew him down.

PHILLIP M. MARGOLIN

'I HAVE TO go,' she said. 'It's very late.'

He looked at the digital clock on his nightstand. It was after midnight.

'Why don't you spend the night? I promise to cook you a terrific breakfast in the morning.'

Valerie looked suddenly worried.

'I can't stay, David. It's . . . I just can't.'

'Why?' David asked, concerned by her sudden change of mood.

'Please, David. It has nothing to do with you. I can't stay. That's all. Can you take me back to Mr. Banks's house? I left my car there.'

David nodded. She stood up and walked to the bathroom, picking up her clothes on the way. He watched her from the bed. She pressed the light switch, and floor-to-ceiling mirrors reflected her in a halo of light. Each part of her body was like a piece of fine sculpture. The long, thin arms, the well-formed legs, the flat, muscular stomach. He wanted to touch her again.

She moved out of his line of vision, and he heard the shower door open. David lay back on the bed and looked at the ceiling. They had been good together sexually. He felt as if he were giving a part of himself when he was inside her, instead of simply taking. He had not felt that way in a long time.

The shower started and David turned his head toward the bathroom door. He didn't want Valerie to leave and he wondered why she had to. The obvious answer was that she was married. That

66

would explain her nervousness at the party. Would it make any difference to him if he found out she was married? No, he decided.

The water stopped and David started to dress. He wondered what it would be like to love somebody. What he and Monica had was not love, but he had never felt as strongly about any other woman. He thought about Gregory Banks and his marriage, which had lasted so long. What was the secret? Was it all chemical? Was he missing something that other men had?

Valerie finished combing her hair and turned off the bathroom light. David put on a pair of slacks. He looked at her while he buttoned his sport shirt. Valerie walked around the room, glancing out the window, fingering objects, not looking at him. He wanted to see her again. There was something about her. He wanted to know if what he felt for her was a product of the magic of the evening or something more.

They rode down from the hills in silence. The view was very beautiful, and neither wanted to break the spell it created. Most of Gregory's guests had left, but there was still noise coming from the big house. Valerie's car was at the foot of the long, winding driveway. David stopped behind it. He turned off the ignition and they sat in the dark.

'I'd like to see you again,' David said.

She looked suddenly nervous, as if she regretted the evening.

'Is something wrong?' he asked.

'David,' she said slowly, 'I don't want you to misunderstand. I enjoyed . . . had a wonderful time . . . being with you. But I'm a little confused just now.'

She stopped. He wanted to hold her. To press her. To make her commit herself. But he knew that would be a mistake.

'All right,' he said. 'I'm glad we spent the evening together, too. If you feel the same way, you know how to get in touch with me.'

Valerie looked down at her lap, then turned quickly and kissed him, opened the door, and walked to her car. David watched her drive off. He was tired and a little down, but he didn't start back immediately.

5

Sunlight streamed through the glass wall of David's bedroom, and he stretched. The warm morning sun made him feel lazy and relaxed. He opened his eyes. A bird was singing and he could see green pines profiled against a clear blue sky. He should have been elated. Instead, he felt a sense of loss. Nothing overwhelming, but real enough to put him off his stride.

In the bathroom he splashed cold water on his face, brushed his teeth, and shaved. He returned to the bedroom and began to perform calisthenics in front of a full-length mirror. He enjoyed watching the play of his muscles as they stretched and contracted. When he broke a sweat, he did some stretching exercises to loosen up his legs. Then he slipped into a pair of shorts and a T-shirt and laced up his running shoes.

David's house was on a three-and-a-half-mile road that circled around the hill back to his front door. His morning run took him past sections of wooded area and other modern homes. There were a few other joggers out and he nodded at them as he went by. This run had become a daily routine for the past five years. His body had become a victim of the sedentary nature of the legal profession. Turning thirty had made him self-conscious about the softening process he was going through. So it was back to the weights and miles of jogging and an attempt to return to the muscle tone of his youth.

It was nine o'clock. He had slept later than usual, but that was okay. He had no court appearances and, at the moment, nothing very pressing to work on other than the Seals case.

Halfway around, David spotted a pretty girl running in front of him. She made him think of Valerie Dodge. Valerie had had a strange effect on him. Perhaps the mysterious way she had ended the evening was responsible for his desire. Perhaps it was the mixture of passion and reticence that had permeated their lovemaking. When they were in bed, she held him so tight; then, just when he thought she was giving herself completely, he would suddenly feel a tension in her that implied a spiritual withdrawal from the act. It had been confusing, yet entrancing, suggesting a mystery beneath the surface of the slender body he was holding.

David sprinted the final quarter mile to his house. He showered and dressed for work. He had decided that he could not wait for Valerie Dodge to call him. He was going to find her.

'BAUER CAMPAIGN HEADQUARTERS.'
    'Joe Barrington, please.'
    'Speaking.'

'Joe, this is Dave Nash.'

'Some party last night, Dave. Tell Greg thanks a million.'

'I'm glad it worked out all right.'

'The senator was really pleased.'

'Good. Look, Joe, the reason I called was for some information. You helped Greg draw up the invitation list for the party, right?'

'Sure. What can I do for you?'

'I met a woman at the party. Her name is Valerie Dodge. Tall, mid-twenties, blond hair. I promised I'd give her the answer to a legal question and I lost her phone number. I called information, but she's not listed.'

'No problem. Give me a minute and I'll get the list.'

'Dave,' Joe Barrington said a minute later, 'doesn't look like I can help you. There's no one named Dodge on the list. Did she come with someone?'

'No. She was alone.'

'That's funny. I'm certain everyone we invited was on the list. Of course, Greg might have invited someone on his own. Or the senator. Do you want me to check?'

'Would you?'

'No problem. It might take a few days, though. We're all backed up here.'

'That's okay. There's no rush. She'll probably call me in a day or so if she doesn't hear from me.'

'Tell Greg thanks. Don't forget. The senator's

going to drop him a line personally, but it might take him some time to get around to it.'

'I'll tell him. Thanks again.'

David hung up and learned back in his chair. No name in the phone book or on the list. Maybe Valerie Dodge wasn't her right name. If she was married, she might have given him a phony. He had to see her again. The more mysterious she became, the greater became David's desire. He closed his eyes and started thinking of ways to track her down. By lunchtime he still hadn't thought of any.

ORTIZ HEARD RON Crosby enter his hospital room. He turned his head toward the door. It took a lot of effort to do even that. His twin black eyes and bandaged nose made him look like a boxer who had lost a fight. His head throbbed and his broken nose hurt even more.

'Ready to get back to work, Bert?' Crosby asked. Ortiz knew Crosby was just trying to cheer him up, but he couldn't smile.

'Is she . . .?' Ortiz asked in a tired voice.

'Dead.'

Ortiz wasn't surprised. No one had told him, but he knew.

'Can you talk about it, Bert?' Crosby asked. He pulled up a gray metal chair and sat down beside the bed. This wasn't the first time he had been in a hospital room interviewing a witness in a homicide. He had been on the force for fifteen years, and a homicide detective for eight of those. Still, it was different when the witness was a fellow cop and a friend.

'I'll try,' Ortiz answered, 'but I'm having trouble getting it all straight.'

'I know. You have a concussion. The doctor said that it's going to make it hard for you to remember for a while.'

Ortiz looked frightened and Crosby held up his hand.

'For a while, Bert. He said it goes away in time and you'll remember everything. I probably shouldn't even be here this soon, but I was gonna drop in to see how you were, and I figured it wouldn't hurt to pump you a little.'

'Thanks for coming, Ron,' Ortiz said. He shut his eyes and leaned back. Crosby shifted on his seat. He was short for a policeman, five eight, but he had a big upper body and broad shoulders that pushed past the edges of the chair back. He had joined the force in his late twenties after an extended hitch in the Army. Last February he turned forty-two, and gray was starting to outnumber black among his thinning hairs.

'I can't remember anything about the murder. I vaguely remember a motel, but that's it. I can remember the car, though,' he said, brightening. 'It was a Mercedes. Beige, I think.'

The effort had taken something out of him, and he let his head loll like a winded runner.

'Did you get a license number or . . .?'

'No, I don't think so. It's all so hazy.'

Crosby stood up.

'I'm gonna go and let you get some rest. I don't want to push you.'

'It's okay, Ron. I . . .' Ortiz stopped. Something was troubling him.

'What does Ryder think?' he asked after a while. 'I mean, does he think I . . .?'

'He doesn't think anything. No one does, Bert. We don't even know what happened.'

Ortiz put his hands to his head and ran them across the short stubble that covered his cheeks. He felt drained.

'What if it was my fault? I mean, they put me with Darlene because she was new, and what if . . .?'

He didn't finish.

'You've got enough to worry about without taking a strong dose of self-pity. You're a good cop and everybody knows that. You worry about getting better and getting your memory back.'

'Yeah. Okay. I just . . .'

'I know. See you, huh?'

'See you. Thanks again for coming.'

The door closed and Ortiz stared at it. The drugs they had given him were making him sleepy, but they didn't get rid of all the pain. They just made it bearable. He closed his eyes and saw Darlene. She had been an annoyance. Really juvenile. Had he screwed up because he had got mad at her? He wished that he could remember what had happened. He wanted to help get the killer, but, most of all, he wanted to know if it was his fault that a young policewoman was dead.

6

The first half of July was cool and comfortable. There was a subdued sun, light breezes, a mad array of flowers, and underdressed girls in eye-catching getups. Then, overnight, the breeze disappeared, the sun went mad, and a thick, unmoving mass of hot air descended on Portland, wilting the flowers and making the girls look tired and worn. To David the oppressive heat was merely a meteorological expression of his mood. The torpid air had a dehydrating effect that wore away the energy of the city, and, in a similar way, David could feel his mental and spiritual energy draining away, like wax slowly dripping down the sides of a candle.

All his attempts to locate Valerie Dodge had failed, and she had not called him. Perhaps David desired her because he could not find her, but her absence gnawed at him, confronting him with the void that was his personal life.

Work provided no escape. It only deepened his depression. The Gault case had brought him many new clients, all guilty and all hoping that he could perform a miracle that would wash away their guilt. His work on their behalf disheartened him. More and more he felt that he was doing something he should not.

The originality that had characterized David's early legal career was giving way to a highly polished routine that let him move through his cases without thinking about them. His success as a lawyer was due to his brilliance and his dedication. Others might not notice, but David knew he was no longer giving his best effort. So far that had made no difference in the results he had achieved. But someday it would. On that day he would know, even if no one else did, that he was no different from the ambulance chasers and incompetents who practiced at the gutter levels of criminal law.

The trial of Tony Seals was scheduled for late July, and David was working on his final preparations when the receptionist told him that Thomas Gault was in the reception room. David had seen little of the writer since the trial, except for a half-day interview for background on the book. David had not felt much like talking about Gault's case, but he was sharing in the proceeds of the book and was obligated by contract to cooperate. The interview had taken place the day after the trial, and a week after that Gault had taken a vacation in the Caribbean, then gone into seclusion to finish the book.

David did a double take when his office door opened. Gault laughed. He loved to shock people, and his appearance provided a low-grade jolt. Below the neck Gault looked the same. It was his head that had changed. His long brown hair had been shorn off, leaving a gleaming skull, and his upper lip sported a Fu Manchu mustache.

'Jesus!' David said, to Gault's delight. 'Have you taken up professional wrestling?'

'I'm changing my image,' Gault answered with a grin.

'Sit down,' David said, shaking his head. 'What brings you to town?'

'The book. My editor wants me to beef up the final chapters, so he suggested that I get a little more of your thinking about the trial.'

'What do you want to know?'

'I don't know. It was his idea. What you ate the morning of the main event. Who does your clothes. Think of something. After all, I'm doing the work, but you're getting part of the profits. Take an interest.'

'Tom, I have no idea what would interest your readers. Give me a hint.'

'You ever play any sports in high school or college?'

David shrugged.

'I ran a little track in college and wrestled some.'

'Okay. Why don't you tell me how trying a case compares to the feeling you get just before a sporting event. How's that?'

David thought for a few minutes before answering.

'I don't think they're that similar,' David said. 'Winning or losing at sports depends on your performance during the sporting event, but a lawyer can't win a case at trial. Or, anyway, not usually.'

'What do you mean?'

'Well, the facts of each case are determined by the time the case gets to you. All the facts might not be revealed, but they're there. So a lawyer wins his case before trial by finding out, through investigation, what the facts are. A lawyer can't change the facts, but once he knows what the facts are, he can deal with them. Try to get the jury to look at them in a certain way. And there is usually more than one way to look at the facts.

'A few years back I represented a man who tried to hold up a minimart. He walked in with a shotgun and told the manager to give him the money or he would kill him. The manager was a feisty little guy, and he whipped out a handgun and shot my client through the neck. When the police arrived, my man was lying in a pool of blood holding the gun, and there were five eyewitnesses who swore that he tried to rob the place. The DA charged my client with armed robbery. Those were the facts I started with. Want to guess the verdict?'

Gault smiled.

"It has to be not guilty, but how did you do it?"

'There were other facts we didn't know about when we started. When they took the defendant to the hospital for surgery, they took a blood sample.

One of the routine checks the hospital makes before performing surgery is to find out how much alcohol a person has in his system. My man was loaded. He had consumed so much alcohol that I was able to get two prominent psychiatrists to testify that a person in his condition would not be able to form the intent to commit the crime, and the district attorney must prove intent as one of the elements of the crime of armed robbery.

'The next step was to find out why my client drank like that. It turned out that his wife had died and he had gone to pieces. When I got him, he was already an alcoholic.

'Finally, we had to figure out why he had been at the minimart in the first place. My investigator asked around, and it turned out that our boy had been blotto that day. Two of his buddies had planned the robbery and sent him inside. He was so drunk, he didn't know what he was doing. In fact, he doesn't remember what happened to this day.

'When we presented all the facts to the jury, they acquitted. It wasn't what we did at trial, but the investigation before trial, that mattered. Getting the facts, then presenting them in a favorable light at trial.'

'And is that what you did in the case of State versus Thomas Ira Gault? Manipulate the facts?' Gault asked with an impish grin.

David looked straight at Gault without smiling. The question had caught him off guard.

'Yes,' he answered.

'You know, David,' Gault said, 'there is something I've always wanted to ask you. All the time you were defending me, and doing such a bang-up job, what did you think? Guilty or innocent? Tell me.'

'Guilty,' David said without a moment's hesitation. Gault threw back his head and laughed loudly.

'Terrific. And you still worked your ass off. David, old buddy, you are a pro. Now, do you want to know something?' Gault asked in a conspiratorial tone.

'What?'

'Is that attorney-client thing – the privilege – is that still in effect?'

David nodded, very tense.

'Anything I tell you is secret, right? No police, nobody else finds out, right?'

David nodded again. Gault leaned back in his seat and grinned.

'Well, I did it, old buddy. Beat the shit out of her. Ah, she deserved it. She was a real bitch. I mean the original bitch. Anyway, I was tanked. Really polluted. But randy. Very hot to trot. And do you know what? She turned me down. The bitch would not spread. I couldn't let her get away with that, could I, Dave? I mean, I was really ready for some exotic stuff. Not your missionary position. No, sir. I was going to dick her good. But she said no dice, so I decked her. It felt great.'

Gault paused for effect. David didn't move.

'Have you ever hit a woman? No? It feels terrific. They're soft. They can't take the pain.'

Gault closed his eyes for a moment, and a beatific expression possessed his features.

'Julie was very soft, Dave. Soft in all the right places. And she adored pain. Loved it. So I gave her the ultimate in pain. I gave her death.'

Gault paused and looked directly at David.

'What do you think of that, Dave?'

David didn't know what to say. He felt sick. Gault's face had hardened into a sadistic mask as he talked, and the handsome features looked twisted and grotesque. Then the face split open and Gault began to shake with laughter.

'Oh, you should see your face. God!' he roared between breaths. David was confused by the sudden change.

'It's not true. I made it all up,' the writer gasped. 'What terrific dialogue. You should see your face.'

'I don't . . .' David started.

'It's a joke, son. Get it? A joke. I didn't kill Julie. She was a bitch, all right, and I'm not broken up about her death. But, shit, she was a human being and I'd hate to see anyone go the way she did.'

Gault stopped and David tried to speak. He didn't know whether he wanted to hit Gault or get a drink.

'You son of a bitch,' he said finally.

'Really had you going, didn't I?'

82

'Jesus.'

'Serves you right for thinking I did it in the first place.'

But David didn't know what to think. There had been something about the expression on Gault's face when he was making his confession . . .

'Aren't you going to say anything, old buddy?' Gault asked, his grin spread across his face.

'I don't know what to say,' David answered, his tone betraying some of the anger that had replaced his initial shock and confusion.

'Aw, come on, Dave. You're not mad, are you?'

'Dammit, Tom,' David said, his face flushed, 'that's not something to kid about.'

'Now, that's where you're wrong, boy-o,' Gault answered. 'The first thing you learn when you are soldiering is that Death is a joke. The ultimate prank, old buddy.'

Gault leaned across the desk. He was talking toward David, but David sensed that Gault was speaking to himself.

'Death is everywhere, and never forget that. The more civilized the surroundings, the harder it is to spot the little devil, but he's there, hiding in the laundromat, peeping out from your microwave oven. He's got more camouflage here in Portland, but he's always present.

'Now, there's two ways of dealing with Death, old buddy: you can fear him or you can laugh at him. But I'll tell you the truth: it don't make no difference how you treat him, because he treats us all the same. So when you're in the jungle, where you see Death every day standing buck naked right out in the open, you get to know the little devil real well and you learn that he is a prankster and not a serious dude at all. And you learn that it's better to die laughing than to live each moment in fear.'

Gault stopped abruptly and sat back in his chair.

'I hope I remember that,' he said. 'Be great in my next book, don't you think? Real profound.'

'Very, Tom,' David said, still unsure of what to make of Gault's confession and disconcerted because of his uncertainty. 'Look, do you mind if we work on the book some other time?'

'Hey, I didn't upset you, did I?'

'No, Tom,' David lied, 'I just didn't expect you and I've got some things to do. Why don't we get together sometime next week?'

'Sounds good,' Gault said, standing. 'I'll give you a call.'

Gault started to leave, then stopped with his hand on the doorknob.

'One thing, Dave. If that had been the truth, if I really had killed Julie, would you have kept it a secret?'

'I never reveal a client's confidence.'

'You're all right, old buddy. And you should take care of yourself. You don't look so hot. Get more sleep.'

Gault winked and he was gone.

7

It took David a long time to calm down after Gault left. Was it all a joke? Gault had a sadistic streak in him. He had enjoyed seeing David wriggle on his hook. But when he was discussing the murder, he seemed so sincere, he seemed to be reliving an experience, not creating one. David didn't know what to think, and the worst thing was that the attorney-client privilege prevented him from discussing with anyone what Gault had said.

The intercom buzzed and David was grateful for the diversion. It was Monica calling from the district attorney's office.

'Can you come over, Dave?' she asked.

'Sure. What's up?'

'I want to talk to you about Tony Seals.'

'What about him?'

'I'll tell you when you get here,' she said with a trace of bitterness. 'And bring your shopping cart. We're giving the store away today.'

A NARROW CORRIDOR led back to the depersonalized cubbyholes that passed for offices at the district attorney's office. Monica had seniority and rated

85

a corner cubbyhole somewhat larger than the rest. Her sole attempt at humanizing her work space was a framed Chagall lithograph that added a splash of color to the white and black of her diplomas.

Monica was working on a file when David entered, and she waved him toward a chair. There were two in front of her desk, and he took a stack of files off one and placed them on the floor, then glanced at the newspaper that was draped over the top file on the other chair. Monica looked up.

'I need Seals's testimony and I'll give him immunity to get it,' she said without ceremony.

David said nothing for a second. He was watching Monica's face. When he was certain she was serious, he asked, 'Why do you need his testimony?'

'Because he is the only one other than Zachariah Small who can testify that Sticks pulled the trigger up on the mountain. Without him Sticks will get off.

'We had an informant who heard the three of them talking after they shot Jessie. Sticks and Zack were bragging about shooting her, and it was pretty clear that it was Sticks who shot from the car.'

'Why don't you use your informant?'

'He's gone. He split shortly after we interviewed him. He's a transient who was staying at the Gomes house when the boys were arrested. I guess he got scared when he realized that we wanted him to testify. I've got the police looking for him, but even if we found him, I'm not sure how much good he'd be to us. He has a police record and he's a drunk.'

David was churning inside. He leaned forward slightly.

'We get complete immunity?'

'Yes.'

David stood up. 'I'll talk to my client.'

THE GUARD LED Tony Seals into the interview room at the county jail. The room was long and narrow, and a row of rickety wooden folding chairs was scattered along its length. There was one Formica-topped table at the far end. David sat in front of it, watching his client walk toward him.

'Buzz me when you're through,' the guard said, pointing to a small black button set in a silver metal box under some steam pipes near the barred door. Then he slammed the door shut and David heard the key turn in the lock.

On visiting day this room was usually jammed full of anxious wives and girlfriends, talking in quiet tones to men they might not be making love to for a long time. But this was early on a weekday, and David and his client were alone.

T.S. smelled worse than the last time they had met. There was a body odor that prisoners at the county jail had that was unique and vile. It was the type of smell you could believe would never be scrubbed away.

David searched his client's eyes as the gangly teen-ager shuffled toward him with a loose, puppetlike gait that made him look as if he had straw where bones should be. The eyes were vacant and as lifeless as his perpetual half smile.

'Hi, Mr. Nash,' T.S. said. He had a soft voice that rarely fluctuated with any emotion.

'Sit down, T.S.'

T.S. did as he was told. He always did. David wondered if he had ever initiated an action in his life. Monica was right. It had to have been Sticks and Zachariah. He was dealing with a boy who lacked free will. Another person's creature who got from point A to point B by suggestion only.

'How've you been?'

'Okay, I guess.'

'I want to ask you a few questions, T.S., and I want truthful answers. This is important, so you have to be straight with me.'

'Sure, Mr. Nash.'

'Who shot Jessie when you were down at the hole? The first shot.'

'That was Zack.'

'You didn't shoot her?'

David detected a flicker of fear.

'Honest, Mr. Nash. I didn't never shoot her.'

'And up on the mountain? Who shot at her there?'

The boy's right hand raised slowly and began to pick at a whitehead on his cheek. The tip of Seals's

88

tongue licked his lower lip, then darted back into his mouth.

'Well?'

'Uh . . . well, there was Zack. He done it first, right after we left her. Then we drove off some and Sticks said we should make sure. So we turned around and Sticks asked Zack if he could take a shot and Zack give him the gun.'

David watched T.S. closely. Remembering anything seemed to exhaust him. He wondered what it would be like to go through life with a brain that worked so slowly.

'T.S., did you ever shoot the gun?'

The hand dropped from the pimple and T.S. looked afraid.

'No, honest. They don't say I done it, do they?'

'I want to know.'

'No, no. Zack said he'd let me try, but I was too bummed out. I said no and Sticks just took another shot.'

'What do you mean, bummed out?'

'I was tired,' T.S. said, sagging back in his chair, as if he had forgotten that he had been frightened only seconds before. He went back to worrying the pimple.

'T.S., just between us, if you hadn't been tired, would you have shot her?'

T.S. considered the question and David wondered why he had asked it. What difference did it make? He had won. T.S. would be a free man after he testified at the trials of his former friends, and David would have earned his fee. Why did he need to know the truth about this idiot boy who would soon be at large again?

'Yeah, I guess,' he said. The pimple burst and white pus squeezed through his fingers. David felt cold and alone. The empty room was suddenly too close, and he wanted to get out.

'The district attorney has offered us a deal, T.S. She feels that she needs your testimony to convict Sticks and Zack. If you are willing to testify against them, she will grant you complete immunity. Do you know what that means?'

T.S. shook his head. His fingers were at work on another pimple.

'It means you go free. That they drop the charges against you for shooting Jessie.'

The fingers still worked, the stare was still vacant.

'I can go home?' he finally asked.

'After you've testified.'

'I have to testify in court?'

David nodded.

'Gee, I don't know,' he said. Seals was trying to piece it together. David leaned back and let him think. He was floating and he needed some air. Dizzy. If he had some water.

'I guess it would be okay,' T.S. said finally. There was no excitement, no elation. David wondered if Seals even cared. For T.S. the world was a torment where everything was too complicated. He was a man made for prison where the rules and regulations set him free from the arduous task of having to make decisions.

'You'll have to get on the witness stand in court and say exactly what happened, and you'll have to take a lie-detector test first, so the district attorney can be sure you're being truthful. Will you do that?'

'If you say so,' the boy said. He had stopped picking his face apart and thought for a second. 'I can really go home?'

'Yes, T.S.'

T.S. smiled, but only for a brief moment. Then he looked at David.

'You know, the guys in here said I was lucky to have you as my lawyer. They said you'd beat the rap for me.'

David stood to go. It was very warm in the narrow room and he needed air badly. He looked down at the idiot boy at the table and saw him back on the streets, the way he'd be in six months or a year. Back on drugs. Doing . . . what? Would he pull the trigger next time? Would there be a next time? David knew there would be, because he could see with his own eyes what Tony Seals was. His hands began to itch as if they were very dirty.

'I THOUGHT YOU'D gone home,' Gregory Banks said.

David was sitting in his office in the dark. His

jacket was folded over the back of a chair on the other side of his desk, and his tie was undone. He had turned his desk chair so that it faced the river, where a tugboat flowed with the current like a firefly tracing the path of a piece of carelessly thrown black ribbon.

'Just thinking,' David said. He sounded down.

'Want to talk, or should I leave?'

David swiveled around and faced his friend.

'Do you ever wonder what the hell we're doing, Greg?'

Banks sat down.

'This does sound serious,' he said, half joking.

'I just made a deal with the DA. Tony Seals is going to get complete immunity.'

'That's great!' Gregory said, puzzled by David's mood. He was close to the Sealses, and he knew what this would mean to them.

'Is it? What do I do six months from now when Tony kills someone and his parents want to hire me because I did such a good job today?'

'The DA made the offer, Dave. You were just representing your client.'

'*Jah, mein Herr*, I vas chust following orders,' David said bitterly.

'Why don't you tell me what brought all this on.'

'I don't know, Greg,' David said. Gregory waited patiently for him to continue. 'I guess I've just been taking a good look at the way I earn my living, and

I'm not sure I like what I see. There are people out there hurting other people. The cops arrest them, the prosecutors prosecute them, and I shovel the garbage right back into the street. You know, that's an apt metaphor. Maybe they should start calling us sanitary engineers.'

'I think you're getting a little melodramatic, don't you? What about that kid you helped out? The college kid who got busted with the marijuana. He was guilty of a felony, right? Should he have been convicted? If you hadn't beaten that case, he wouldn't be in medical school. And you beat that case using the same legal arguments you used to get that heroin dealer off last year. You can't have two systems of justice.'

'Maybe not, Greg. Your arguments, as always, are very logical. That's what makes you such a good lawyer. But I just made a deal today that is going to permit a very sick young man, who made a young girl dig her own grave and left her to die, to walk out of jail scot-free.

'You know, when I got into this business, I saw myself as a knight in shining armor defending the innocent, the unjustly accused. How many innocent people have I represented, Greg? After a while you realize there aren't any innocent men, only a lot of guilty ones who can pay pretty good for a smart lawyer. So at first you rationalize what you're doing, but eventually you're just in it for the money.'

'Look, Dave, I know what you're going through.

I've been through it, too. Anyone who practices criminal law and has a conscience has to deal with the conflict between that idealized crap they teach you in law school and the way the real world is, but the picture you're painting isn't accurate either.

'You are a good lawyer and you do good, honest work. There are innocent people who get arrested. There are people, like that college kid, who are guilty but shouldn't be convicted. In order to help them, you have to help people like Tony Seals. It's the system that's important. It's the only thing that keeps this country from being Nazi Germany. You think about that.'

'I do, Greg. Look, I know what you believe and I respect you for it. My problem is, I don't know what I believe in anymore. I know what I used to believe in, and I'm beginning to think I sold that out when the money started getting too good.'

Gregory started to say something, then changed his mind. He remembered the agonies he had gone through over this same question. He never had to find an answer, because he'd stopped taking criminal cases, except those that interested him, when he'd started doing more and more work for the union. Greg had made his fortune by winning big verdicts in personal-injury cases and dealing tough at negotiating sessions for union contracts. Getting out of criminal law was no problem for him.

David was different. He had no interest in any other area of the law. He had tried to branch out, but he had always come back to his criminal practice. And why not? He made a good living at it and he loved what he did. Only now he was beginning to question his worth because of his work.

'You want to go get a drink?' Gregory asked. It was quiet in the evening offices. A few associates staying late to work on problems assigned by the partners made an occasional disturbance in the dark rhythms. David stood up and put on his suit jacket.

'I think I'll just go home.'

'I could tell Helen to set another place for dinner.'

'No, I'd rather be by myself.'

'Okay. Just promise me you won't let this drag you down.'

'I'll try,' David said, making an effort to smile.

After David left, Gregory walked back to his office. He looked at his watch. It was late. He was working too damn late recently. He'd have to cut that out. He sighed. He'd been telling himself that since he started practice, what was it, over twenty years ago. That was a long time, twenty years.

He sat at his desk and started to proofread the brief he had been writing. Poor David. There were advantages to being in your fifties. Growing up was hell and you never really stopped. You thought you did when you got out of your teens. Then you found out that the crises were just starting.

David was a good boy, though. A sound thinker.

What he needed was a case he could believe in. There had been too many hard cases lately. He needed to feel his worth again. A good case would come along. It was the law of averages.

PART II

THE LAST INNOCENT MAN

1

Judge Rosenthal looked across the courtroom toward the clock that hung above the empty jury box. The last witness had just been excused, and there was plenty of time before lunch.

'You might as well argue now, gentlemen,' he said to the two attorneys seated at opposite tables in front of the bench. Walter Greaves struggled to his feet. He had been fighting a battle with arthritis, and, the judge reflected sadly, he seemed to be losing. That was too bad. He'd known Wally for thirty years, and he had a genuine affection for him.

The judge let his eyes wander over to opposing counsel. Larry Stafford provided a perfect contrast to Greaves. He looked so healthy that he made the judge self-conscious about his own physical condition. There had been an upsurge of work during the past few weeks, and he had been passing up his noontime squash games. He was suddenly aware of the pressure of his waistband against his belly. The pressure made him feel guilty and uncomfortable, and he tried to take his mind off it by listening to Greaves's argument.

When Greaves sat down, the judge nodded

at Stafford. The young lawyer had been before Rosenthal on a few occasions representing Price, Winward, Lexington and Rice, Portland's largest law firm. Rosenthal considered him to be conscientious and thorough, if not exceptionally bright.

Stafford was dressed in a lightweight plaid suit that was conservative enough for the courtroom, yet sufficiently summery to fit in with the unseasonably mild September weather. Stafford was just under six feet in height, but his slim, athletic build made him look taller. When he spoke, the pure white of his teeth contrasted with his deep tan. The boy was good-looking enough to be an actor, Rosenthal thought.

'As the Court is aware, and I set this out in full in my trial memorandum, the Uniform Partnership Act permits a limited partner to have some degree of control over the conduct of the business with which he is involved. Mr. Tish has done nothing more than the limited partners did in the Grainger case or the Rathke case. I don't want to go into this too much more, because I'd just be repeating the brief, but I don't see where the plaintiffs have established liability. If the Court has any questions . . .'

'No, Mr. Stafford. I'll tell both of you gentlemen that this question is too close for me to make a decision now. I've read your briefs, and I want some time to do some independent research before resolving this. I'll try to have a written opinion in a week or so. If you have any supplemental authorities, you can submit them in letter form. Anything further?'

The attorneys shook their heads.

'Then we'll adjourn. Have a nice lunch, gentlemen.'

The judge rose and disappeared through a door behind his seat. Larry Stafford started collecting his notes and putting them into his file in an orderly manner. The notes, written in a neat, precise hand, were set out on index cards. Andrew Tish, Stafford's client, asked for an opinion on how the case had gone. Stafford tucked a law book under his arm and hefted his attaché case as he shook his head and started for the courtroom door.

'No way of telling with Rosenthal, Andy. The guy's bright, and he'll give a lot of thought to the case. That's about all I can say.'

Walter Greaves was waiting in the hall outside the courtroom.

'Larry.'

Stafford stopped and asked Tish to wait for him.

'I talked with my people, and they're willing to come down on the settlement offer.'

'I'll tell Tish, but I'm going to advise him to hang tough.'

'I'm just conveying my client's offer.'

Stafford smirked and walked down the hall that led to the elevators. The courthouse had four corridors that ran along the sides of an empty central shaft. Greaves picked up his briefcase and walked toward the rear of the building. He did not like dealing with Stafford. He was too cocky. Very . . . superficial – that was the word. Nothing under the surface. Come on like Mr. Nice Guy one minute, then you find out you've been double-crossed. And in this case it had not been necessary to do some of the borderline ethical things the boy had done. Hell, Stafford had him dead to rights. His clients were just trying anything they could to prop up a dying business. Greaves shook his head and moved aside to get out of the way of a young man dressed in jeans and a work shirt. This young man had a dark complexion, a shaggy black mustache, and thick black hair and he was staring down the corridor toward Judge Rosenthal's courtroom.

'AND THEN WHAT happened, Officer Ortiz?'

'My job was to wait outside the residence in case any of the suspects attempted to escape. The other officers went inside to execute the search warrant, and Officer Lesnowski and I waited near the front of the building.'

'Did you actually take part in the search?'

'No, I did not.'

'What happened then?'

'Shortly after, Officers Teske and Hennings exited the residence with the two prisoners and a bag containing evidence. Officer Teske gave me the evidence bag, and he and Hennings drove to the station house with the prisoners.'

'Did you talk with either of the prisoners or look in the bag?'

'No, sir.'

'I have no further questions, Your Honor.'

Judge McDonald nodded toward the public defender, who was conferring with his client, a teenage black man accused of possession of cocaine. Ortiz relaxed. He had been cross-examined by this asshole before, and he expected the interrogation to be long and stupid, even though he had no information of interest to anyone.

But the prospect of cross-examination didn't bother him. He was happy just being back at work. First there had been the stay in the hospital, then the vacation he had not really wanted to take. The department had insisted, though. It wanted him to rest and get his memory back, because his memory was the only thing the department had left in the Darlene Hersch case.

He had dropped in on Crosby before going to court, and nothing had changed. No fingerprints, no other witnesses, no leads. Crosby had moved around the edges, not wanting to ask the question directly. Probably under the orders of some department shrink. So Ortiz had answered the unspoken question. Nothing had changed. He still had trouble sorting out what had happened. His memory was getting better every day, but it blurred and faded, and even when his idea of things seemed clear, he could not be sure if what he was seeing was what had really happened.

The public defender was still gabbing, and Ortiz shifted in his chair in the witness box. Thinking about his memory and that night had spoiled the feeling of peace he had experienced when he had started giving testimony. It was Darlene that troubled him. He was afraid of the pictures he would see when his memory came back. Afraid that he had been responsible for her death. Everyone assured him that it wasn't so, but how did they know? How could they be so sure of what had happened that night?

The public defender looked up from his notes. Ortiz waited for the questions, grateful for a chance to escape from his own thoughts.

'Officer Ortiz, what happened to Officer Murdock and Officer Elvin after Teske and Hennings left the scene?'

'They remained in the residence.'

'Thank you, I have no further questions.'

'You're excused,' the judge said. Ortiz was surprised he had gotten off so easily. Maybe the schmuck was learning.

Jack Hennings, Ortiz's partner, looked up from his newspaper when the courtroom door opened.

'You're on,' Ortiz said.

Hennings handed the paper to Mike Elvin and went through the door. Ortiz turned toward Elvin to ask for the sports section when he noticed two men talking at the other end of the corridor. His hand started to shake and his chest felt suddenly constricted. The two men concluded their conversation, and the older man walked toward him. Ortiz did not see him. His eyes were riveted on the younger man – the blond. He had started down the hall that led to the elevators, but Ortiz was seeing him in a different place. He was remembering a man with curly blond hair walking quickly along the landing that ran outside the rooms at the Raleigh Motel, and he was seeing a face spotlighted for a moment in the doorway of the motel room where Darlene Hersch had died.

The older man passed him, and the blond disappeared around the corner.

'Tell Jack to wait for me,' he said to Elvin. Elvin looked up, but Ortiz was already halfway down the corridor.

There was no one in the hall when Ortiz reached the corner. He looked up at the floor indicator. Both elevator cars had reached the ground floor. Ortiz walked back toward Judge Rosenthal's courtroom. The law student who served as the judge's clerk was reading a textbook in the empty courtroom and munching on a sandwich.

'Excuse me,' Ortiz said. The boy looked up.

'There was a lawyer in here just now, with blond hair. Can you tell me who he is?'

'Why do you ask?' the boy asked suspiciously.

Ortiz realized that he was dressed for undercover work and looked as grubby as the degenerates he had to mix with. He walked across the room and flashed his badge.

'Now, can you tell me his name?'

The boy studied his badge, then hesitated. Ortiz knew he was thinking about the constitutional rights his professors had told him he had.

'I don't know if – ' the boy began.

'You'd better,' Ortiz said softly, and there must have been something in his tone, because the boy spoke.

'Stafford. Larry Stafford.'

'And where does he work?'

'The Price, Winward firm. It's in the Standard Plaza Building.'

Ortiz put his badge away and headed for the door. Halfway there, he stopped and turned.

'This is official police business, you hear, and I don't want this mentioned to anyone. If it gets back to me that you opened your mouth, you're in serious trouble.'

There was a pay phone near the elevators. The phone book had two listings for Lawrence Dean Stafford. Ortiz wrote them both down; then he called homicide. Ron Crosby answered.

'This is Bert Ortiz, Ron. I want you to check something for me. I need the make of car for Lawrence Dean Stafford, 22310 Newgate Terrace.'

'Why do you want to know?'

'Just do it for me by this afternoon, okay? I'll be back to you.'

'Does this have something to do with the Hersch case?'

'Everything.'

THE LUNCH HOUR crawled by and Ortiz made his second call to Crosby shortly after one.

'I've got your information,' the detective said quietly. The tension on the other end of the line was the tip-off. Crosby had struck pay dirt. 'There are two cars registered to Lawrence Dean Stafford. The first is a Porsche and the second is a Mercedes-Benz.'

Ortiz said nothing. He was cradling the phone and staring at the wall of the phone booth, without seeing it or feeling the plastic thing in his hand. He was back on Morrison Street and the Mercedes was right in front of him.

'Is this your man, Bert?'

'I think so, but I have to see his face.'

'You saw the killer's face?'

'Before I blacked out. I know the man's face.'

'Where are you? I'll be right over.'

'No. Let me handle this. You get a DA and have a judge on standby to issue a search warrant. I want to be sure.'

'What are you going to do?'

'Follow him. If it's the car, I'll know. Then we can search for the clothes. But I want it all legal. I don't want this one to slip away.'

*

107

'PRICE, WINWARD, LEXINGTON and Rice,' the receptionist said in a pleasing singsong.

'I'd like to speak to Larry Stafford.'

'Who shall I say is calling?'

'Stan Reynolds. I was referred to Mr. Stafford by an old friend.'

'Please hold and I'll see if Mr. Stafford is in.'

There was a click and the line went dead. Ortiz held the receiver to his ear and waited. Thirty seconds later there was another click.

'This is Larry Stafford, Mr. Reynolds. Can I help you?'

'I hope so. I'm in a kind of a bind and I was told you're the man to see. I run a small construction company. Spec housing. I'm doin' pretty good now financially, but I'm beginnin' to have some hassles with my partner, and I need some advice fast.'

'Well . . .' Stafford said, and Ortiz could hear paper rattling, 'I've got a spot open tomorrow at . . . Let's see. How about three o'clock?'

Ortiz was taking in the voice and trying to size up the man. The voice had strong, confident qualities, but there was a slick gloss to the tones, as if the timbre and pitch were learned, not natural.

'Gee, I was hopin' I could see you today.'

'I'm afraid I have a pretty full schedule for the rest of the afternoon.'

'I see,' Ortiz said. He paused, as if thinking, then asked, 'How late will you be at your office?'

'My last appointment should be over at seven.'

Ortiz paused again.

'Well, I guess I can wait until tomorrow.'

'Good. I'll see you then.'

They hung up and Ortiz stepped out of the booth. He was across the street from the Standard Plaza. The light changed and he crossed the street. It took him ten minutes to find the beige Mercedes in the underground garage. It was near the fire door toward the rear of the second parking level. He checked the license number against the number Crosby had given him; then he left the building. All he had to do now was wait for seven o'clock.

ABNER ROSENTHAL WAS a small, dapper man with a large legal reputation. He had made a fortune as a corporate lawyer, then taken an enormous cut in salary to become a circuit-court judge. It was common knowledge that he had passed up several opportunities to be appointed to the state supreme court because he enjoyed being a trial judge. Rosenthal especially liked criminal cases, and he had developed an expertise in the area of search-and-seizure law. The police usually sought him out when they needed a search warrant in a particularly sensitive case.

The doorbell rang just as the judge was finishing dinner. His teenage son started to stand, but Rosenthal waved him down. Monica Powers had called him earlier to alert him that there was a breakthrough in the Darlene Hersch case.

PHILLIP M. MARGOLIN

'Sorry to bother you, Judge,' Monica said when the door opened. 'Do you know Ron Crosby and Bert Ortiz?'

'I've met Detective Crosby before,' the judge said as he led them into his den. 'I don't believe I know Officer Ortiz.'

As soon as they were seated, Monica handed the judge the search warrant and the affidavit Ortiz had sworn to in support of it. The affidavit set out all the information that Ortiz felt supported his belief that Lawrence Dean Stafford had murdered Darlene Hersch and that evidence of that crime could be found in Stafford's house. The judge looked grim when he finished reading it. He looked at Ortiz long enough to make the policeman feel uncomfortable.

'Are you aware that Larry Stafford was in my courtroom this very day, Officer Ortiz?'

'Yes, sir.'

Rosenthal reread a section of the affidavit.

'I've read this, but I want you to tell me. Are you positive that Larry Stafford is the man you saw at the motel?'

Ortiz's mouth felt dry. Was he positive? Could he have made a mistake? No. He had waited outside Stafford's office at seven. He had seen Stafford leave the office. He had seen the face of Darlene's killer.

'Larry Stafford killed Darlene Hersch,' Ortiz answered, but there was a slight quiver in his voice.

'And you, Miss Powers?'

110

'I don't like this any more than you do, Judge, but I've worked with Officer Ortiz before, and I trust his judgment.'

The judge took a pen out of his pocket.

'I'm going to sign this warrant, but you'd better keep a tight lid on this if you don't make an arrest. This case is going to be sensational. If you're wrong,' he said, looking directly at Ortiz, 'the publicity alone will be enough to destroy Larry Stafford's career at a firm like Price, Winward. Do you understand me?'

'Yes, sir,' Ortiz said.

No one spoke when Rosenthal signed the warrant. Monica picked up the documents and they left, Monica for home and Ortiz, Crosby, and a second carload of men for Larry Stafford's house.

NEWGATE TERRACE WAS a long, winding, tree-lined country road fifteen minutes from down-town Portland. At uneven intervals driveways led the way to expensive homes, few of which were visible from the street. Stafford's home was at the end of a stretch of straight road. A row of tall hedges screened the house from view, and the policemen were not able to see it until they had driven a short distance up the driveway. The house was a two-story Tudor design painted a traditional brown and white. The grounds had the well-manicured look of professional care, and there were several large shade trees. The driveway circled in front of the house, and Ortiz imagined the

PHILLIP M. MARGOLIN

Mercedes parked in the garage that adjoined it on the left.

The young woman who answered the door was puzzled by the appearance of two carloads of uniformed policemen at her doorstep.

'Mrs. Stafford?' Ron Crosby asked.

'Yes,' the woman answered with a tentative smile.

'Is your husband home?'

'Yes.'

'Could you please ask him to come to the door?'

'What's this all about?'

'We have a matter to go over with your husband. I'd appreciate it if you would get him.'

The woman hesitated for a second, as if hoping for more of an explanation. She got none.

'If you'll wait here, I'll get him,' she said, and walked toward the end of the hall, disappearing around the back of a staircase that led upstairs from the foyer. Ortiz watched her go and his stomach tightened. In a few moments the man who killed Darlene Hersch would come down that hall.

Ortiz was in uniform, and he had placed himself at the rear of the small group of policemen. He wanted a long second look at Stafford before the lawyer got an opportunity to recognize him. Crosby and two policemen had stepped into the foyer to await Mrs. Stafford's return. A moment later Larry Stafford, dressed in Bermuda shorts and a red-and-black-striped rugby shirt, walked down the carpeted corridor. His wife trailed behind, more visibly worried now.

'What can I do for you?' he asked with a wide smile. Ortiz concentrated on the face. There was so much light in the hallway, and there had been so little in the motel room. Still, he was sure. It was him.

Crosby handed Stafford the search warrant. Ortiz watched him carefully as he read it. If Stafford was nervous or upset, he did not show it.

'I'm afraid I don't understand . . . What did you say your name was?'

'Crosby. Detective Ron Crosby, Mr. Stafford.'

'Well, Detective Crosby, I don't understand what this is all about.'

'That is a search warrant, Mr. Stafford. It is an authorization by a judge to search your house for the items listed in the warrant.'

'I can see it's a search warrant,' Stafford said with a trace of impatience. 'What I want to know is why you feel it is necessary to invade my privacy in the middle of the night and rummage through my personal effects.'

'I'd prefer not to go into that right now, Mr. Stafford,' Crosby said quietly. 'If you'll just permit us to do what we came for, we won't take much of your time.'

Stafford scanned the warrant again.

113

'Judge Rosenthal signed this warrant?' he asked incredulously.

'Yes, sir.'

Stafford said nothing for a moment. There seemed to be a private war waging inside him. Then he relaxed.

'Search if you want to. I'm sorry if I gave you a hard time. It's just that I've never had anything like this happen before. I'll even make it easy for you. I own several sport shirts of this type,' he said, indicating the list of clothing set out in the warrant, 'and at least three pair of tan slacks. Why don't you come up to my room and I'll show you. Then, if you're not satisfied, you can search the house.'

Stafford was not reacting the way Ortiz had expected him to. The man was too self-possessed. Maybe he was wrong. After all, he had gotten only a fast look at the murderer's face, and he was dazed and in pain at the time. And there was the lighting. No, there had been enough light. The globe outside the motel room was very bright. Still, it had been so fast.

Stafford started to climb the stairs to the second floor with his wife close behind. Ortiz stayed to the rear as several officers followed Crosby. Two men stationed themselves in the foyer.

Stafford's bedroom was toward the rear of the house. It was bright and airy and had a decidedly masculine feel about it. A sliding glass door

114

led to a small balcony, and Ortiz glanced out into the darkness. A twin bed sat against the north wall. It was unmade, and the edge of one of the blankets touched the hardwood floor. A large walk-in closet occupied the east wall, and an expensive-looking chest of drawers stood to their right as the party entered the room. Stafford pulled out one of the middle drawers and stood back.

'My sport shirts are in here. My slacks are in the closet.'

Crosby signaled to Ortiz and the policeman stepped over to the closet. He opened the louvered doors and started to examine several pairs of slacks that hung on a long row of wooden hangers. He pushed several aside before stopping at a pair of tan slacks. He wasn't positive, but they were close. It was the shirt he could be sure about. The flowered pattern was distinctive.

He finished sorting through the hangers, then walked back down the line and selected the tan pants. He looked at Stafford. The man had not changed his expression of detached interest, and he had given no indication that he recognized Ortiz.

'Let me see the shirts,' he said to Crosby. The detective stepped back, and Ortiz carefully lifted one shirt after another out of the drawer, placing them in a neat pile on top of the chest of drawers. Midway down, he stopped. It was

115

sitting there. A shirt of brown and forest-green with a leaf-and-flower design. The shirt that the man who killed Darlene Hersch had been wearing. Ortiz called Crosby aside, and the two men conferred in the corridor. Mrs. Stafford stood on one side of the room, nervously shifting her attention between her husband and the door to the hallway. Crosby and Ortiz reentered the room. They looked grim. There were two other policemen with them. That made a total of six officers, and the large bedroom was beginning to shrink in size.

'Mr. Stafford, I am going to have to place you under arrest.'

Mrs. Stafford blanched, and her husband's composure began to slip.

'What do you mean? Now, see here. I . . .'

'Before you say anything, Mr. Stafford, I have to advise you concerning your constitutional rights.'

'My rights! Are you insane? Now, I've cooperated with you and let you into my home. What nonsense is this? What am I being arrested for?'

Crosby looked at Stafford, and Ortiz watched for a reaction.

'I am arresting you for the murder of Darlene Hersch.'

'Who?' Stafford asked, his brows knitting in puzzlement. Mrs. Stafford's hand flew to her mouth, and Ortiz heard her say, 'My God.' Crosby began reciting Stafford's Miranda rights.

'You have a right to remain silent. If you choose to—'

'Wait a second. Wait a second. Who is Darlene Hersch? Is this a joke?'

'Mr. Stafford, this is no joke. Now, I know you're an attorney, but I am going to explain your rights to you anyway, and I want you to listen carefully.'

Mrs. Stafford edged over to her husband with a slow, sideways, crablike movement. Stafford was beginning to look scared. Crosby finished reciting Stafford's rights and took a pair of handcuffs from his rear pocket.

'Why don't you change into a pair of long pants and a long-sleeved shirt?' Crosby said. 'And I'm going to have to cuff you. I'm sorry about that, but it's a procedure I have to follow.'

'Now, you listen to me. I happen to be an attorney—'

'I know, Mr. Stafford.'

'Then you know that as of right now you are going to be on the end of one hell of a lawsuit.'

'Getting excited is not going to help your situation, Mr. Stafford. I'd suggest that you keep calm and have your wife contact an attorney.

'Mrs. Stafford,' Crosby said, turning his attention to the lawyer's wife, 'you had better contact an attorney to represent your husband. He will be at the county jail within the hour.'

117

The woman acted as if she had not heard Crosby. Stafford started toward her, stopped, and looked at Crosby.

'May I talk to my wife in private for a moment?'

'I can send most of my men out, but someone will have to stay in the room.'

Stafford started to say something, then stopped. He seemed to be back in control.

'That would be fine.'

Stafford waited to go to his wife until all but one policeman had left. She looked confused and frightened.

'Larry, what's going on?'

Stafford took her by the shoulders and led her to the far corner of the room.

'This is obviously some mistake. Now, call Charlie Holt. Tell him what happened and where I am. Charlie will know what to do.'

'He said murder, Larry.'

'I know what he said,' Stafford said firmly. 'Now, do as I say. Believe me, it will be all right.'

Stafford changed his clothes and his wife watched in silence. When Stafford was finished, Crosby put on the handcuffs and escorted the prisoner downstairs. Ortiz watched Stafford closely. He said nothing as they led him to the car. He walked with assurance, his back straight and his shoulders squared. Mrs. Stafford stood alone in the open doorway. Ortiz watched her shrink in the distance as they drove away.

2

'There's a Mr. Holt to see you, Mr. Nash,' the receptionist said. "He says it's urgent."

David looked at his watch. It was eight-thirty. He had been at the office since seven working on a brief that was due in two days, and he was only half-done. He was tempted to tell Charlie to come back, but Charlie would not be at his office this early unless there was an emergency. He sighed.

'Tell him I'll be right out.'

He finished editing a paragraph and carefully moved his work to one side. He placed an empty legal pad on his blotter, straightened his tie, and put on his suit jacket.

Charlie Holt was pacing in front of the bar that separated clients from the well-endowed redhead who served as the receptionist at Banks, Kelton, Skaarstad and Nash. Only Charlie was not looking at the girl. His eyes were straining toward the swinging doors that opened onto the lawyers' offices. Charlie was a tall, balding securities lawyer who had never lost the military bearing he had acquired in the Marines. His movements were always sharp and jerky, as if he were on parade. It was an exhausting experience spending

time with Charlie: you always felt like a passenger
in a sports car driving on a winding mountain road
at top speed.

David pushed through the swinging doors and
Charlie rushed toward him.

'Thanks, Dave,' Holt said quickly, pumping
David's hand. 'Big trouble. Sorry to interrupt so
early.'

'That's okay. What's up?' David asked as he led
Holt back down the corridor to his office.

'Larry Stafford, one of our associates. Do you
know him?'

'I think I met him at the bar-association dinner
last month.'

Charlie sat down without being asked. He looked
at the floor and shook his head like a man who had
given up hope.

'Really shocking.'

'What is?'

Holt's head jerked up. 'You didn't read it in the
papers?'

'I've been here since seven.'

'Oh. Well, it's front page. Bad for the firm.' He
paused for a moment and thought. 'Worse for Larry.
He's been arrested. Wife called me last night. In tears.
Doesn't know what to do. Can I help? I went out to
the jail, but I'm no criminal lawyer. Hell, I'd never
even seen the jail before this morning. Your name
naturally came to mind, if you'll take it.'

'Take what, Charlie? What's he charged with?'

'Murder.'

'Murder?'

Holt nodded vigorously.

'They say he killed that policewoman. The one who was pretending to be a prostitute.'

David whistled and sat down slowly.

'He's very upset. Made me promise to get you out there as soon as I could.'

Holt stopped talking and waited for David to say something. David started to doodle on the legal pad. A lawyer. And that murder. That was a hot potato. Lots of press and TV coverage. A good investigation, too. The police were not going to go off half-cocked and look bad later. They would make damn sure they had a good case before they moved. And it would be better than damn good before they arrested an associate from the biggest and most influential law firm in the city. Hell, half the politicians in town had received sizable contributions from Seymour Price.

'Who's footing the bill, Charlie? This will cost plenty.'

'Jennifer. Mrs. Stafford. They have savings. She has family. I asked her and she said they could manage.'

'What do they have on him, Charlie?'

Holt shrugged. 'I don't know. I told you, I'm no criminal lawyer. I wouldn't even know who to ask.'

'What do the papers say?'

'Oh, right. Something about an eyewitness.

Another policeman. Jennifer says they searched the house and took some of Larry's shirts and pants.'

'That's right,' David said, remembering one of the newspaper stories he'd read. 'Bert Ortiz was working with her and got knocked unconscious. But I didn't know he'd seen the killer.'

'You know this Ortiz?'

'Sure. He's a vice cop. He's been a witness in several cases I've tried.'

'Will you go out and see Stafford?'

David looked at the half-finished brief. Did he want to get involved in a case this heavy right now?

'Jennifer swears he didn't do it. Says they were home together the night the girl was killed.'

'She does? Do you believe her? After all, she is his wife.'

'You don't know Jenny. She's a peach. No, if she says so . . .'

David smiled, then laughed softly. Holt looked at him quizzically.

'I'm sorry, Charlie. It's just that you don't run across too many innocent men in this business. They're about as rare as American eagles.'

David felt a surge of excitement at the thought. An honest-to-goodness innocent man. It was worth a look. He'd finish the brief tonight.

'AM I GLAD to see you,' Larry Stafford said. The guard closed the door of the private interview room, and David stood up to shake hands. Stafford was dressed in an ill-fitting jumpsuit.

'Sit down, Larry,' David said, indicating a plastic chair.

'How soon can you get me out of this place?' Stafford asked. He was trying to keep calm, but there was an under-current of panic flowing behind his pale-blue eyes and country-club tan.

'We'll be in front of a judge later this morning, but this is a murder case, and there's no requirement that the judge set bail.'

'I . . . I thought they always . . . there was always bail.'

'Not on a murder charge. If the DA opposes bail, we can ask for a bail hearing. But there's no guarantee that the judge will set an amount after the hearing, if the DA can convince the court that you may be guilty. And even if the judge does set an amount for bail, it could be high and you might not be able to make it.'

'I see,' Stafford said quietly. He was trying to sit straight and talk in the assured tone he used when conferring with attorneys representing other people. Only he was the client, and the news that he might have to remain in jail caused a slight erosion in his demeanor. A slumping of the shoulders and a downcasting of the eyes indicated to David that the message was starting to get through.

'On the other hand,' David said, 'you are an attorney with a good job. You're married. I doubt the district attorney's office will oppose bail, and if they do, I'm pretty sure most of the judges in the courthouse would grant it.'

Stafford brightened as he clutched at the straw David had held out to him. David did not like to build up a client's hopes, but in this case he was certain that his evaluation of the bail situation was accurate.

'How have you been treated?' David asked.

Stafford shrugged.

'Pretty well, considering. They put me by myself in a small cell in the, uh, "isolation." '

'Solitary.'

'Yes.' Stafford took a deep breath and looked away for a second. 'All these terms. I never . . . I don't handle criminal cases.' He laughed, but it was forced laughter, and he moved uncomfortably on the narrow seat. 'I never wanted to get involved in it. Now I wish I'd taken a few more courses in law school.'

'Have the police tried to interview you yet?'

'Oh, yeah. Right away. They've been very polite. Very considerate. Detective Crosby. Ron is his first name, I think. Treated me very well.'

'Did you say anything to him, Larry?'

'No, except that I didn't do anything. He . . . he read me my rights.' Stafford laughed nervously again. 'Just like television. I'm still having a hard time taking this seriously. I half believe it's some fraternity prank. I don't even know anything about the case.'

'What did you say to the police?' David asked quietly. He was watching Stafford closely. People who were not used to the police or prison situations often talked voluminously to police detectives who were trained to be polite and considerate. Once the prisoner was cut off from his friends and family, he would open up to any concerned person in hopes of getting support. The voluntary statements of helpless men were often the most damaging pieces of evidence used to convict them.

'I didn't say anything. What could I say? I don't know anything about this.'

'Okay. Now, I want to say a few things to you and I want you to listen very carefully. I am going to explain the attorney-client relationship to you. I know you are a lawyer by profession, but right now you are a prisoner charged with murder, and the lawyer in you is not going to be functioning very well, because people are never very objective when they are dealing with their own problems.'

Larry nodded. He was leaning forward, concentrating on every word.

'First, anything you tell me is confidential. That means that not only won't I tell anyone what you say to me, but I cannot, by law, reveal the contents of our conversations.

'Next, you should tell me the truth when we discuss this case. Not because I will be offended if you lie to me, but because if you tell me something that is not true, I may go off half-cocked in reliance upon what you've said and do something that will hurt your case.'

David stopped and let the point sink in. Stafford looked very uncomfortable.

'Dave . . . look, I want to get one thing clear. I'm not going to lie to you, because I didn't do anything. I have nothing to lie about. This whole thing is one ridiculous mistake, and I can promise you that I am going to sue those bastards for every cent in the city treasury when I'm finished with this business. But there is one thing I want to get straight between you and me. I . . . I have to be sure that the lawyer who represents me believes me. I mean, if you think I'm lying . . . well, I don't lie, and when I say I'm innocent, I am innocent.'

David looked straight at Stafford, and Stafford returned his stare without wavering.

'Larry, what I'm telling you I tell every one of the people I represent, and I tell them for a reason. Let me make one thing clear to you. You don't want a lawyer who believes you. You want a lawyer who will clear you of the charges against you. This isn't Disneyland. This is the Multnomah County Jail, and there are a large number of well-trained people in this county who, at this very moment, are conspiring to take away your liberty for the rest of your life. I am the only person who stands between you and prison, and I will do everything in my power, whether I believe you or not, to keep you out of prison.

'If you want someone to hold your hand and say

that they believe you and tell you what a good guy you are, there's a baby-sitting service I know of that can take care of that. If you want to get off, that's another matter, and I'll be glad to take your case.'

Stafford looked down at the floor. When he looked up, he was flushed.

'I'm sorry,' he said, 'it's just that . . .'

'It's just that you're scared and cut off from your family and friends, and you're confused and you want to know that someone is on your side. Well, I'm on your side, Larry, and so is your wife and Charlie Holt and a lot of other people.'

'I guess you're right. It's just so . . . so frustrating. I was sitting in my cell and thinking. I don't even know how this happened.'

'It has happened, though. And that's what we have to deal with. Can you tell me where you were on the evening of June sixteenth and the early-morning hours of June seventeenth?'

'Is that when the murder occurred?'

David nodded.

'What day of the week was that? A weekday or weekend?'

'June sixteenth was a Thursday.'

'Okay. Without my appointment book and talking with a few people, I couldn't say for sure, but I probably worked at the office and went home.'

'How late do you usually work?'

'I put in pretty long hours. I'm still an associate at Price, Winward. Hoping to make partner pretty

soon, but you know what that's like. And I had a
fairly complicated securities case I was working on
about that time. I was probably at the office until
seven at least. It could have been later. I really can't
say until I see my book.'

'Who would have that?'

'Jennifer. My wife.'

David made a note on a yellow lined legal pad.

'Let's talk about you for a bit. How old are
you?'

'Thirty-five.'

'Education?'

'I went to law school at Lewis and Clark,' Stafford
said. David nodded. Lewis and Clark was a private
law school located in Portland.

'I was back east for my undergraduate work.'

'Are you from the East Coast?'

'That's hard to answer. My father was in the
military. We traveled a lot. Then my folks got
divorced, and I lived with Mom on Long Island,
New York, until I went into the Army.'

'You were in the service?'

Stafford nodded.

'Was that before or after college?'

'After college and before law school.'

'Did you go to work for Price, Winward right
after law school?'

'Yes. I've been there ever since,' Stafford said.
David noticed something peculiar in the way Stafford
answered, but he moved on.

'Larry, have you ever been convicted of a crime?'

'I had some trouble in high school. Minor in possession of beer. But that was cleared up.'

'I'm only interested in criminal situations after the age of eighteen where you were either found guilty by a jury or by a judge or pleaded guilty.'

'Oh, no. I never had anything like that.'

There was a knock on the door and the guard stuck his head in.

'He's got to go to court soon, Mr. Nash.'

'How much time have I got, Al?'

'I can give you five minutes.'

'Okay. Just knock when you're ready.'

The door closed, and David started collecting his material and placing it in his attaché case.

'We'll finish this later. I'll meet you at the courthouse.'

'I'm sorry about that business before. About . . .'

David stopped him.

'Larry, you're under more pressure now than I've ever been, and I think you're holding up very well, considering. I'm going to try to find out what the DA has on you, then I'll meet with you again and we'll start plotting strategy. Try to relax as much as you can. This is out of your hands now, and there isn't much you can do. So try not to brood about the case. I know that that's impossible advice to follow, but you pay me to do your worrying, and you'll be wasting your money if you do that part of my work for me.'

Stafford smiled. It was a broad, brave smile. He grasped David's hand in a firm grip.

'I want to thank you for taking this case. I feel much more confident now with you on it. You've got quite a reputation, if you don't know that already. And one more thing. I know you said it didn't matter, and I believe you, but I want you to know that I am innocent. I really am.'

THE PHONE RANG just as Monica was leaving her office. She hesitated for a moment, then answered it.

'Monica, this is Ron Crosby.'

'Oh, hi, Ron. I was just on my way up to arraign Stafford, and I'm going to be late. Can I call you back?'

'No. Hold on. This is about Stafford. Does he get out on bail today?'

'I talked it over with the boss, and we're not opposing bail if David asks for it.'

'I see. Look, I may be onto something and . . . I don't think he should be out.'

'Why not?'

'Do you remember when we were talking? We figured Stafford was getting a little on the side without risking the dangers and entanglements of an affair. So he picks up a prostitute and panics when he finds out she's a policewoman.'

'That's what I think,' Monica said. 'His wife is the one with the money. If there was a divorce, it would hurt him more than her.'

THE LAST INNOCENT MAN

'Right. That's what everyone was thinking. We saw Darlene as a policewoman. But she was posing as a prostitute. Maybe she was killed because Stafford thought she was a prostitute.'

'I don't get you.'

'I did some checking on Stafford. He's never been convicted of a crime or even arrested for one, but I did come up with something. This isn't the first time Larry Stafford's had problems with a whore.'

THE GUARD OPENED the steel door of the holding tank and told Larry it was time to go to court. He was polite and more deferential than he had been with the other prisoners. It made Larry feel uncomfortable. Another guard opened the door that connected the holding area to the courtroom. Larry hesitated at the threshold. He wanted to crawl inside himself and disappear. David had arranged for him to have the dignity of his own clothes, so that he did not have to parade in the uniform of a prisoner before all these people he knew, but the clothes did not prevent him from feeling shame and that nauseated feeling in the pit of his stomach that had grown worse since his arrest.

There was an embarrassed quiet when Stafford was led into the courtroom. Other lawyers looked away. The judge, a man he had appeared before only last week, occupied himself with a loose stack of papers. The bailiff, a young night student with whom he had sometimes chatted during court recess, would not look at him.

David hurried to Stafford's side and began telling him what would happen. Larry wanted to see Jennifer, but he could not bring himself to look at the packed courtroom. He felt he could hold himself together if he stared forward. He wanted to numb all feeling, freeze his heart, and melt away.

They were through the bar of the court now and standing in front of Judge Sturgis. An attractive woman was reading the charge against him, but he could not associate the words she was saying with himself. It was some other Larry Stafford she was talking about. And all the time, he concentrated on a spot just above the judge's head and tried to stand erect.

'Your Honor, I am David Nash, and I will be representing Mr. Stafford in this matter.'

'Very good, Mr. Nash.'

'Your Honor, I would like to raise the matter of bail. Mr. Stafford was arrested last night. As the Court knows, he is a member of the bar, he is married, and he is practicing with a well-respected firm . . .'

'Yes, Mr. Nash,' the judge interrupted. He turned toward Monica Powers.

'Is there any opposition to the setting of bail at this time, Ms. Powers?'

'Yes, Your Honor. The State would be opposed to the setting of bail at this time.'

David started to say something, then thought better of it. Instead, he addressed the Court. 'We would like to have a bail hearing scheduled as quickly as possible then, Your Honor.'

Monica turned toward him.

'I should tell counsel that we are taking this case directly to the grand jury this afternoon, and we expect to arraign Mr. Stafford in circuit court in one to two days.'

'We'll set a hearing date anyway, Ms. Powers,' Judge Sturgis said. 'You can reset the hearing in circuit court if an indictment is handed down, Mr. Nash.'

'Do I have to stay in jail?' Stafford whispered.

'Yes,' David said. He looked at Monica, but she seemed uncomfortable and looked away from him, he thought, intentionally.

'But I thought—'

'I know. I don't know what's going on, but I'll find out as soon as this is over.'

The clerk set a hearing date and David marked it on his folder. The next case was called and Monica started to leave. David touched her elbow.

'Can I talk to you for a second?'

She looked undecided, then nodded.

'I'll wait for you in the hall,' she said, then hurried out.

'Larry, I'll be in touch soon. I want to find out why there was opposition to your bail.'

'You've got to get me out of here,' Stafford said.

The guard was gesturing Stafford back toward the holding area, and a new prisoner was being led into the courtroom. 'You don't know what it's like in that place.'

'We'll have a hearing on the bail in a few days and get this cleared up. I—'

'I don't know if I can take it in that stinking hole for two more days. I want out now, dammit. That's why I hired you.'

David stopped and looked directly at Stafford. His voice was quiet, but firm.

'Larry, you have to start adjusting to the fact that, guilty or innocent, you are accused of a crime. You may not be able to get out of jail. The DA may convince the judge that bail is inappropriate. You have to get hold of yourself or you are going to be a mess by the time we get to trial.'

Stafford was breathing heavily, and David could see the rapid beating of a pulse near his temple. Suddenly, he sagged and his breathing quieted.

'You're right. I'm sorry. I should know enough about the courts to know that nothing is going to happen right away. There's no reason it should be any different because I'm the one in trouble.'

'Good. I'm glad you understand that. I'll see you soon, Larry.'

MONICA WAS STANDING in the hall near the elevators.

'What was that all about?' David asked.

'Our office is opposed to your client's release on bail.'

'You made that quite obvious in there,' he said, pointing over his shoulder. 'I want to know why. Stafford's no junkie who's going to split the minute the jail door opens. He's married, with a job—'

'I know all that. It makes no difference.'

'Why? What have you got on him?'

'You'll get all your discovery in the normal course when he's arraigned in circuit court,' Monica said abruptly. Something was upsetting her.

'I know all about discovery procedures, Monica. I'm asking you now, as a colleague who's—'

'Look, David, I'm putting you on notice. This one is different. No breaks and nothing that isn't procedure according to the books.'

'Whoa. Slow down. I've always been square with you, haven't I?'

'Yes. And this has nothing to do with you or me. This one is different, and I mean it. There is more to this case than you know.'

'Like what?'

The elevator door opened and Monica stepped inside.

'I can't discuss it and I won't. I'm sorry.'

David watched the door close and turned back toward the courtroom. Monica had never acted this way before, and it troubled him. When they had a case together, they discussed it. They tried to be as honest with each other as the rules of the game

135

allowed. David's initial impression of Larry Stafford had been favorable, but Monica had said that there was more to the case than he knew. Did that mean that she had conclusive evidence of Stafford's guilt? Had Stafford lied when he'd said he was innocent?

The courtroom door opened and someone called his name. He looked up and saw Charlie Holt approaching. He had not noticed him in the packed courtroom.

'What was this about no bail?' Charlie asked.

David did not answer. He was staring at the beautiful woman who was following Charlie.

'Oh, sorry,' Charlie said. 'Dave, this is Jennifer Stafford.'

Only it wasn't. It was Valerie Dodge.

'I'M SORRY, DAVID. I didn't want to lie to you, but . . .' Her voice trailed off and she looked at her hands, clasped tightly in her lap. David sat across from her. They had both managed to carry on a normal conversation on the way to his office. Charlie was too distracted to notice the tension between them. David asked Charlie to stay in the waiting room, and they both walked to his office in silence. When David closed the door, Jennifer had taken a chair without looking at him.

'I don't know if I should stay on this case,' he said.

She looked up, startled.

'Oh, you must. Please, David. Larry needs you.'

'I'm not sure that I'm the best person to represent your husband.'

'Why? Because we slept together? Please, David. I don't know why I . . . We'd quarreled and . . .' She shook her head. 'I never did anything like that before. You have to believe me.'

'I do believe you. That doesn't matter. A lawyer is supposed to be objective, uninvolved. How am I going to do that?'

She looked down at her hands again, and David leaned back in his chair, trying to maintain control. The shock of meeting her in the courthouse was wearing off, and a deep depression was setting in.

'When Charlie suggested your name . . . at first I was going to say no, but I couldn't. Larry has to have the best lawyer. I can't let him . . .'

She stopped. David turned his chair slightly so she would not be in his line of vision.

'Do you love him?'

She looked up but didn't say anything.

'I asked you if you love your husband.'

He didn't really want to know. He had asked the question to hurt her. He felt confused and betrayed.

'Please don't,' she said. Her voice was almost a whisper, and he was afraid that she would cry.

'Do you love your husband?' David repeated forcefully.

'Does it matter? Do you ask that of every wife

137

who comes to you for help? Isn't it enough that I'm asking you for help?'

He still could not face her. She was right and he saw that. He was being a fool. A child. And she was asking for help. But to give her that help, he would have to build a barrier between them that might never come down. He swiveled the chair back toward her. She was sitting erect and watching him.

'I could give you the names of several other attorneys. All very competent.'

'No, I want you. I believe in you. I know you can clear Larry.'

'Who is Valerie Dodge?' he asked. She blushed and smiled.

'Dodge is my maiden name. The other one . . . Valerie . . . There's a TV show I watch. I didn't know what to say and that was the first name I thought of.'

David laughed. She hesitated a second to make sure that his laughter was real; then she laughed. A nervous laugh. Grateful that the tension had been broken.

'I tried very hard to find you. Called Senator Bauer's campaign committee, scoured the phone books.'

'I thought about you, too. There were times I wanted to . . . But I couldn't. Larry and I . . . we've had problems. He works very hard and . . . What happened that night. It just happened. But you can't let that interfere with Larry's case. Whatever

138

I feel for him, if it's love or . . . he is my husband and . . .'

She stopped and they looked at each other. Now it was his turn to avert his eyes. He felt very tired.

'I want to think, Jennifer. I'm mixed up now and I want some time to clear my head.'

'All right.'

'I'll call you in the morning and let you know what I decide.'

He stood up and she followed. He held open the door and she started to leave. They were close. Within inches of each other. His hand poised on the doorknob, the scent of her all around him. He wanted to hold her. She sensed it and pretended not to notice. The moment passed and he opened the door. When she was gone, he sat at his desk without moving for a long time.

3

David had not slept well. There had been clear skies and a bright slice of moon, and he had watched the stars from the darkness of his living room when he found he could not sleep. What was there to it? A woman he had slept with one time. Why should she matter, when none of the others he had taken to bed had mattered? He knew he would not find the answer with logic, the lawyer's tool.

What should he do? The answer was obvious. Get out. Obvious on paper, that is. But not in his heart, where the decision was being made. And it was not all that obvious, anyway, because one factor muddied everything over. What if Larry Stafford was innocent? Charlie Holt had told him that Jennifer said she had been with her husband the night Darlene Hersch was murdered, and Jennifer had told him when they were walking to his office from the courthouse that Larry was innocent. Stafford had said it too, and David believed him. On the other hand, was the man who had cuckolded the defendant the best man to represent him?

David had to give that a lot of thought. Now that he had found Jennifer, he did not want to let her go. He wanted to know if there was anything more possible between them. He had sensed that possibility when they had parted at his office.

Did he want the case because of Jennifer? Did he care about Larry Stafford at all? If it was just Jennifer, he knew he would have to give it up. But it wasn't just Jennifer, David told himself. If Larry Stafford was innocent, David could not stand by and see him convicted. There was more to this case than just a chance to see Jennifer again. Hadn't he felt the excitement when Charlie Holt had told him that Stafford might be innocent? David thought about Ashmore and Gault and Anthony Seals. When their cases had concluded, he had felt a sense of guilt, not pride. This was a case he could be proud of. He was the best criminal lawyer in the state and one of the best in the country. It was about time he started using his abilities the way they were meant to be used.

THERE WAS A note from Monica in his message box the next morning. An indictment had been returned, and a date for the arraignment had been set in circuit court. David made a note to himself to set a time for a bail hearing. The first thing he did when he reached his office was call Jennifer Stafford. She answered after the first ring.

'I'll represent Larry if you want me to.'

'Yes,' she answered after a brief pause. 'Thank you. I was afraid you wouldn't . . . Larry is very high on you. We talked about it yesterday evening.'

'You didn't tell him I was thinking about not taking the case?'

'Oh, no. He doesn't know anything about us.'

There was silence on the line.

'You haven't . . .?' she started.

'Of course not.'

There was another pause. Not an auspicious beginning. They could not relax with each other.

'Larry said that you have his appointment book at home,' he said.

'I think so. I'll look.'

'I'll need it as soon as possible. And the fee,' he added, feeling uneasy about asking her for money.

'Of course; Charlie told me. I'll go to the bank.'

Again, dead air. Neither of them knew how to fill the space.

'I'll let you know when the bail hearing is set,' David said, unwilling to let the conversation end.

'Yes.'

'And don't forget the book. It's important.'

He was repeating himself.

'If . . . if I find the book, should I bring it down this morning?'

Did that mean she wanted to see him? He felt very unsure of himself.

'We can set an appointment.'

'I could leave it with your secretary. If you're busy.' She hesitated. 'I don't want to bother you. I know you have other cases.'

'No. That's all right. If you find it, come down.

I'm pretty open this afternoon, and I have to talk to you anyway for background.'

'Okay. If I find it.'

They rang off. He leaned back, breathed deeply, and composed himself. This was no good. There was too much adrenaline involved. He wasn't thinking straight. Like some high-school kid with a crush. Stupid. When he felt he had himself in hand, he dialed Terry Conklin, his investigator.

'How you doing, Terry?'

'Up to my ass. And you?'

'Same thing. That's why I called you. I have a real interesting one. It'll probably take a lot of your time.'

'Gee, I don't know, Dave. I hate to turn you down, but I just picked up Industrial Indemnity as a client, and I've had to hire another guy just to handle their caseload.'

David was disappointed. Terry had been an intelligence officer in the Air Force and a policeman after that. When he got tired of working for someone else, he quit the force and started his own agency. David had been one of his first clients, and they were good friends. As Terry's reputation grew, he acquired several insurance companies as clients. The money end of his business was in investigating personal-injury claims, and he had little time now for criminal investigation, his first love. But he and David had an understanding if the case was big enough, and he had never let David down yet.

PHILLIP M. MARGOLIN

'It's the policewoman who was murdered at the Raleigh Motel,' David said. He was laying out the bait.

'Oh. Yeah? Some of my police friends were talking about that. They got someone, huh?'

'You don't read the papers?'

'I was in New Orleans last week.'

'My, my, aren't we getting to be the cross-country traveler. Business or pleasure?'

'A little of both. You representing the accused?'

David smiled. He was interested.

'Yeah. They arrested a lawyer from the Price, Winward firm.'

'No shit!'

David relaxed. He had him.

'Can you recommend someone to work on the case? I'd like someone good.'

'Hold on, will you? Just one minute.'

Terry put him on hold and David laughed out loud. When Terry got back on the line, they made an appointment to meet after work and drive to the Raleigh Motel.

JENNIFER SHOWED UP at three. She was dressed in a conservative gray skirt and a white blouse that covered her to the neck. Her hair was swept back in a bun. With glasses she would look like a librarian in one of those forties movies, whose hidden beauty was revealed when she let her hair down.

'I brought the book,' she said, holding out a

144

pocket-sized notebook with a black leather cover. David reached across the desk and took it, careful not to let their hands touch. He flipped through the pages until he came to June 16. Stafford had had an appointment at nine forty-five with someone named Lockett and another appointment at four-thirty with Barry Dietrich. David recognized Dietrich's name. He was a partner at Price, Winward who specialized in securities work. That would tie in with what Larry had told him at the jail. There were no other entries for the sixteenth, and David made a note to contact Dietrich.

'Is that any help?' Jennifer asked.

'It could be. Larry met with one of the partners on the day of the murder. I'll find out how late they worked.'

Jennifer nodded. She looked ill at ease, sitting erect with her hands folded in her lap, making an extra effort to look businesslike. David appreciated her discomfort. He felt rigid, and the conversation had an artificial quality to it.

'I want to talk to you about your relationship to Larry. Some of the questions I'm going to ask will be very personal, but I wouldn't ask them if the answers weren't important to Larry's defense.'

She nodded again, and he noticed that her hands clasped tighter, turning the knuckles of her left hand momentarily white.

'How long have you known Larry?'

'Just over a year.'

145

'How did you meet?'

'I was teaching school with Miriam Holt, Charlie's wife. She introduced us. Larry and Charlie play a lot of handball together.'

'How long after that were you married?'

'A few months. Four.'

It came out as an apology, and David looked down at his notes, sensing her embarrassment. Whether the jury found Larry innocent or guilty, this would be an ordeal for her. And it would never really stop. If Larry was convicted, she would be the wife of the young lawyer who had killed a policewoman he thought was a prostitute. Why had he needed a prostitute? They would look at her and wonder. What was wrong with her that she had driven him to that?

And if he was acquitted? Well, you never were, really. The jury might say you were not guilty, but the doubts always remained.

'Where do you teach?'

'Palisades Elementary School.'

'How long have you been teaching?'

She smiled and relaxed a little.

'It seems like forever.'

'Do you enjoy it?'

'Yes. I've always liked kids. I don't know. It can be hard at times, but I really feel it's worthwhile. Larry wanted me to stop teaching after we were married, but I told him I wanted to keep on.'

'Why did he want you to stop?'

Jennifer blushed and looked down at her hands. 'You have to understand Larry. He's very tied up in this manhood trip. It's just the way he is.'

'Has Larry ever cheated on you?'

There was a sharp intake of breath, and Jennifer looked directly at David.

'No,' she said firmly. 'And I think I would have known.'

'Has he ever struck you?'

'No,' she said after a moment's hesitation.

'Has he or hasn't he?'

'Well, we've quarreled, but he's never . . . No.'

'Do you consider Larry to be normal sexually?'

'What do you mean, "normal"?' she asked hesitantly.

David felt uneasy and unsure of himself. He had asked this type of question often enough in the past, but it had always been strictly for professional reasons. He was asking now as a professional, but there was something more. He wanted to know what the relationship between Larry Stafford and his wife was really like. He wanted to know how he stacked up sexually to the man he was representing. He wanted to know if Jennifer responded to her husband with the passion she had exhibited during their lovemaking.

'Are his sexual preferences unusual? Does he have any peculiarities?'

'I don't see why, what that would . . . Can't we talk about something else? This is very hard for me.'

'I know it's hard for you, but this case is heavily

147

concerned with sex, and I want you prepared for the questions the district attorney is going to ask you in open court.'

'I'll have to . . .? I couldn't . . .'

Jennifer took a deep breath, and David let her compose herself.

'Our sexual relationship is . . . just normal.'

Her voice caught, and David again watched her hands, tense and entwined, clasp each other rigidly.

'I don't know what you want me to say,' she said so softly that he had to strain to hear her.

'David, that evening you and I . . . It is true that Larry and I were having problems, but they had to do with his work, not our sexual relationship. He was working very hard. He didn't make partner last year and it deflated him. At first he just gave up. It was right after we got married, and he was talking about leaving the firm and trying something else: government work or going out on his own. Then he changed his mind and decided that he would be accepted if he just worked harder. Even harder than before. He was leaving early and coming home late. He was drinking, too. I hardly saw him at all, even on the weekends. And when I did see him, it seemed we were always quarreling.

'The evening I met you . . . I just blew up at him. Called him at the office. He came home all upset. I'd interfered with his work. Couldn't I understand? I told him I did understand. That I thought he considered his work more important than me. I walked out. Then I met you and . . . and it just happened. I wanted to hurt him, I guess. But it isn't . . . wasn't sex. We were . . . all right.'

She stopped, out of words, her energy spent. David didn't know what to say. He wanted to take her in his arms and comfort her, but he knew he couldn't.

'Besides,' she said, 'I don't see what any of this has to do with Larry's case. I told Charlie, Larry couldn't have killed that girl. He was home with me on that evening.'

'You're certain?'

'Yes. I would know. I mean, if he was out with another woman . . . He was with me.'

'You would swear to that in court?'

'Yes. I don't want Larry to go to prison. He couldn't take it, David. He couldn't take the pressure.'

'He seems to be holding up pretty well.'

'You don't know him like I do. He puts up a good front, but he's a little boy underneath. He's very good at seeming to be in one piece, but I know him well enough to see the cracks beneath the surface.'

David put down his notepad. The short interview had taken its emotional toll on both of them.

'I guess that's enough for now. I'm going to visit the motel after work and try to talk to the desk clerk. I'll let you know if I turn up anything.'

She stood, and he walked her to the door.

'I want to thank you for taking the case. I know it

was a hard decision for you. And I know that Larry will be safe with you.'

He didn't know what to say. She solved the problem by leaving quickly. He watched her walk away, hoping that she would turn and give him some sign, but she didn't and he returned to his desk, more confused than ever about their relationship.

There was a glass and a bottle of good bourbon in David's bottom drawer. He took his bourbon neat. It was some time since he had felt the need for a midday drink, but he had the feeling that there would be many more before he was through with the Stafford case.

TERRY CONKLIN WAS medium height, a bit chubby, and had a wide and continuous smile. He looked like the least dangerous person in any gathering, and people trusted and talked to him. That's what made him so valuable as an investigator.

Terry turned his Dodge station wagon into the parking lot at the Raleigh Motel. The wagon was strewn with debris left by Conklin's five children. It was a far cry from the flashy sports cars James Bond drove, and Terry liked to joke that it was part of his cover.

Terry had spent some time that afternoon in the morgue at the *Oregonian* reading everything he could find about the Hersch case. He had photocopied the clippings for David, who was finishing the last one as they pulled up in front of the motel office.

'Any help?' Conklin asked as he shut off the engine.

'They don't give me much more than I already know. Say, before I forget, the bail hearing's tomorrow and they'll probably put Ortiz on. Can you make it?'

'No problem,' Terry said as they headed toward the motel office.

Merton Grimes was an old man, stooped and slow to move. The cold weather was still holding off, but Grimes had on a heavy plaid shirt, buttoned to the neck, and a pair of soiled gray slacks. He was standing over a pot of coffee when David entered, and David had to cough to get his attention. Grimes looked put out and took his time shuffling across the room. David could see a section of the back room through a half-open door. There was a small couch covered by an antimacassar. A lamp rested on a low end table casting a dim light on the green-and-white fabric. David could hear the muffled sound of a TV whose volume had been turned low, but he could not see the screen.

'Mr. Grimes?' David asked. The old man looked immediately suspicious. 'My name is David Nash. This is Terry Conklin. I'd like to talk to you about the murder that occurred here a few months ago.'

'You reporters?' Grimes asked in a tone suggesting that he would not be upset if they were.

'No. I'm a lawyer. I represent the man who's been charged with the crime.'

'Oh,' Grimes said, disappointed.

'I'd like to see the room if I could and talk about anything you might know.'

'I already told what I know to the police. Damn place was like a circus for a week,' he said, nodding at the memory. 'Reporters and cops. Didn't do business no harm, though.'

He laughed and it came out more of a snort. The old man wiped his nose with the back of his hand and turned to a pegboard on the wall behind the desk counter. It took him a moment, but he found the key he was looking for. He started to reach for it, then stopped and turned back. He had a crafty look on his face, and David knew exactly what was coming next.

'You know, I ain't sure I should be doin' this. You representing a criminal and all. I don't know if the cops would like it. I could get in trouble.'

'I can assure you this is perfectly legal . . .'

'All the same . . .'

'And, of course, we would pay you for your time.'

'Oh, say, that's mighty nice of you,' Grimes said with a smirk. David wondered how much dough he'd pulled in from the press for exclusive tours. He laid a twenty-dollar bill on the countertop. Grimes looked at it for a moment, probably figuring if there was any way to get more; then his fingers made the fastest move David would see all evening, and the bill was gobbled up and stuffed into his trouser pocket.

'We can talk while we walk,' Grimes said, taking the key off the peg and shuffling toward the door. Conklin held it open, and he and David followed Grimes across the parking lot toward the motel rooms.

'She sure was a nice-lookin' gal,' Grimes said as they started up the metal stairs to the second landing. 'Didn't look like no hooker to me. I got suspicious right off.'

'You get plenty of hookers here?' Terry asked with a straight face.

'What's that supposed to mean?'

Terry shrugged.

'You said she didn't look like one. I just supposed . . .'

The old man weighed his answer for a second, then snickered.

'Yeah, we get our share. I don't take no cut, you understand. But there's a few that likes our accommodations. Cops don't care, so why should I?'

'Did you ever see the fella who was with the dead girl before that night?'

'Like I told the cops, he was out in the car and I didn't pay no attention to him. She come in and I was readin'. Then she took up most of my attention, if you know what I mean. Nice tits, as much of 'em as I could see. I just didn't have no interest in the john.'

'So you didn't get a good look at him at all?'

153

'I didn't say that. I seen him, but he didn't make no impression. And it was only a little look, when he come tearin' out of here after he killed her.'

'What do you remember seeing?'

'Nothin' much. A man in a car. I already been through this with the cops.'

'I know,' David said, 'and I appreciate your taking the time to talk to us now.'

They were on the landing and Grimes was leading the way toward a room at the end. Terry looked around, filing the layout away in his mind for future use. Grimes stopped and inserted his key in the door of the next-to-last room. The door opened. A large globe light to the right of the door hung above David's head and cast a pale-yellow glow over the door. Grimes put his key in the lock and pushed the door open.

'There she is. Course it's cleaned up now. It was some mess then, I can tell you.'

Grimes stepped aside, and David entered the unlit room. He turned and saw the neon signs on the boulevard. A reminder of the life outside. Here, in the sterile, plastic room, there was no sign of life or death. Just a twentieth-century motel limbo devoid of feeling. The shadowy figures of Grimes and Conklin wavered in the doorway like spirits of the dead. Grimes reached around the wall and found the light switch.

'There isn't much we can learn here,' Terry said

when he had toured the bedroom and bathroom. 'The DA will have pictures of the scene.'

David nodded.

'The papers say it was some young lawyer,' Grimes said.

'That's right.'

'That fits with what I seen. Fancy car he was drivin' and the long hair.'

'You saw his hair?' David asked.

'I said so, didn't I?'

'I must have misunderstood you. I thought you said he didn't make an impression on you.'

'He didn't. But I seen the hair. Brown hair.'

'You're certain about that?' David said, casting a quick look at Conklin.

'I'm gettin' along, but I ain't senile. Say, you think they'll put it in the papers when I testify?'

'No doubt, Mr. Grimes,' Terry said. Grimes smiled and nodded his head.

'I was in the papers once before. They had a robbery here and they listed me as the victim. I got the clipping in my desk.'

'I think I've seen all I want to. How about you?' David asked Conklin. The investigator just nodded. He and David walked onto the landing, and Grimes switched off the light and locked the door.

'Thanks for the tour,' David said when they reached the office.

'Anytime.'

'See you in court,' Conklin said.

The old man chuckled and shook his head. 'That's right,' he said. 'That's right.'

He was shuffling toward the back room as they drove away.

4

The main entrance to the county courthouse was on Fourth Avenue. David entered through the back door on Fifth. The rear corridor was jammed with police officers waiting to testify in the three traffic courts located there. Lawyers in three-piece suits huddled with straggly-haired dopers and stylishly dressed young women about defenses to their traffic citations. Court clerks shuffled people back and forth between the courtrooms and the large room where the fines were paid. An old lawyer listened patiently to the complaints of a young member of the bar, and an even younger district attorney tried to understand the testimony of a police officer as he prepared to try his seventh straight speeding case.

David pushed through the crowd and into the narrow alcove that housed the jail elevator. The courthouse jail was used to hold prisoners who had court appearances and for booking new arrestees.

The elevator stopped at seven, and David stepped up to a thick glass window and called through an intercom to a guard who was seated at a control panel.

'I'd like to see Larry Stafford. Do you have an empty booth?'

'Try two, Mr. Nash,' the guard said over his shoulder. David signed his name in the logbook. The guard pressed a button and a floor-to-ceiling steel gate swung open. David walked into the narrow holding area and waited for the gate to close. As soon as it clicked shut, the guard pressed another button. There was an electronic hum, and the solid-steel door at the other end of the holding area swung open. David walked to a door that opened into the conference area. Several identical booths were set up side by side. Each booth was divided by wire mesh that started halfway up from the floor. There was a chair on each side of the mesh and a ledge underneath it.

David took some papers out of his attaché case and read them while he waited for the guard to bring Larry Stafford. Stafford arrived a few minutes later, smiling and looking thinner than he had at the arraignment.

'It's good to see you, Dave,' he said through the mesh. There was no tremor in his voice, as there had been the last time they were together.

'How are you getting along?' David asked.

Stafford shrugged.

'I guess you can get used to anything. In a way, it's not all that bad. No clients yelling at me. No partners making demands. Plenty of sleep. If the food was a little better, I'd recommend the place.'

David smiled. Stafford seemed to have developed a sense of humor, and that was essential if he was going to get through his ordeal.

'You do look a little thinner than when I saw you last.'

'Yeah, well they cut down on all those fancy sauces here. It definitely helps the waistline.'

David took the appointment book out of his attaché case and held it against the wire mesh.

'We have some time before the bail hearing, so I want to go over some stuff. Does this help you remember any more about the night of the murder?'

Stafford read over the entry for June 16.

'Right. I was going to talk to you about that. I talked to Jenny and she mentioned the book. Call Dietrich. He'll tell you. We had a conference that night. Remember I told you about that securities case? Well, we were together until six, six-thirty. You can check the time sheets we keep at the firm for billing clients.'

'Okay,' David said, making a notation on his pad, 'but that doesn't help us too much. Hersch started her shift around ten-thirty, and she was killed about midnight.'

'Oh,' Stafford said, momentarily dejected. Then he brightened.

'It would still be good circumstantial evidence that I'm innocent. I mean, it doesn't make sense, does it, for me to have a normal business day, confer on a

159

securities case, then slice up a policewoman. I mean the two are pretty inconsistent, aren't they?'

'Not necessarily. There are plenty of businessmen who use the services of prostitutes. Why should you be any different?'

'Okay,' Stafford answered eagerly, 'I've been thinking about that angle. But it won't work. Jenny will testify that we're happily married. You've seen Jenny, haven't you? What jury would believe that a guy married to someone as good-looking as that would waste his time with a whore? Right? It doesn't fit in.'

Stafford sat back and smiled, satisfied that he had won his case. David looked up from his notes and waited a moment before speaking. He noticed that his palms were damp, and for the moment he felt certain that he was more unsure of himself than was his client.

'A man married to a good-looking woman might seek the services of a prostitute if he and his wife were having difficulties with their marriage.'

Stafford continued to smile. He nodded his head to acknowledge the point.

'If. But there's no "if" about Jenny and me.'

'No difficulties at all? No arguments, no sexual difficulties or money problems? You'd better be straight with me on this, Larry, because putting you and Jenny on the stand will open the door for the district attorney, and if there's dirt, you can bet she'll find it.'

David thought about his evening with Jenny as he waited for Stafford to answer. A mental image of her, naked and in his bed, appeared, and he fought to erase it.

'We have spats. Who doesn't?' Stafford paused. 'Look, I'm going to level with you. Jenny and I have had our problems. What marriage doesn't? And you know what they say about the first year being the toughest.'

David thought back to his first year of marriage. It had not been pleasant for either of them. Vicious words, said for the sole purpose of hurting. Slammed doors and backs turned in anger.

'Hell, it was both our faults. I'm not an easy guy to live with sometimes. I didn't make partner last year and it really hurt me. Two other guys who were hired the same year I was made the grade, and I was pretty depressed for a long time. I don't suppose that was easy for Jenny to take.'

'How are you two sexually?'

Stafford reddened slightly. The question seemed to make him uneasy.

'I don't know. I'd say we do okay. I'm maybe more demanding than some guys. You might say I dig sex a little more than Jenny. She's more conventional in her, uh, tastes. Nothing I'd call a, uh, problem though.'

Stafford hesitated. He looked upset.

'Will . . . will they be asking about that at the trial? Our sex life, I mean?'

161

'It could come up. Why?'

'I don't know. It's just embarrassing, I guess. I don't mind talking to you. You're my lawyer and I trust you. It would be different in front of all those people.'

David glanced at his watch. The bail hearing was set for two and it was ten of.

'It's almost time to go to court,' he said, 'so I'm going to stop now. But I want to ask you one more question. You remember how surprised I was that the district attorney's office opposed bail at the arraignment? Well, I talked with Monica Powers after court, and she acted very peculiar. She hinted that they had some kind of surprise evidence I didn't know about. Do you have any idea what that might be, Larry?'

'Surprise evidence,' Stafford repeated. 'I can't think of . . .' He stopped for a moment, and David got the distinct impression that something was troubling his client.

'Look, I didn't do it, so what could they have? It doesn't make any sense.'

'You do some thinking on this, okay, Larry? I don't like surprises, and it looks like Monica is planning one. Remember what I told you about being straight with me. If you've done something that can hurt us, I want to know right now.'

'Dave, I have been one hundred percent square with you. There's nothing.'

'You're sure?'

'Absolutely. Say, how do my chances look today?' Stafford asked anxiously.

'I don't know. It depends on what kind of showing the State makes. One point for our side is that Jerry Miles is the presiding criminal judge this month.'

Stafford brightened. 'He's pretty liberal, isn't he?'

'He's good and he's fair. Keep your fingers crossed. I hope you'll be out of here by this evening.'

They shook hands and David buzzed the guard. Stafford was still waiting in front of the door when the guard let David out. On the elevator ride up to the courtroom, David tried to analyze his feelings about his client. He felt uncomfortable around Stafford. The man appeared to be open and honest, but David could not help feeling that Larry was using the same technique on him that David used on a jury. Or did he just want to feel that way? He had to face one very unpleasant fact: he wanted Jenny, and Larry Stafford was his rival for Jenny's affections.

David tried to stand back from his problem and be objective. Was Stafford lying to him? Was he really guilty? Were his uneasy feelings about Stafford generated by his emotional involvement with Jenny? He had given Larry a chance to lie today, and Stafford had not taken it. Although reticent at first to discuss his private life, Larry had eventually been candid about his marital problems, and he had told David about his failure to make partner. And then there was Jenny. She swore she was with Larry on the night of the murder. She would not lie to him.

By the time the elevator doors opened, David was starting to feel better about his case. Jenny would make a good witness, and there was Grimes's testimony about the hair. The jury might not be totally convinced of the accuracy of the motel clerk's observations, but his testimony, combined with other evidence, could create the reasonable doubt needed for an acquittal. Now all David had to do was find those other pieces of evidence. He hoped some of them would be provided by the testimony at the bail hearing.

PRESIDING CRIMINAL COURT was at the far end of the corridor from the bank of elevators David had used. He was halfway to the courtroom when he saw Thomas Gault grinning at him from a bench near the courtroom doorway.

'You're just the man I wanted to see,' Gault said. David stopped and looked at his watch. Court would start in a moment, and he really did not want to talk to Gault anyway. Ever since Gault had shaken him with his false confession, David had gone out of his way to avoid the writer.

'I'm sorry, Tom, but I'm due in court.'

'The Stafford bail hearing, right?'

'Right.'

'That's what I want to talk about. I'm covering the case for *Newsweek*.'

'The magazine?' David asked incredulously.

'The same. They gave a lot of coverage to my trial, so I convinced them that it would be a neat gimmick to have someone who was just acquitted of murder cover a murder case. Hell, I'm their murderer-in-residence now. Besides, I did those articles on Cambodia and the article on the mercenaries for them.

'So what do you say? Is Stafford guilty? Come on. I need a scoop to beat out the local yokels.'

David couldn't help laughing. Gault was a leprechaun when he wanted to be, and his humor could be infectious.

'No scoops and no comment. How would you have liked it if I'd blabbed to reporters about your case?'

'But, Dave, I had nothing to hide. Can you say the same for Stafford? If I don't get facts from you, I'll have to make something up. I've got deadlines.'

'No comment,' David repeated. Gault shrugged.

'Suit yourself. I'm only trying to make you famous.'

'And I appreciate the effort, but I really do have to go.'

'At least say something memorable, old buddy. I've gotta have some snappy copy.'

David shook his head and laughed again. He opened the door and entered the courtroom. Gault followed him and took a seat in the back of the room where he would not be noticed.

'THIS IS THE time set for the bail hearing in State versus Lawrence Dean Stafford, case number C94-07-850. The State is represented by Monica Powers,' Monica said, 'and the defendant is present with his attorney, David Nash.'

'Are you prepared to proceed, Mr. Nash?' Judge Autley asked.

'Ready, Your Honor,' David answered stiffly. Clement Autley was the worst judge they could have gotten. Almost seventy, Autley was so erratic that many attorneys filed affidavits of prejudice against him rather than risk his unpredictable rulings at trial and subject themselves and their clients to his very predictable temper tantrums. Autley was not supposed to be on the bench today. Jerome Miles was. But Miles had the flu, and Autley had been shipped upstairs for the week.

'You may proceed, Mr. Nash.'

'Your Honor, I believe the burden is on the district attorney.'

'You're asking for bail, aren't you? Your motion, your burden,' Autley snapped.

'If I might, Your Honor,' David said, careful to maintain his composure and to address the judge formally. He had once seen Autley, in a fit of anger, hold a young lawyer in contempt for not using the proper court etiquette. 'Article one, section fourteen of the state constitution states that, and I quote, "Offenses, except murder and treason, shall be bailable by sufficient sureties. Murder or treason shall not be bailable when the proof is evident or the presumption strong."

'In *State* ex rel. *August v. Chambers*, our supreme court held that if the State seeks to deny bail to a person charged with murder, it has the burden of proving that there is proof of, or a presumption of, the defendant's guilt which is evident or strong. In light of the Chambers case, it appears that the State has the burden, not Mr. Stafford.'

Judge Autley glared at David for a moment, then turned rapidly toward Monica Powers.

'What do you say to that?'

'I'm afraid he's right, Your Honor,' Monica said nervously. It was widely known that the one thing Autley hated more than young defense lawyers was any kind of woman lawyer.

'Then why are you wasting the Court's time? I have a busy schedule. You see all these people waiting here, don't you? Why did you let him go on and on if you agreed with what he said?'

'I'm sorry . . .' Monica started, but Autley waved a hand toward her.

'What's your evidence?'

Monica tendered to the judge a copy of the indictment charging murder. His bailiff, an elderly woman who had been with him for years, handed the document to him.

167

'I believe the indictment in this case should be sufficient. It establishes that the grand jury, after hearing testimony, decided that there was sufficient proof to indict for murder.'

Judge Autley scanned the document for a moment; then he handed it back to the bailiff.

'Bail denied,' he said without looking up. 'Next case.'

David was on his feet, waving a law book toward the judge.

'Your Honor.'

'I've ruled, Mr. Nash. Next case.'

'Your Honor, last month in the Archer case the Oregon Supreme Court ruled on this specific question and held that an indictment is not sufficient evidence to support a denial of bail in a murder case. I have the case here, if the Court would read it.'

'What case?' Autley asked, annoyed that the matter was not over.

'Archer, if you'd take a look.'

'Give it to me. But if this case isn't on point . . .' He let his voice trail off, leaving the threat dangling over David's head.

David handed the law book to the bailiff. Stafford leaned forward to say something, but David touched his leg and he sat back. Autley read the page twice, then turned his anger on Monica Powers.

'Don't they teach you the law anymore? Didn't you know about this case?'

'Your Honor, I—'

'You'd better have more than this, young lady,' Autley said, waving the indictment toward Monica, 'and you'd better produce it fast.'

'We do have further evidence, Your Honor. Officer Ortiz is prepared to testify.'

'Then call him.'

Monica gestured toward the first row of spectator seats, and Bert Ortiz rose from his seat next to Detective Crosby. He pushed through the gate that separated the spectators from the bar of the court and stopped in front of the bailiff.

'Do you swear to tell the truth, the whole truth, and nothing but the truth, so help you God?' the bailiff asked.

'I do,' Ortiz replied.

'Then state your name and spell your last name.'

Ortiz sat down in the witness box and spelled his last name for the court reporter. His throat felt dry as he did so, and there was none of the air of self-assurance about him that he usually had when he testified. He felt uncomfortable reliving the events of the murder.

'Officer Ortiz,' Monica asked, 'how are you employed?'

'I'm a police officer with the Portland Police Bureau.'

'How long have you been so employed?'

'It will be seven years this coming February.'

'Were you so employed on the evening of June sixteenth of this year?'

169

'I was.'

'And what was your assignment at that time?'

'I was working in a special vice unit. We were using policewomen disguised as prostitutes to arrest males who were soliciting prostitution.'

'Could you be more specific for the Court?'

Judge Autley leaned toward Monica and waved an impatient hand.

'I know what he means. Don't insult the Court's intelligence. Now, get on with this.'

'Very well, Your Honor. Officer Ortiz, who was your partner that evening?'

'Darlene Hersch, a policewoman.'

'When did you begin work?'

'The shift started at ten-thirty, but we weren't out on the street until about eleven-thirty. We had a meeting first.'

'Officer, please tell the Court what happened from the time you began work on the street until the time Darlene Hersch was murdered.'

Ortiz leaned forward slightly. There was tension in his shoulders and a tight feeling in his stomach. He looked down at the railing of the witness box and quickly ran his tongue across his dry lips.

'I was in our car in a parking lot on the corner of Park and Morrison, and Officer Hersch was on the far corner. Shortly after I started my surveillance, a beige Mercedes-Benz stopped and Darlene – Officer Hersch – got in. It drove off and I followed.'

'Were you able to read the license number of the car at that, or any other, time?'

'No.'

'Go on.'

'Officer Hersch was not supposed to enter a vehicle if asked. She was supposed to decoy the subject back to the lot, where we would make the arrest. She had strict orders not to do that.'

Ortiz stopped. He realized that he was trying to justify his actions by putting Darlene in a bad light. He looked up. Monica was waiting for him to continue. There was little sound in the courtroom. For the first time in a long time, he noticed the faces watching him.

'Officer Hersch got into the Mercedes and I followed the car to the Raleigh Motel. I saw Officer Hersch enter the motel office, and I saw the car drive around back. I parked in the lot of a fast-food place next door and took up a surveillance post.'

'To this point had you been able to see who was driving the Mercedes?'

'Not really. I had a look at him when Officer Hersch got into the car, but he was too far away. It was the same when he was letting her off at the motel office.'

'Go on.'

'Well, Officer Hersch was new. She didn't have much street experience. I started to worry about her being alone with the, uh, the subject.'

Ortiz paused again. He wanted to look for Crosby

171

but was afraid. Would the older man condemn him for letting things go as far as they had? He had been wrong. He should never have let Darlene go into that room alone. Even if it meant losing the collar, he should have stopped it as soon as he reached the motel. Should have parked in the motel lot and gone straight up to the room.

Ortiz looked over to the defense table. They had dressed Stafford in a suit. Very Ivy League. He looked more the lawyer than Nash. Their eyes met, and Stafford's face, for a brief instant, reflected contempt. There was no fear in his eyes, only ice. Humorless, emotionless, unlike Ortiz's own, which wavered with confusion and self-doubt. Ortiz looked away, defeated. And in that moment he felt the sick feeling in his stomach turning to hate for the man who had taken Darlene Hersch's life. He wanted that man. Wanted him more than he had ever wanted any other man he had hunted.

'I saw the subject walk along the second-floor landing and enter the room Officer Hersch had entered.'

'What did the man look like?'

'He was tall. About six feet. Athletic build. I would say he was in his late twenties or early thirties. I didn't see his face, but he had curly blond hair, and he was wearing tan slacks and a flowered shirt.'

'What happened after the man entered the motel room?'

'I . . . I crossed over to the motel lot and started up

the stairs. When I was halfway up, I heard a scream. I broke down the door, and then I was struck several times. I remember crashing into the bed. I must have hit the metal leg, because I passed out.'

'Before you lost consciousness, did you get a look at your assailant?'

'I did.'

'Do you see that man in this courtroom?'

Ortiz pointed toward Stafford. This time his hatred made him strong and he did not waver. David watched his client. If the identification upset him, he did not show it.

'The man I saw in the motel room is sitting beside counsel at that table,' Ortiz said.

'Officer Ortiz, if you know, what type of car does Mr. Stafford drive?'

'Mr. Stafford drives a beige 1991 Mercedes-Benz, model 300 SEL.'

'Is this the same car that you saw at the corner of Park and Morrison and later at the Raleigh Motel?'

'Yes.'

'At a later point in time, did you have an opportunity to search the defendant's home?'

'On September fifth we obtained a search warrant for Mr. Stafford's home. Detective Crosby, myself, and several other policemen arrested Mr. Stafford and conducted a search for clothing.'

'What did you find?'

'A shirt identical to that worn by the person I

saw at the Raleigh Motel, and tan slacks that were very similar to those worn by the killer.'

'I have no further questions,' Monica said.

'Officer Ortiz,' David asked, 'you were a full city block away from the Mercedes when you first saw it, were you not?'

'Yes.'

'As I understand your testimony, Officer Hersch was supposed to lead a person back to you if she was propositioned and you would then arrest him in the lot?'

'Yes.'

'And you were watching Officer Hersch from your car?'

'Yes.'

'Was the engine on?'

'In the police car?'

'Yes.'

'No.'

'And you were surprised when Officer Hersch got into the Mercedes?'

'Yes.'

'Park is one-way going south, is it not?'

'Yes.'

'Where was Officer Hersch when she got into the Mercedes?'

'At the corner of Park and Morrison.'

'Did the Mercedes turn up Park?'

'No. It proceeded down Morrison.'

'In order to follow it, wouldn't you have to go

up Park to Taylor, then back down Tenth?'

'No, sir, I went down Park the wrong way.'

'Then turned on Morrison?'

'Yes, sir.'

'How far away from the Mercedes were you when you spotted it again?'

'Two blocks, about.'

'And did you maintain that distance?'

'Yes.'

'You were too far back to read the license plate?'

'Yes.'

'Where was the Mercedes when you reached the motel?'

'I believe it had just stopped in front of the motel office.'

'Why didn't you get the license number then?'

'At that point I didn't realize it would be important. Besides, I was going too fast.'

'When did you next see the Mercedes that night?'

'I didn't. It was gone by the time I parked.'

'Let me see if I have this straight. You first saw the car from a distance of one city block, then you followed it from a distance of approximately two city blocks, and, finally, you saw it briefly as you passed by the motel lot?'

'Yes.'

'Now, you testified that the car you saw was a beige 1991 Mercedes-Benz, model 300 SEL, did you not?'

'Yes.'

'How do you know that?'

Ortiz looked perplexed.

'How do I know . . .?'

'The model and year and color?'

'That's the car Mr. Stafford drives.'

'Yes. But did you know the year and model and color on the night of the murder?'

'I . . . The color was beige. I could see that.'

'And the year and model?'

Ortiz paused.

'No. I only knew it was a beige Mercedes on that night.'

'So it could have been an '89 or an '85 Mercedes?'

'I later saw Mr. Stafford's car and it was the same one.'

'Do you know what a 1989 Mercedes looks like?'

'No.'

'Or an '85?'

'No.'

'The only time you saw the killer's face was just before you passed out, is that correct?'

'Yes.'

'Where were you and where was he, when you saw his face?'

'I was lying on my back on the floor looking up, and Mr. Stafford . . .'

'Your Honor, I move to strike that response,' David said. 'He's saying it was Mr. Stafford. That's a conclusion a jury or judge will have to draw.'

'Oh, let him go on, Mr. Nash. I've been around.'

Judge Autley turned to Officer Ortiz and smiled. David didn't like that. It was rare that anyone was graced with an Autley smile, and if the judge was bestowing one on Ortiz, that didn't bode well.

'Just say "suspect," Officer, and Mr. Nash won't get all bent out of shape.'

'Thank you, Your Honor,' Ortiz said. 'I was lying on my back on the floor, my head was against the bed, and the suspect was standing in the doorway.'

'Could you step down to the easel and draw a picture for us?'

Ortiz turned to the judge and the judge nodded. There was an easel with drawing paper and felt-tipped colored pens propped against the wall. Ortiz pulled the easel closer to the witness stand and picked up a black pen.

'This would be the doorway,' he said, tracing a rectangle on the paper. 'I was here, against the bed.' He drew a stick-figure bed and a stick-figure man. The man's head rested against a leg of the bed with its eyes facing the door.

'The door was open. It opened inward and it was half-open, about where I'd kicked it. I guess it must have swung back a ways. He was standing at the door frame, leaning into the room.'

'How far in?'

'Not much. I think his body was at a slight angle, and his right leg and arm were outside the door, but the left leg and his left arm were inside the room a bit.'

'And where was his head?'

'Leaning down toward me. Looking at me.'

'You are certain?'

Ortiz looked directly at David. Then he looked at Larry Stafford.

'I will never forget that face.'

David made some notes, then directed Ortiz back to the stand.

'Were you seriously injured?'

'I was in Good Samaritan Hospital for a day or so.'

'What hospital?'

'Good Samaritan.'

'How long did you view the killer's face?'

'I don't know.'

'A long time?'

'No.'

'How long did the man stand there?'

'A few seconds. Then he bolted.'

'So you saw him for a few seconds?'

'Yes.'

'Less than a minute?'

'Maybe five, ten seconds. But I saw him.'

David consulted his notes. He looked at the judge.

'Nothing further, Your Honor.'

Judge Autley looked at Monica Powers.

'Any further witnesses?'

'No, Your Honor. The State feels that it has met the standards set out in the case law. Officer Ortiz is a trained police officer. He has identified the man he saw at the Raleigh Motel as being the defendant. His testimony is corroborated by the fact that the defendant drives a car similar to the car seen at the motel and has similar clothes.'

'Mr. Nash?'

'Your Honor, I don't feel that a five-second identification by a man who had just been struck sufficiently hard to require hospitalization is the type of proof that creates a presumption of guilt that is evident or strong as is required by the Chambers case.

'Furthermore, Officer Ortiz can only say that the car was a Mercedes. He embellished that description with information he learned later.'

'Have you made your record, Mr. Nash?'

'I do have several character witnesses here to testify in the defendant's behalf.'

'You won't need them. Officer Ortiz is not your ordinary witness, Mr. Nash. He is a trained and experienced policeman. I think his testimony is sufficient and I am going to deny bail.'

David saw Stafford sag for a moment beside him. Monica was collecting her papers and Ortiz was starting to leave the witness stand.

'I can take this up to the supreme court on mandamus, Larry. If we—'

'It's okay,' Stafford said in a defeated voice. 'I knew we were dead when I saw Judge Autley. You did a great job, Dave.'

'Do you want me to come back and see you?'

'No. It's all right. Just get the trial date set as soon as you can. I don't know if . . . Just set the trial date soon.'

Stafford walked over to the guard, who led him back to the holding area. David saw Terry Conklin fold a secretarial notebook and head for the door of the courtroom. Jennifer was waiting just outside the courtroom.

'He's not getting out. The judge denied bail,' David said bitterly. He was disappointed. He had wanted to win, because he wanted Jennifer to see him win and because he thought that Stafford should be out. But he had lost, and it was starting to get to him: the shock of the court's rapid-fire decision was just wearing off, and the fact that bail had been denied was just seeping through.

'He didn't seem to even listen,' Jennifer said incredulously. 'He didn't even let you put on our witnesses.'

'I know. I'll petition the supreme court for a writ of mandamus, but I doubt they'll grant one. They rarely reverse a discretionary decision of a judge unless there's a gross abuse.'

'Well, isn't this . . .?' Jennifer started.

David shook his head. 'No. He just gave a lot of credence to Ortiz's testimony. Another judge might not have. That son of a bitch. Maybe I should have . . .'

David stopped himself.

'Look, Jenny, I'm going to meet with my investigator. I know we lost this time, but I developed several important points during my examination of Ortiz. Points that could win us the trial. And that's the important thing.'

'Won't it be the same at trial? They'll take his word because he's a policeman. They won't believe . . .'

David put his hand on her shoulder before he realized what he was doing. Jennifer looked startled, and he recalled the first time they had touched; saw her standing with her forehead pressed against the cold glass of his windowpane. He released his hand slowly. She looked away.

'At trial we'll have a jury and it will be different,' he said, but his thoughts were elsewhere. 'Juries are very fair. They do make the State prove its case, and I think the State is going to have a harder time than it thinks, if I'm right about a few things. Now, let me get to work, okay?'

'Yes. Of course. I . . . Thank you, David.'

'Don't thank me. So far all I've done is lose.'

'You'll win in the end. I know.'

They both stood in the hall, unwilling to break away. When David finally turned and walked over to Terry Conklin, he felt very depressed.

IT TOOK ONLY a few minutes with Conklin to restore his spirits. They walked from the courthouse to the Shingle Tavern, discussing the case as they went. Conklin had spotted the same thing David had, and the fact that his investigator had been thinking along the same line sent his adrenaline pumping. If they were right, David would have an excellent shot at an acquittal.

'When can you get on it?' David asked excitedly.

'I'll do it this evening, if I can find the man I need.'

David sipped his beer, then bit into his ham sandwich.

'I want Ortiz's medical records. Do you know anyone at Good Sam?'

Conklin thought for a moment. 'It might cost a few bucks, but I think I can swing it.'

'Don't worry about the money. There are a few other things. See if I'm right on the Mercedes and check the shirt.'

'I'll do that this week.'

'Good. You know, Terry, I'm starting to feel very good about this case. Very good.'

RON CROSBY WORKED the long, sauce-covered noodles around his chopsticks until he had them where he wanted them. Then, with a swift, stabbing movement, he jabbed the rolled noodles into his mouth.

'This place makes the best Chinese food in town,' he said. A piece of chewed noodle slipped out of the side of his mouth, and he nudged it back with his chopstick.

'How does it look, Ron?' Ortiz asked. He was toying with his food and had eaten little of it.

'Nash is smooth. That's why he does so well. He scored a few points, but Stafford's still in jail, isn't he?'

'Only because Autley was on the bench. He wouldn't let the pope out on bail. I'm not fooling myself. I made a lousy witness, and Nash didn't take the gloves off like he will at trial.'

Crosby put down his chopsticks. 'What's bothering you, Bert?'

'Nothing. It's just . . . Well, I feel responsible for . . . If I'd acted sooner, Darlene might still be alive. And now . . . I want that bastard, Ron, and I'm afraid I'll screw up again and Nash will get him off.'

'You didn't screw up the first time. Nobody thinks you did. Hersch was green and she was trying to prove how tough she was. She's dead because she broke the rules. And Nash isn't going to get Stafford off, anyway.'

Something in Crosby's tone made Ortiz look up.

'What's that supposed to mean?' he asked.

'Eat your noodles and I'll tell you,' Crosby answered, pulling a folded police report from his inside pocket. 'Do you know a pimp named Cyrus Johnson?'

'T.V.? There isn't a vice cop in town who doesn't know that asshole.'

'Check out this report,' Crosby said, handing it to Ortiz, 'then have a talk with T.V. It might prove interesting.'

CYRUS (T.V.) JOHNSON was probably the easiest person to find in the city of Portland. Every evening he parked his pink Cadillac outside the Jomo Kenyatta Pool Establishment so junkies would know where to make their connections, and his whores would know where to bring their take. T.V. was not the biggest pimp or pusher in Portland, but he was the most notorious. He had once had the temerity to be interviewed as part of a locally produced television special entitled *Drugs in Our Schools*, and thus the sobriquet.

Ortiz parked his car in front of the Cadillac and tried to make out T.V. through the haze of smoke that obscured the activity going on behind the storefront window. He could not see Johnson, but that didn't matter: he knew exactly where he was. T.V. always held court from an expensively upholstered armchair he had had the owner install in the rear of the pool hall. The armchair, surrounded as it was by the room's shabby furnishings, was a symbol of T.V.'s affluence, and it was understood that heavy penalties attached if anyone else used it.

Ortiz snaked his way around the players and their extended cues, aware that the noise level dropped as soon as he neared a table. A few players turned to watch him, but none moved out of his way. It was

184

a game that Ortiz was used to playing. You trained yourself to suppress the anger that the defiance kindled inside you. A white face in a place like the Kenyatta usually meant cop, and the men who played their pool here had no use for him.

T.V., as usual, was dressed in one of his flamboyant outfits. He hadn't always dressed like the stereotype pimp before his television appearance, and it was only by coincidence that he had been wearing an ankle-length fur coat and garish gold jewelry when the television cameras had happened along. But the word was that T.V.'s television performance had been the high point of his life, and since that day he had dressed to fit the part in case the cameras should call again.

T.V.'s nostrils flared as Ortiz approached, and he sniffed the air.

'We havin' bar-be-cue tonight, Kermit?' he asked the large man standing to his left, in an exaggerated Negro accent.' 'Cause I believe I smell pig.'

The large man fixed Ortiz with a cold, challenging stare. Ortiz recognized Kermit Monroe, a bodyguard who had played pro ball for Detroit before injuring a knee.

'You seem to be in good spirits, T.V.,' Ortiz said calmly.

'Why, sho' nuff, massah. We colored folks is always happy.'

'Do you think you can cut your routine long enough for us to have a little talk?'

185

The grin faded and T.V. eyed him suspiciously. Ortiz was no stranger. He had busted T.V. twice, but neither rap had stuck. The last time Ortiz had split T.V.'s lip. T.V. was vain about his looks and had not shown up at the pool hall for a week. He had also taken out his anger on one of his girls and sent her to the hospital. T.V. held Ortiz responsible for the girl's lost earnings, as well as his humiliation.

'Whatcho want to talk about?'

'In private,' Ortiz said, gesturing toward Monroe.

'Uh-uh. I got nothin' to say to you I can't say in front of my friends.'

'Why don't you piss off, Ortiz?' Monroe said. His voice was deep and smooth. Ortiz didn't show it, but he was afraid. He knew Monroe would not hesitate to kill a policeman. He might even enjoy it.

'I want some information about a white man who had some dealings with you and one of your girls a few years back,' Ortiz said, ignoring Monroe and pulling a mug shot of Larry Stafford out of his pocket. He noticed Monroe's hand move inside his leather jacket when his own hand moved.

'Girls? What girls he talkin' about, Kermit?' T.V. asked Monroe over his shoulder.

'I heard Ortiz don't like girls. I hear he likes little boys,' the bodyguard said with a sneer.

T.V. took the photo and studied it. If he recognized Stafford, it did not show.

'This is your boyfriend, Ortiz?' T.V. asked.

'You like to do it with boys, Ortiz?' Monroe

186

asked, echoing his boss. There was no emotion in his voice.

'Do you know him?' Ortiz asked T.V.

T.V. smiled. 'I ain't never seen this white boy, massah.'

'I think you have.'

Ortiz noticed that the noise in the pool room had stopped. He suddenly regretted his decision to come alone.

'You sayin' I'm lying, Ortiz?' T.V. asked. Monroe moved a step closer to Ortiz. T.V. took another look at the mug shot.

'You know, Kermit, this looks like that white boy who offed the lady pig. I read about that in the papers. The word is that Ortiz here fucked up. The word is she's dead because of you.'

He directed his last shot at Ortiz, and it scored. Ortiz could feel his stomach tighten with a mixture of rage and anguish. He wanted to strike out, but his own uncertainty about his role in Darlene's death sapped him of his will. T.V. read the uncertainty in Ortiz's eyes, and a triumphant smirk turned up the corners of his lips. Ortiz stared at him long enough to collect himself. Then he took the picture back.

'It's been nice talking to you, T.V. We'll talk again.'

He turned his back on Monroe and Johnson and walked back through the maze of black figures. There was laughter behind him, but the ebony faces in front of him were blank and threatening.

His hand was shaking as he turned the key in the ignition. He felt dizzy and slightly nauseated. He had made a fool of himself. He knew it. Suddenly he was filled with rage. That black bastard was going to talk to him. That son of a bitch would tell him what he wanted to know. And he knew just how to make him tell.

David looked down at the stack of papers scattered across his desk. He had brought home a legal memorandum in the Stafford case to proofread, but he was too tired to go on. He closed his eyes and massaged his eyelids. The pressure felt good.

He stood up and stretched. It was ten-thirty. He looked out his den window. A pale-yellow half-moon was peeking around the side of the hill.

It was two weeks after the bail hearing, and the case was starting to shape up nicely. Conklin had secured a copy of Ortiz's medical file, and it had proved interesting reading. His idea about the Mercedes had panned out, too. Most important, Terry Conklin had finally got around to taking the shots he wanted at the motel. The pictures had not been developed yet, but Terry was confident that they would show what they both thought they would.

David had learned a lot about Larry Stafford, too. He and Terry had talked to people who knew Larry. A picture had emerged of a person who was always under a little more pressure than he could handle. Larry was a striver, never secure with what he had, always reaching for the pot of gold at the end of the rainbow.

Larry's father had divorced his mother when Larry was in his teens. Larry stayed with his mother, who was never able to cope with the destruction of a life she had built around one man.

Larry's father was a military man and a stern disciplinarian. Larry idolized him. Although there was no truth to it, Larry half believed that his father had left because Larry had not lived up to his expectations. He had spent the rest of his life trying to prove himself.

Larry had not just joined the Army, he had joined the Marines. In college and law school he had studied constantly, pushing himself to the point of exhaustion. Socially it had been the same story. He read all the books on self-improvement, drove the latest sports cars, often piling up debts to get them, and dressed according to the latest trends. Anyone who did not know Larry well would assume that he had achieved the success he sought, but Larry had achieved only a state of perpetual fear that drove him toward goals he could never reach.

David had come to feel sorry for Stafford. Jenny was right when she said he was like a little boy. He had no idea of what was really important in life, and he had spent his life running after the symbols of success. Now, just as he had grasped those symbols, they were going to be stripped away.

Stafford had married wealth and beauty, but his

marriage would not last. Jenny was protective of her husband, but David knew that it was out of a sense of duty, not love. He felt sure that when the trial was over, no matter what the outcome, Larry Stafford would lose his wife.

Larry would never make partner at Price, Winward, either. David had talked to Charlie Holt about that. Before his arrest there had been no clear consensus among the partners. Stafford did not have a first-class legal mind, but he did well in matters that required perseverance. Stafford's arrest had unbalanced the scales. The firm could not afford the publicity. If acquitted, Larry could look forward to a year more as an associate to give the appearance that the firm was fair, but it would be made clear to him that there would never be an offer of a partnership.

The doorbell rang and David went to answer it. Jennifer Stafford was waiting when he opened the door.

'Can I come in?' she asked, a bit unsure of herself.

'Of course,' he said, stepping aside.

Jenny was dressed in jeans, a black turtleneck, and a poncho. Her long hair was tied back in a ponytail. She looked very beautiful.

'I was going to call,' she said hesitantly, 'but I was afraid you would tell me not to come.'

'Don't be silly,' he said a little too quickly. 'I've been locked up with my law books all evening, and I can use some human companionship.'

191

David watched her wander across the living room. There was a fire in the fireplace, and Jenny stood in front of it, her back to him.

'Can I get you a drink?' David asked.

'Please.'

The liquor was in another room and he wanted a chance to settle down. Jenny had not been to his house since the night they had made love. Now she had come to him, and he was very unsure of himself. There had not been a moment since he had seen her again at the courthouse that he had not wanted her, but there was an unspoken understanding between them that made any personal discussions taboo.

Jenny was sitting in front of the fire, leaning against a large pillow, when he returned with her drink. He sat beside her, listening to the logs crackle and watching the flames twist and curl.

'How have you been?' he asked.

'Busy. School's back in session. I've had lesson plans to prepare, and they've given me a class of exceptional children. They really keep you on your toes.'

'Have you had any problems because of the case?'

'No. Actually, everyone has been very kind. John Olson, our principal, told me I could stay out for the whole trial.'

'That's great.'

'My folks have been unexpectedly supportive, too.'

'Why, didn't you expect them to be?'

'Mom's never approved of Larry. You know how mothers are.' Jenny shrugged. 'Anyway, Mom even volunteered to go to the jail with me on visiting day.' Jenny laughed suddenly.

'What's so funny?'

'Mom at the jail. You wouldn't understand unless you knew her.'

Jenny laughed again. The laugh was warm and open, without a trace of the self-consciousness that had characterized their relationship from the start. David wanted to hold her very much at that moment. She must have sensed this, because she stopped and her smile faded.

'David, I want you to be honest with me. Are you going to win? Will Larry be acquitted?'

'I think so. The State's whole case rests on Ortiz, and I think I'm going to be able to take him apart.'

David expected Jenny to ask him how he planned to get to Ortiz, but she didn't. Instead, she stood up and walked toward the window. He rolled onto his side and watched her.

'If Larry was convicted . . .' she started. 'If you didn't do your best to . . .'

She didn't finish. He stood up and walked over to her. When he spoke, his voice was firm.

'But I wouldn't do that and you wouldn't want me to. That's not the solution to our problem, Jenny.'

'David, I—'

193

He stopped her by placing the tips of his fingers against her lips.

'We're both under a lot of pressure, Jenny. I should never have taken this case, but I did. I've tried to kid myself, but a lot of the reason was so I could see you again. That's a very bad reason, but there it is and there's nothing I can do about it.'

'Oh, David,' she said, and it sounded like the sigh of a lost soul. David put his arms around her and they stood there, her head on his shoulder, not holding tight, but holding soft and caring.

'You don't know how much I've wanted you,' she said, 'but I couldn't hurt Larry. After that evening . . . I felt so confused and guilty. And I didn't know what the evening meant for you. You were so self-assured, as if you had done . . . been to bed with other women so often. I was afraid that it had just been sex for you and that I would make a fool of myself.'

'It was never just sex,' David whispered.

'Then Larry was arrested and Charlie told me to hire you. It made it worse for me, but Larry needed you.'

'And I need you, Jenny, very much.'

She looked up at him. She was frightened. They both were. Then their lips met, and they sank down on the soft carpet and made love in front of the fire.

Afterward she slept curled up in his arms. When David was certain he would not wake her, he eased her down and covered her with a blanket. Flame shadows played across her face, and she looked as peaceful as a sleeping child.

David put another log on the fire; then he sat across from Jenny so he could see her. She had come so close to saying something he did not want to think about. He could lose the trial, and their problems would be solved. But he would not. He would win an acquittal for Larry Stafford by trying the best case he had ever tried.

What kind of life could he and Jenny have together if he intentionally lost Larry Stafford's case? Even if no one else ever knew, they would know, and that knowledge would destroy them.

Jenny said that Larry was innocent, and Terry Conklin's pictures would prove it. Larry Stafford would be acquitted. Then Jenny would make her choice. A free choice.

PART III

TRIAL BY JURY

1

'Nice of you to drop by,' Larry said sarcastically as soon as the guard shut the door to the private visitor's room.

'Don't, Larry,' Jennifer began. She wanted to say more, but her courage failed her. Larry started to say one thing, changed his mind, and shook his head.

'I'm sorry. It's just with the trial starting . . . I just thought you'd visit more.'

Jennifer did not answer. She turned and walked to the far end of the narrow room. Larry followed her and touched her arm.

'I said I'm sorry, kitten. I'm all wound up.'

'I know,' she said quietly. He had lost weight, and he looked sad and defeated. She did not want to hurt him any more than he had already been hurt, but she knew she would have to.

'Larry, I don't know if I can go through with it.'

Larry paled, just staring, his mouth partly open.

'What . . . what do you . . .?'

'It's no good. They'll see that I'm lying and it will make it worse for you.'

'No. No. You'll do okay,' Stafford said desperately. 'Nash believes you, right? He's a pro. If we've got him fooled, the jury will be easy.'

Jennifer tried to say something. To talk to him. But her stomach was cramped with fear and self-loathing, and she felt short of breath. Larry just stared at her, afraid to speak. The silence in the room terrified him.

'Jenny, they can't prove anything,' he said finally. 'How will they know?' He stopped. He was pleading. 'Besides, it's the truth. I told you that, didn't I? I swore to God.'

Jenny still could not speak. She could see the panic in his eyes.

'Goddammit,' he said, his voice rising, 'you can't change your story now. You'll crucify me.

'Say something. It's your fault I'm here. Do you want to bury me now?'

His voice rose in pitch and cut through her. She started to cry.

Larry grabbed her roughly by both arms. His fingers dug into her flesh, hurting her.

'Answer me, Jenny. Do you want me to die? Because that's what's happening to me here. I couldn't stand prison, locked away, I can't stand it now. The noise, the smells. This filth.'

He raised his arm like an accusing angel and pointed at the room.

'Do you hate me so much that you want me to live the rest of my life like some animal?'

She started to cry, turning her head from him, not wanting him to hold her or comfort her. He was right. She did not hate him. She was only tired of him. Disillusioned by the destruction of the love that she had once felt for him. She couldn't let him end up in a place like this. Not even if he had . . . She could not complete the thought, because if Larry had killed that woman, then she was partly to blame.

'All right,' she whispered, her voice catching in her throat. 'All right.'

Stafford let her go. He was afraid and alone, and he could see the strands of his slender lifeline unraveling before his eyes.

ORTIZ SLOUCHED DOWN in the passenger seat of the unmarked police car. He had on a heavy jacket and a sweater, and he was still cold. Beside him Jack Hennings blew into his cupped hands, then tucked them under his armpits for warmth.

'I can't believe it's this fucking cold,' he complained.

'Tell me about it,' Ortiz mumbled. He leaned forward and wiped a space on the windshield clean where it had fogged over.

'I don't see why we can't just bust in and arrest him,' Hennings said.

'I told you why. My snitch said T.V.'d have it on him. I'm not going to risk missing it in a search and have that asshole laughing at me up and down the avenue.'

'I'd rather have every nigger in the city laughing at me than have to sit out here for another hour.'

'Besides, Kermit is probably in there with him, and I want to be sure where he is when we move.'

'Monroe's a pussy,' Hennings said. Hennings was big and talked tough, but Ortiz doubted he'd be able to take Kermit Monroe one on one.

'If you think it's so easy, Lone Ranger, why don't you go over there all by yourself and call me when it's over?'

Hennings grinned. 'Don't get so nervous, Bert. I know karate.'

'Oh, Jesus, that's all I need.'

'Besides,' Hennings said, holding up the Magnum he had placed on the seat of the car, 'the man won't be doin' much wrasslin' with his balls in China. Now, if—'

Ortiz sat up. The door to Johnson's house opened, and two men were illuminated by the porch light. From where they were sitting, it was easy to make out Johnson in his ankle-length fur coat.

'Let's go,' he said, and the two policemen left the car. Johnson and Monroe talked as they walked to the curb. Ortiz and Hennings moved quickly, trying to attract as little attention as possible as they approached. Monroe turned his back to them and opened the passenger door for his boss. The howling wind muffled the sound of footsteps. Monroe turned and made a move for his gun. He stopped when he saw Hennings poised in a shooting stance.

'Freeze!' Hennings shouted.

Johnson stood with his hands half-raised and a stunned expression on his face. Then he bent his head and squinted into the dark and cold.

'Is that you, Ortiz?'

'Shut up and spread against the car.'

'What the fuck you doin', man? I'm clean.'

'I said, against the car. Both of you.'

'I ain't humiliatin' myself in no—'

Ortiz hit Johnson in the solar plexus as hard as he could, then kicked him in the crotch. The pimp looked as if he were going to be sick. He slipped to his knees. A quick look of surprise crossed Hennings's face. Monroe started to lower his hands.

'Just try it, fuck face. I'd love to waste you,' Ortiz said, swinging his weapon in Monroe's direction. The big man looked uncertain for a moment, then slowly leaned against the car as he had been told.

'Now, spread,' Ortiz commanded, pulling Johnson to his feet and shoving him against the car. Hennings kept a few paces back and Ortiz frisked Monroe. He handed a gun and a switchblade to his partner. Hennings placed them in his pocket. While Hennings's attention was distracted, Ortiz slipped the plastic baggie from his pocket and palmed it. Johnson was still doubled over and in pain, but he was doing his best to spread-eagle in order to avoid another beating. There were no wisecracks now, Ortiz thought with satisfaction. No bad-mouth.

Ortiz reached around in front of the pimp and

pretended to search inside his coat for a weapon. Suddenly, he pulled his hand out of T.V.'s pocket and waved the baggie toward Hennings.

'Bingo,' Ortiz said.

T.V. turned his head. His eyes opened wide when he saw what Ortiz was holding.

'What's that?' he asked, surprise distracting him from his pain.

'Your passport to the penitentiary, T.V. Now, move over to that police car so we can escort you downtown.'

'You planted that!' T.V. said incredulously.

'Shut up,' Ortiz said softly.

'You in on this too, pig?' T.V. asked Hennings.

'Didn't you hear Officer Ortiz tell you to shut your face?' Hennings asked.

Ortiz jerked Monroe's hands behind him and cuffed the big man. He made sure that the cuffs were too tight. He gave T.V. the same treatment.

'I'm going to read you your rights, gentlemen,' Ortiz said as the prisoners were hustled to the police car.

'You are really a sick son of a bitch, Ortiz. You plant that shit on me, then talk about rights.'

Ortiz read the Miranda rights to the prisoners, then motioned them into the back of the police car. There were no handles on the inside of the back door, and a wire screen separated the back seat from the front. Hennings drove and Ortiz leaned back. Monroe looked out the back window, accepting his fate silently. Johnson slouched beside him with a sullen expression on his face. The whole thing was unfair. He expected a beating now and then. He had seen police lie on the witness stand when an arrest was legitimate but the defendant would escape on a technicality if the truth came out. But this was different. It was . . . was . . . unfair.

Johnson looked through the mesh at the back of Ortiz's head. Ortiz wanted something. He had a feeling about it. Something he wanted bad enough to break the rules. He'd wait and see what it was. If he could, he'd do what Ortiz wanted; then he would wait for his chance.

'WHY YOU PLANT that dope, Ortiz?' T.V. asked when they were alone in the interrogation room.

'I didn't plant any dope on you, T.V. My inform-ant said you'd have it on you and you did. Anyone who watches television knows you're a notorious pusher. Why wouldn't you be carrying narcotics?'

'My lawyer gonna tear that story apart. You got no case on me.'

'Oh, yeah? When you talk to your lawyer, ask him how he's going to do that. A court won't order me to tell you the name of an informant. It's the law, T.V.'

T.V. was silent for a moment. His eyes darted nervously from one side of the room to the other, as if looking for some way out of his predicament.

'You ain't nothin' but a crooked cop, Ortiz.'

'Try and prove that in court. You think a jury will take the word of a nigger pimp against mine? You're gonna do ten hard years on this, T.V., unless . . .'

T.V. looked up from the floor. 'Unless what?'

'Unless you tell the truth about what that white man did to your whore friend.'

'You still on that kick?' Johnson asked, surprised.

'The truth, T.V., will set you free.'

'How? How you gonna arrange for me to beat this rap?'

'I found the evidence, I can lose the evidence. You play ball with me, and this case will disappear like one of Houdini's card tricks. But you fuck with me, and I'll see you in the penitentiary doing hard time. My word.'

'Your word ain't worth shit,' Johnson said in a sudden burst of anger.

'Maybe,' Ortiz said with a broad smile, 'but it's all you've got.'

Johnson stood up and walked to the far wall. He turned his back on Ortiz. It was quiet in the soundproof room.

'And suppose I tell you what I know? Is that all?'

'No. You tell the jury. You testify.'

'I gotta . . . I don't know if I can do that.'

'Well, you better decide fast. The trial starts tomorrow and you don't have much time.'

2

A fog bank drifted across the sand, obscuring the terrain of the endless beach. Monica stopped, terrified and alone. She turned slowly, looking for a landmark, but the fog had made subtle changes and she felt lost.

The fog lifted for a moment, and a figure, half-shrouded by the mist, floated away from her. She ran after it, lifting her legs high to avoid the sand that clutched at her ankles. She must not fall or the sand would suck her down.

The fog was drifting back and her quarry was slipping into the shadows. She ran faster, the pounding of her heart drowning out the cadence of the incoming tide. Faster. She was losing ground. Faster. She was falling, screaming, flailing helplessly as she hurtled downward into darkness.

Then the beach was gone, and the only part of her dream that remained was the beating of her heart.

Monica looked around the room. It was her bedroom and she was sitting up in her bed, drenched in sweat. The clock read six A.M. She could try to sleep for another half hour, but she was too wound up.

Monica turned on the light and went into the

bathroom. The face she saw in the mirror was pale and had bags under the eyes. Not good, she thought, but it would not get better if she did not get a decent night's sleep.

She had been exhausted during jury selection, and her opening statement lacked the punch of David's emotional declaration of his client's innocence. Monica had watched the jurors as she outlined the evidence she would produce at trial. They had listened attentively, and she was convinced that they were responsible people who would convict Larry Stafford if they believed he was guilty. But would they believe that, or would David fool them?

Fool them. That was an odd way to describe the function of the defense bar, but Monica felt it was an accurate description. When they had lived together, David often talked of himself, self-deprecatingly, as a magician whose job it was to make people see what was not there and to conceal what was there. Monica believed that Larry Stafford killed Darlene Hersch, and she was afraid that David would make her evidence disappear with a wave of his verbal wand.

Monica opened the refrigerator and took out a container of orange juice. She put a kettle of water on the stove and tried to decide between cold cereal and frozen waffles. She settled for two pieces of whole-wheat toast.

Judge Rosenthal had been chosen to preside at the trial, and David did not object, even though

Rosenthal had issued the search warrant. Jury selection had taken longer than expected because of the difficulty in finding twelve Portland residents who had not formed an opinion about the 'Policewoman Murder.' Monica and David had agreed on a jury shortly before noon on the second day of trial. They had concluded opening statements after lunch, and she had presented the testimony of Dr. Francis R. Beauchamp, the medical examiner, before Judge Rosenthal had called a halt to the proceedings for the day.

The coffee was bitter and Monica grimaced as it went down, but she needed the caffeine. The toast was burned, too. Shit! She felt like smashing something. Not a good way to begin the most important day of the State's case. She tried to calm down.

Monica was always tense when she was in trial, but it was worse when she tried a case against David. She was a highly competitive woman who enjoyed winning. When Monica tried cases against other attorneys, she thought of them strictly in business terms. She could never think of David that way. Even after all these years she was still a little in love with him, and she knew it, so she overcompensated whenever they were matched against each other, and ended up pushing herself harder than she had to, out of fear that her feelings for him would influence her performance.

There was an added reason for her anxiety this morning: Ortiz and his surprise witness. Last night, after court recessed, she had been making notes on Beauchamp's testimony when Ortiz and Crosby came into her office. She was in a foul mood and wanted to leave, but the two policemen seemed excited.

'Beauchamp was pretty convincing, I hear,' Crosby said, settling into a chair. Dr. Beauchamp was a frustrated actor with a knack for describing fatal wounds that made them appear more revolting than a color photograph ever could.

'All Beauchamp established was that Darlene Hersch was struck in the abdomen and neck, then had her throat slit. He didn't establish who did it,' Monica replied testily.

'I don't think pinning this on Stafford is going to be a problem anymore,' Ortiz said with a confident smile.

'I'm glad to hear that, Bert. I thought we had problems.'

Ortiz's face clouded over. 'Why do you say that?' he asked.

'The case is flimsy. No offense, Bert, but all we have is your ID based on a few seconds' observation after you had been struck on the head hard enough to require hospitalization. I'm beginning to think we may have moved too fast on this one.'

'You can stop worrying, because I've got the man who is going to do it to Mr. Stafford.'

Monica put her pen down and waited for Ortiz to continue. Ortiz had a tendency to be dramatic, and he paused to heighten the tension.

'Remember Ron called you when Stafford was arraigned and asked you to oppose bail?'

'Yes,' she said, turning toward Crosby. 'You said that another officer was certain that Stafford had beaten up a prostitute and was going to try to find the police reports. I also recall being put off by you every time I've asked you about that report,' she added angrily. 'I put myself on the line at the bail hearing because of your assurances.'

'You have every right to be angry, Monica,' Crosby said sheepishly. 'Tracking down our witness just took longer than we thought.'

'You have a witness who saw Larry Stafford beat up a prostitute?'

'Exactly,' Ortiz said.

'Who is it?' Monica asked.

'Cyrus Johnson.'

'Cyrus – Jesus, Bert. I'm not going to vouch for the credibility of a known pimp and dope dealer.'

'Who else would be able to testify about Stafford's sex habits? It's the fact that he's a pimp that makes him credible.'

'Bert, you've seen David operate. Do you know what he'd do to Johnson? The man sells dope to schoolchildren, for Christ's sake.'

'If you're afraid of Nash, you shouldn't be trying this case,' Ortiz said, suddenly very angry.

Monica jumped to her feet. 'Get out of my office,' she shouted. 'I'm not going to take that shit.'

Crosby put his hand on Ortiz's elbow and Ortiz was immediately contrite.

'I'm sorry. I didn't mean . . . I think you're a hell of a good lawyer. It's just . . . well, the case means a lot to me and I want to make sure Stafford doesn't get away.'

Monica sat down and leaned back in her chair. The outburst had taken a lot out of her.

'Apology accepted. The case is getting to me, too.'

'Will you at least talk to Johnson and read this police report?' Crosby asked, placing the report in front of her.

'Yeah. I didn't really want to go home, anyway. But you two are going to stand me dinner. I'm starving.'

THE INTERVIEW WITH Johnson created more problems than it solved. The man was smooth, and she could not determine if he was telling the truth. True, the story he told her was the same story he had told the police two years ago, but he had reason to lie to the police then, and he was in trouble, and obviously anxious to deal now. Monica wanted to convict Stafford, but she would not put on testimony she believed might be perjured.

Even if the story was true, she did not know if she could get Johnson's testimony into evidence. Johnson would be testifying that Stafford had committed a prior criminal act, and the rules of evidence forbade the introduction of that type of evidence, with only a few narrowly defined exceptions. Monica was not convinced that Johnson's evidence fell under any of them. David was an expert on the rules of evidence, and she would have to research the question of admissibility thoroughly, because she knew how hard David would fight when he learned about Johnson.

Monica finished combing her hair and put on her coat. Her key witnesses, Grimes and Ortiz, were scheduled to testify today. If they survived David's cross-examination, she might not have to put on Johnson.

'AND WHAT HAPPENED then, Mr. Grimes?' Monica asked. The motel clerk had just taken the stand and had been preceded by several laboratory technicians, a supervisor from the Motor Vehicles Division who established Stafford's ownership of the Mercedes, and Detective Crosby, who testified about the search of Stafford's house.

'I gave her the key and she left. I went back to readin', and the next thing I know, I hear these screams.'

David leaned forward and began making notes about Grimes's testimony on a yellow legal pad. Larry Stafford sat beside him at counsel table, looking businesslike in a conservative dark-blue three-piece suit. David had intentionally dressed more casually than his client to give the jury an initial visual impression that Stafford, not he, was the defense attorney.

'Where were the screams coming from?' Monica asked. David heard Stafford shift nervously in his seat. He glanced at his client and caught him looking over his shoulder at the crowded courtroom. Stafford was looking for his wife, and David felt a slight pang of conscience that momentarily dampened his otherwise expansive mood. David knew where Jenny was and why she was late for court this morning. They had spent the night together, and she had returned home to change while he dressed for court.

'Did you notice Jenny this morning?' Stafford whispered, as if reading David's thoughts. There was an edge to Larry's voice, and an air of tension around him that David had noticed since the start of the trial. David expected a person on trial for murder to be nervous, but he sensed that there was something else eating at his client and that it concerned Jenny.

'She'll be along,' David whispered back. 'And don't look so down in the mouth. Take notes and concentrate on the witnesses, like I told you. I don't want the jury to see your interest lag for one second.'

'I couldn't tell who was screamin' at first,' Grimes continued, 'so I went outside in the lot. The motel rooms are behind the office, and I had to go around the corner of the building. That's when I seen this guy come bustin' out of twenty-two.'

'Did you get a good look at the person you saw running away?'

'No, ma'am, I didn't. He was runnin' too fast and there's a lot of shadow up there.'

'Go on.'

'Well, by now the screamin' had stopped, and I looked up at twenty-two to see if anyone'd come after the one that run out. I seen the door was wide-open, but no one was comin', so I started across the lot to see what's what. Just then this car came from the rear parking lot. It was the same one the girl'd come in, but she wasn't in it.'

'Who did you see in that car?'

'It was a man drivin', but I didn't get a clear look at him.'

Monica stood up and walked across to the witness box. 'Mr. Grimes, I hand you what has been marked as State's exhibit number five, and I ask you if you recognize the car in that picture.'

Grimes took the color photograph of Stafford's Mercedes and studied it carefully.

'I can't say for sure, but it's like the car that girl came in.'

'Thank you,' Monica said, returning the exhibit to the bailiff. 'After the car left the lot, what did you do?'

'To tell the truth, I wasn't too anxious to find out why there'd been all that screamin', but I got to thinkin' that someone might be hurt up there, so I went up to the room. That's when I seen 'em.'

215

'Who was that?'

'Well, the lights were out, so I didn't see her at first. The man was lyin' with his head against the bed. He was bleedin' and I thought he might be dead. Then I seen he was breathin', so I went to use the phone. That's when I saw her. You see a lot workin' in the hotel business, but that was terrible. I ran outa there and called the cops from my office.'

'And did the police come?'

'A few minutes later. An ambulance came too.'

'Thank you, Mr. Grimes. I have no further questions.'

'Mr. Nash,' Judge Rosenthal said, nodding in David's direction.

David took a final look at the report Detective Crosby had made of his interview with Grimes, and Terry Conklin's report of their interview. It was quiet in the courtroom, and David could hear a juror shifting in his seat and the nervous drumming of Stafford's fingers on the wooden table.

'Just a few questions, Mr. Grimes. As I understand your testimony, you did not get a good look at the man who was driving the Mercedes while Darlene Hersch was registering.'

'That's right.'

'And you did not get a good look at him when he ran out of the room where the murder was committed?'

Grimes nodded.

'Did you get a look at him as he drove out of the parking lot, after the murder?'

'Like I said, not a clear look.'

'Did you see his hair well enough to describe it to the jury?'

Monica had been going over her notes and listening to David's examination with half an ear. Now she lowered her pen and concentrated. She could tell from David's tone that something was up.

'Yeah, I seen his hair,' Grimes answered. 'Just for a second, but I seen it.'

'Did the driver of the Mercedes have blond curly hair like Mr. Stafford?'

Grimes leaned forward and studied Larry Stafford.

'Could he turn around?' Grimes asked, turning toward the judge. 'I only seen him from the back.'

'That's up to Mr. Nash,' Rosenthal replied.

'Certainly,' David said, and Larry stood up and turned his back to the witness stand.

'I don't remember it lookin' like that,' Grimes said decisively.

'How would you describe the driver's hair?'

'Well, like I said, I only seen it for a second, but it looked brown-colored to me, and he had one of them cuts that came down a ways.'

'Thank you. I have nothing further.'

Monica reread the police report on Grimes rapidly. There was nothing about hair color in the report. She turned to the third page and saw why. The son of a bitch was going back on his statement to the police. This was bad, because Grimes had the appearance of an honest witness. His testimony about the hair color could be crucial in a close case.

'Mr. Grimes,' Monica asked, 'how well lit is the parking lot at the Raleigh?'

Grimes tilted his head back and furrowed his brow. 'Not too good over by the side near Tacoma Street, but there's plenty of light from that McDonald's. Bothers some of the customers sometimes.'

Monica felt her stomach tighten. Damn, she'd just made it worse. She hated surprises in trial, and this was a bad one. She decided to back off on the lighting.

'Was the murderer's car moving fast when it left the lot?'

'I'll say. It just come whippin' around that corner. He screeched his tires when he did that, and that's why I looked over.'

'So you just had a brief view of him?'

'Right. Like I said, I wasn't concentratin' on him much. I was lookin' up at the room.'

'Do you remember being interviewed by Ronald Crosby, a Portland police detective, on the evening of the murder?'

'Was that the fella that bought me coffee?'

'I wouldn't know, Mr. Grimes.'

'Nice fella. He even sprung for a doughnut. Not as tight as some a them cops I know.'

Someone laughed in the back of the courtroom,

and the judge rapped his gavel. Monica waited for the jury's attention to return to the witness stand.

'You never told Detective Crosby that the man had long brown hair, did you?'

'He never asked.'

'But he did ask you if there was anything about the man you could remember, did he not?'

'I don't recollect the whole conversation.'

'Do you remember saying that the man did not make much of an impression on you and Detective Crosby asking you if you remembered his hair, eyes, or anything else about him and your answering "No"?'

'That sounds right. Only I was talkin' about when the girl come in. He never asked about when the fella drove off.'

Monica looked as if she were going to ask another question, then thought better of it.

'Nothing further,' she said.

Judge Rosenthal looked at David, who merely smiled and shook his head.

'Nice going,' Larry whispered.

'That's what you pay me for. If I do as well with the next witness, we'll be in good shape.'

'Who's the next witness?' Stafford asked David.

'The State calls Bertram Ortiz,' Monica said.

DIRECT EXAMINATION WAS easy for Ortiz. The questions were almost identical to the direct examination during the bail hearing, and he had gone over his answers with Monica several times. First he described the stakeout and the beige Mercedes. Then he recounted his surveillance during the drive to the motel. He told the hushed courtroom of his violent encounter with the man who had murdered Darlene Hersch, his reaction when he saw Larry Stafford in the courthouse corridor, and the results of the search at Stafford's house. Then, as the jurors leaned forward, caught up in the tension of the moment, Ortiz turned toward the defense table and pointed his finger at the defendant. Direct examination was over, and Monica nodded to David.

Ortiz turned toward the defense table and waited for cross-examination to begin. His hand had been steady, and there had been no tremor in his voice when he identified Larry Stafford, because he had learned from dozens of experiences on the witness stand to control his nerves, but the fear of what David might do to him was there.

David did not rush his questions. He smiled at Ortiz and leaned back in his chair. He wanted Ortiz to wait, and he wanted to build on the tension that already permeated the courtroom.

'Officer Ortiz,' he asked finally, 'what day was Darlene Hersch killed?'

'June sixteenth,' Ortiz answered tersely. He was determined to answer only what he was asked and to volunteer nothing. The less he said, the less information Nash would have to work with.

'Thank you,' David said politely. 'And when

did you see Mr. Stafford in the courthouse hall-way?'

'Early September.'

'Some three months after the murder?'

'Yes.'

David stood up and walked to an easel that the clerk had placed between the witness stand and the jury box. David flipped the cover page from a large drawing pad over the top of the easel and revealed the diagram of the motel room that Ortiz had drawn at the bail hearing.

'During a prior hearing in this case, I asked you to draw this sketch and to indicate your position and the killer's position at the moment you saw his face, did I not?'

'Yes.'

'And is this an accurate representation of those positions?'

Ortiz studied the drawing for a moment, then nodded.

'I believe at the hearing you stated that, at the moment you saw the killer's face, his left arm and leg were inside the room a bit and his body was at a slight angle, with the right arm and leg outside the door?'

'Yes.'

'Good. Now, you were struck immediately upon entering the motel room, were you not?'

'Yes.'

'The lights in the room were out?'

'Yes.'

'You fell, twisted, and your head struck the bed?'

'Yes.'

'How long would you say you had a good view of the killer's face?'

'A few seconds.'

'Five to ten?'

'A little more than that.'

David picked up the transcript of the bail hearing, consulted an index card, and flipped to a page.

'At a prior hearing in this case, did you not testify as follows:

'"Q: So you saw him for a few seconds?

'"A: Yes.

'"Q: Less than a minute?

'"A: Maybe five, ten seconds. But I saw him."'

'I think that's right.'

'So the only time you saw the killer's face was for five or ten seconds after you had been struck on the head and before you lost consciousness?'

'Yes, but I saw him clearly. It was Stafford,' Ortiz blurted out. Monica expected David to object to the unresponsive answer, but David merely smiled.

'You are certain of that?' David asked. Monica was puzzled. Why was David giving Ortiz a chance to repeat so damaging a statement?

'Positive.'

'Yes. I believe, at the prior hearing, I asked you,

"You are certain?" and you replied, "I will never forget that face."'

'Yes, I said that,' Ortiz answered nervously. He had forgotten that he had given that answer at the bail hearing.

'But the impossible happened, did it not?'

'What do you mean?'

David strolled over to the far end of the counsel table and picked up a stack of papers.

'Were you hospitalized after the blow to your head?'

'Yes.'

'Was Dr. Arthur Stewart your treating physician?'

'Yes.'

'How long were you in the hospital, Officer Ortiz?'

'About a week.'

'How long did you continue to see Dr. Stewart for problems relating to the blow to your head?'

Ortiz could feel the sweat forming on his brow. Why didn't the bastard ask the question Ortiz knew he would ask?

'I stopped two weeks ago.'

'Mid-October? Is that when he released you?'

'Yes.'

'You had a concussion, did you not?'

'Yes.'

David paused and the smile disappeared. 'And you could remember nothing about what happened inside that motel room from June sixteenth until September? Isn't that true?'

'I remembered parts of what happened. It was—'

'Mr. Ortiz . . . Pardon me. Officer Ortiz,' David said, his voice cutting like a knife, 'I have here copies of your medical records from Good Samaritan Hospital. On September third, did you visit Dr. Stewart?'

'Uh, I . . . It could have been that date. I had an appointment in early September.'

'You don't remember?' David asked with a smirk.

Ortiz felt his body tighten. He wanted to strike out at David. He felt like a butterfly pinioned on a board, waiting for dissection.

'Objection,' Monica said, standing. 'Mr. Nash is arguing with the witness.'

She could see the danger signs and had to give Ortiz a chance to collect his thoughts.

'Yes, Mr. Nash,' the judge said, 'just ask your questions.'

'Very well, Your Honor. Officer Ortiz, did you not tell Dr. Stewart during your September visit, a few short days before you arrested Larry Stafford, that you could not remember what happened inside the motel room and that you could not remember what the killer looked like?'

Ortiz did not answer immediately. He stared at David and at Stafford. Stafford stared back.

'Well, Officer?' David asked sharply.

'Yes.'

'You had amnesia, did you not?'

'Yes, if that's what you call it.'

'What do you call it?'

'I mean . . .'

Ortiz stopped. David waited a moment, watching the jury.

'Officer, if I understand your testimony, you first saw the Mercedes from a distance of one city block?'

'Yes,' Ortiz answered quickly, grateful that the subject had been changed.

'Then you followed it from a distance of approximately two city blocks?'

'Yes.'

'And, finally, you saw it briefly as you drove by the motel lot?'

'Yes.'

'Those were the only times you saw the car that evening?'

'Yes.'

'And you did not know what model and year the car was until you checked with the Motor Vehicle Division?'

'I . . . It's the car I saw,' Ortiz answered weakly.

David picked up three color photographs from his table and walked over to the witness stand. Monica drummed the tip of her pen on her desk. Ortiz was in trouble, and she did not know how much longer he would be able to stand up under

David's questioning. She had Dr. Stewart on call to testify that Ortiz, and others with amnesia caused by a concussion, could recall with complete accuracy events they had forgotten. But for the jury to believe in Ortiz's recall, they had to believe in Ortiz.

'Will you study these three photographs, please?' David asked Ortiz. The policeman shuffled the photos until he had viewed all three.

'Would you tell the jury what they are?'

'They appear to be a beige Mercedes-Benz.'

'Same type that Mr. Stafford drives?'

'Yes.'

David smiled at Ortiz and took back the pictures.

'I have no further questions.'

Monica could not believe it. She had seen David tear witnesses apart and she knew his technique. He always softened them up, as he had Ortiz, with questions that would shake their confidence. Then he progressed from point to point, ending with a series of questions that involved a major point in their testimony. The questions about Ortiz's amnesia had been expected, but she also expected more. Ortiz had been touched by David, but not badly shaken. She wanted him off the stand quickly, while he was still basically intact.

'No further questions,' Monica said.

'Call your next witness.'

'Dr. Arthur Stewart, Your Honor.'

*

ORTIZ WANTED TO discuss the case as soon as she left the courtroom, but she told him to wait until they got to her office. Dr. Stewart had been excellent and David had not scored many points. She had rested the State's case at the end of his testimony without calling Cyrus Johnson.

'But why?' Ortiz demanded when he and Monica and Crosby were alone.

'Because it wasn't necessary and I did not want to risk it.'

'You haven't shown any motive. Johnson can establish that this guy is an S-M freak.'

'Or make it look like we're trying to railroad him with perjured testimony. Look, Bert, we already have a motive. He is a member of a big law firm, but not a partner. He is married to a wealthy woman. If he is arrested for prostitution, his career and marriage could be over. What more do we need? Besides, you were terrific.'

Ortiz shook his head. 'I don't know. That business with the amnesia. Don't you think . . .?'

'I was in the courtroom, Bert,' Crosby said. 'You came off just great, and that doctor cleared that whole business up. I was surprised how easy Nash went on you.'

'Yeah. That has me worried, too. Why do you think he let up?'

'I don't know,' Monica said, 'but let's not look a gift horse in the mouth.'

'If it was a gift,' Ortiz said. 'That son of a

bitch has something he's not telling you about. I can feel it.'

Monica shrugged. 'I'm not going to worry about it now.'

'And you can still use T.V. in rebuttal, right?' Ortiz asked.

'Bert, I don't trust him. He'll do anything to get out of this dope charge.'

'I don't think so,' Ortiz said, shaking his head vigorously. 'It's too much of a coincidence.'

'Well, if the case goes as well as it has so far, it will all be academic.'

'MR. STAFFORD CALLS Patrick Walsh, Your Honor,' David said, and the clerk left the courtroom to summon the witness. David took the opportunity to collect the exhibits he would use and to review his notes on Walsh's testimony.

The defense was going well. David had started by calling several of Larry's friends and business associates, who testified to his good character. They had painted a picture of a newly wed, young professional who possessed a sense of humor and a dedication to his work. Monica, through cross-examination, brought out the fact that Larry had been passed over for partner by his firm, but Charlie Holt, the witness, had handled that line of questioning well. David thought this revelation had provoked sympathy from the jurors.

David used Barry Dietrich, the partner with whom

Larry had met on the evening of the murder, to bridge the gap between the character witnesses and those witnesses who would establish Stafford's defense. Dietrich was not enthusiastic about testifying. With the exception of Charlie Holt, the partners at Price, Winward had been reluctant to get involved in the case. However, once on the stand, Dietrich had done well.

The courtroom door opened, and a tall, angular red-headed man with a slight limp walked to the stand. David looked back toward him and noticed Jenny seated on the aisle at the rear of the courtroom. They had been together often during the last month, treating each moment alone as if it might be their last. David loved Jenny. He knew that now. Often, when they were lying together, David wondered what would happen to them when the trial ended. If Larry was free, would Jenny go back to him? David was weak and vulnerable at such moments. He would hold Jenny, afraid of what might happen if he let her go.

'Mr. Walsh, how are you employed?' David asked once the witness had been sworn.

'I'm a zone distribution manager for Mercedes-Benz of North America.'

'What does a zone distribution manager do?'

'For sales purposes Mercedes has divided the United States into zones and subzones, and I'm in charge of sales in the San Francisco zone, which covers the Pacific North-west and Northern

California. I order all the cars for the zone and distribute them to the dealers in the subzones.'

David picked up the photograph of Larry's Mercedes and handed it to the witness.

'How long have you been with Mercedes-Benz, Mr. Walsh?'

'It will be twenty-two years this April.'

'I've just handed you a photograph which has been marked as State's exhibit five, and I ask you if you can identify that car for the jury.'

'Certainly. This is our model 300SEL, 1991. It is beige in color.'

'What does 300SEL mean?'

'The 300SEL is a four-door sedan with a gas engine. Three hundred is the engine size. *S* means the car is one of our super-class models, the largest sedan we sell. *E* means the car has fuel injection. *L* stands for a long wheel base.'

'Do you also sell a 300SE model?'

'Yes, we do. That model looks identical, but it's four inches shorter.'

'Thank you. Now I am handing you three other photographs,' David said, handing Walsh the pictures he had shown to Ortiz on the preceding day. 'Can you identify the cars in those pictures?'

Walsh studied the photographs, then stacked them and turned toward the jury as David had instructed him to do at their pretrial meeting. He held up the top photograph.

'This photograph, which is marked defendant's exhibit seven, is a beige Mercedes-Benz.'

'Is it a 1991, 300SEL?'

'It is not. It is a 1981, 300SD.'

Several of the jurors leaned forward, and Monica cocked her head to one side, focusing her attention on the witness.

'And exhibit eight?'

Walsh held up a picture of another beige Mercedes.

'This is a 1985, 300SE model.'

There was a stir in the courtroom.

'And the final car?'

'Exhibit nine is a 1987, 420SEL.'

'If I told you that a person who had viewed those photographs had described all three cars as being the same type as the defendant's 1991, 300SEL, would you be surprised?'

'Not in the least. From 1981 to 1991 Mercedes-Benz made several models in that basic body style that were, with minor differences, very similar. From 1981 to 1983 there was a model 380SEL, a four-door long-wheel-base sedan. From 1981 to 1985 there was the model 300SD. In 1984 and 1985 there was a 500SEL and the 380SE. From 1986 through 1991 we had a model 560SEL, which was similar in appearance to the 300SEL and the 420SEL. And we had a diesel engine car in 1986 and 1987 with the same body. In 1990 and 1991 we had diesel models 350SD and 350SDL.'

'With all these cars looking so similar, how were

you able to tell that the three cars in exhibits seven, eight, and nine were not the 300SEL?'

'Exhibit seven shows a 1981, 300SD. The most obvious difference is that the 300SD is four inches shorter. If you look at the front and back doors and windows, you can see that they are roughly the same size in the 300SD, but the back door and window of the 1991, 300SEL are longer than its front door and window because of the longer wheel base. This difference is obvious to me but would not be noticeable to someone who is not familiar with Mercedes-Benz body types.

'The 1985, 380SE in exhibit eight is also shorter, and the wheel design is different. The 1991 car has a solid disk where a hubcap would normally be, but the 1985 car has a concave disk with a center hub about the size of the fuel-tank cap.'

'Mr. Walsh, what discernible difference is there between the 1991, 300SEL and the 1987, 420SEL, the car in exhibit nine?'

'Mr. Nash, there is no difference at all. Not even an expert can tell the difference between those two cars. I knew they were different only because I supplied you with the photograph.'

'Was there any difference in the number of cars sold for the four models in the four photographs?'

'No. They all sold roughly the same in all four years.'

'And what color was the most popular color for the four models we have been discussing?'

'Beige.'

David turned and smiled at Monica. To the witness he said, 'Thank you, Mr. Walsh. I have no further questions.'

'AND HOW ARE you employed, Mr. Waldheim?' David asked the distinguished-looking businessman who had just taken the witness stand. Across from David, Monica listened with one ear as she carried on a hurried conversation with Detective Crosby. Walsh's testimony had hurt, and she wanted Crosby to start looking for ways to rebut it. She was painfully ignorant about cars and had asked no questions of Walsh. That meant that, as of the moment, Ortiz's testimony about the Mercedes was virtually worthless.

'I am the vice president in charge of menswear for Sherwood Forest Sportswear.'

'Where are your headquarters located?'

'Bloomington, Illinois.'

'And that is where your office is?'

'That is correct.'

From a pile of exhibits David selected the shirt that had been seized from Stafford's house and brought it to Waldheim.

'I hand you what has been marked as State's exhibit twenty-three and ask you if you recognize this shirt.'

Waldheim took the shirt and examined it. 'Yes. This is part of last year's summer line.'

'Would you tell the jury how many of these shirts your firm distributed nationally?'

Waldheim turned slightly and addressed the jury.

'Last year was a very good year for menswear. This particular shirt was one of our most popular items. I checked our records before flying here, and I would say that we sold some five thousand dozen of this shirt nationally.'

'How many shirts are five thousand dozen, Mr. Waldheim?'

'Well, one thousand dozen equals twelve thousand shirts, so . . . let me see . . . sixty thousand shirts.'

'And that is a round figure?'

'That is correct. The actual number was in excess of five thousand dozen.'

'Mr. Waldheim, are you aware of the shirt patterns used by your competitors?'

'Certainly. We have to keep tabs on the competition.'

'To your knowledge does Sherwood Forest, or any other shirt manufacturer, make a shirt with a pattern similar to this shirt?'

'Yes. That forest pattern was so successful, especially in this area of the country, that we put out another similar line, and so did two of our competitors.'

'Thank you, Mr. Waldheim. Nothing further.'

Monica had been doing some calculations while David questioned Waldheim. There is a rule of cross-examination which holds that an attorney should never ask a witness a question unless she knows the answer. Monica had a question she wanted to ask, and Waldheim's testimony was so damaging that she decided to break the rule.

'Mr. Waldheim, your company distributes shirts nationally, doesn't it?'

'Yes.'

'How many of the shirts you were just shown were distributed in this state?'

'Uhmm, something in excess of one hundred dozen, I believe. The shirt did very well here.'

'And of those one hundred dozen, how many were distributed in Portland?'

'I'm not certain, but I would guess more than half.'

'So we are talking about approximately six hundred shirts in the metropolitan area?'

'A little more than six hundred. Yes.'

'Nothing further.'

Monica was troubled. She had softened the impact of Waldheim's testimony a little, but six hundred shirts was still a lot of shirts, and there were all those knockoffs from other companies. David was starting to cut away the basis for Ortiz's identification, and if he did that successfully . . .

There was a stir in the courtroom and Monica looked around. While she had been lost in thought, David had called his next witness – Jennifer Stafford.

*

JENNIFER WALKED TO the stand without looking at David, but she did pause momentarily by Larry's side. The look she gave him was one the jury could not see and David could not read.

Jennifer took the oath, then seated herself in the witness box. She sat erect, her hands folded primly in her lap. There was a trace of tension at the corners of her lips, and a tightness about her that betrayed her uneasiness. When David addressed her, she jerked slightly, as if she had experienced a minor electric shock.

'Mrs. Stafford, are you employed?'

'Yes,' she answered softly. The court reporter glanced at the judge, and Judge Rosenthal leaned toward the witness.

'You'll have to speak up, Mrs. Stafford,' he said gently.

'Yes, I am,' Jenny repeated.

David noticed that Larry was leaning toward Jennifer, listening to her testimony with an intensity that David had not noticed when the other witnesses were on.

'Where do you work?'

'I teach second grade at Palisades Elementary School.'

'How long have you been teaching there?'

'This will be my third year.'

'How long have you and Larry been married?'

'A little less than a year,' she answered, her voice breaking slightly from the strain. David waited for her to compose herself. He fought the urge to go to her and hold her.

'Can you remember when you first saw your husband on June sixteenth of this year?'

'Yes. We got up together and ate breakfast. Then Larry went to work.'

'Was he acting unusual in any way?'

'No.'

'When did you next see him?'

'Around eight o'clock, when he came home from work.'

'Was it unusual for Larry to work so late?'

'No. His job was . . . is very demanding. He would often keep late hours.'

'Tell the jury what happened after Larry came home.'

'We just watched some television. I can't even remember what. Then we had a snack and went to bed.'

'You and Larry sleep together?'

'Yes,' Jennifer said, blushing and looking at her lap.

'Where was Larry when you woke up the next morning?'

'In bed.'

'Do you have any reason to believe that he left your bed at any time that evening?'

'No. I'm a light sleeper, and I would have heard him if he got up.'

David paused. He had established Larry's alibi.

PHILLIP M. MARGOLIN

There was no reason to ask any more questions, and he wanted to make Jenny's ordeal as easy as possible. He turned toward Monica.

Monica acknowledged David's nod. Jennifer Stafford had been very believable, and her alibi would be difficult to break down. She did not know what to do to attack it, and she was beginning to feel helpless. She had put an investigator on the Staffords and had come up with nothing. She risked a look at David. He was chatting with the defendant, looking very sure of himself. Monica felt herself tighten with anger. She could not lose this case. She had to do something. But what?

'Mrs. Stafford, you are a wealthy woman, are you not?'

'Objection,' David said, standing.

'This goes to motive, Your Honor,' Monica replied.

'We went through this before, Mr. Nash, in chambers. You may have your objection.'

'Thank you, Your Honor,' Monica said. 'Are you a wealthy woman, Mrs. Stafford?'

'I don't know what you mean by that. I am well-off financially.'

'If neither you nor the defendant were working, could you get by?'

'Larry wouldn't accept my money. He—'

'That doesn't answer my question, Mrs. Stafford.'

'I don't need to work,' Jennifer said stiffly.

238

'But your husband does?'

'He has saved money from his job. He works very hard and—'

'Your Honor,' Monica interrupted, 'would you please instruct the witness to confine her answers to the questions?'

'Yes, Mrs. Stafford. Answer only the question put to you.'

'I'm sorry,' Jennifer answered nervously. Monica was pleased with the course of the questioning. Stafford's wife was becoming defensive, and that would help cast doubt on her credibility.

'You purchased your house for four hundred seventy-five thousand dollars, did you not?'

'Yes.'

'Mr. Stafford could not have purchased the house without your money, could he?'

'No,' Jennifer answered. She was angry and David began to worry.

'In fact, if you and he were divorced, it would seriously alter his lifestyle, wouldn't it?'

'Objection,' David said.

'Sustained. That is highly speculative, Ms. Powers.'

'I withdraw the question,' Monica said, satisfied that the jury had got the point.

'Mrs. Stafford, do you love your husband?'

David looked up. He knew that her answer would mean nothing, but he tried to read something in her eyes: a message he hoped he would see there.

239

Jennifer hesitated a second and Monica noticed. She wondered if the jury had, and she turned in its direction.

'Yes,' Jennifer answered softly.

'Would you lie to help him?'

'Yes,' she answered, 'but I did not lie, because I did not have to. Larry was with me, Miss Powers. He couldn't have murdered that poor woman.'

DAVID SELECTED THE Georgetown for lunch because it was dark and the individual wine-red booths provided privacy.

'I was so frightened,' Jenny said.

It was the first time they had met during the day someplace other than his office. David reached across the narrow table and touched Jenny's hand.

'You were fine.'

'And Larry?' she asked.

'He was fine, too. The trial is going very well.'

Judge Rosenthal had called a recess for lunch as soon as Larry had finished testifying. Stafford had been nervous but had handled himself well. On direct, David had limited himself to asking the defendant where he had been on the evening of the murder and filling in items of his biography that had not been provided by other witnesses. On cross, predictably, Monica had delved into Larry's feelings about not making partner and asked about his relationship with his wife. Stafford was well prepared to handle this line, as David, playing the role of district attorney, had grilled him far worse in the jail than Monica did on the stand. David enjoyed Monica's frustration as it became clear that she was making little headway. Her final questions concerned Stafford's sex life, and David felt they were sufficiently embarrassing so that the overall effect was to create sympathy for his client. When Monica asked her final question, 'Have you been with a prostitute in the past two years?' Larry's answer – 'Why would I do that, when I have a wife like Jenny, who loves me?' – had caused several of the jurors to nod their heads in approval.

'Do you . . . will you win, David?' Jenny asked.

'It's impossible to say, but I feel good about the case. I believe in Larry. I could see his sincerity when he testified. I'm a pretty good judge of people, and if I'm getting these impressions, I'm sure the jurors are, too.'

Jenny looked down at the table for a moment. She seemed troubled.

'What's the matter?' David asked.

'I've decided, David,' Jenny answered in a hushed voice. David felt his heart leap. Was she saying goodbye? Was this the end of his dream?

'No matter what happens, I'm going to ask Larry for a divorce. Then, if you want me . . .'

'Want you? God, Jenny, you don't know what this means to me. I love you so much . . . Don't cry.'

Jenny's head was lowered, but even in the dim light he could see tears coursing down her cheeks.

'I hope I'm not interrupting anything,' a voice

from behind David said. Jennifer looked up, startled, and David turned rapidly. Thomas Gault was standing over the table, a sly grin looking diabolical in the frame of his Chinese mustache.

'I saw you two over here and thought maybe I'd get me a scoop.'

'Gault,' David barked angrily, 'this is a private meeting.'

'But you and the lady are public people. I have my duty as an agent of the press to seek headlines wherever.'

Gault stopped suddenly when he noticed Jenny's tears. The smile disappeared.

'Say, I am sorry. I didn't realize . . . It's so dark in here.'

He whipped out a handkerchief and held it toward Jenny. She looked at David, puzzled.

'It's okay,' Gault said. 'I've been there. Had my own trial. For murder, too,' he said with a trace of pride. 'But Dave got me off and he'll clear your husband. Don't you worry.'

Jenny continued to stare at the handkerchief, which drooped from the end of Gault's hand like an ill-cared-for flag. David saved the situation by proffering his own, which Jenny took quickly.

'Look, Tom, Mrs. Stafford is upset and we would like a little privacy.'

'Sure thing. And I am sorry. Didn't mean to . . . you know.'

'Sure. And, Tom, if you want a scoop, come to court this afternoon. My last witness is going to be a doozy.'

Gault brightened.

'Now, that's the spirit. I'm givin' you great press, buddy. Sorry again, Mrs. Stafford. Your husband's got a great lawyer.'

Gault left and the couple said nothing for a moment. Then Jenny asked David, 'What's going to happen this afternoon?'

David felt a surge of excitement and smiled. 'Oh, I'm going to hammer the final nail into the State's coffin. But I don't want to talk about that now. I want to talk about us.'

'MR. CONKLIN, DURING your years as an investigator have you developed an expertise in the area of photography?'

'I have.'

'Would you tell the jury what training you have in this field?'

Terry turned toward the jury and smiled. He was an old hand at being in the witness box and appeared to be completely relaxed.

'I received my initial training in the Air Force, then studied by correspondence through the New York Institute of Photography. For a short time, after the Air Force and before I went into police work, I owned a photo studio and worked as a cameraman for KOIN-TV.

243

'When I was with the Lane County Police Department, I set up their photo lab, and, since going into private practice, I have done all of the accident and special photography for several law firms in town.'

'Have you ever won any prizes for your work?'

'I've won several awards over the past ten years. In fact, I won the blue ribbon in two categories at the last Multnomah County Fair.'

'Did I contact you with regard to assisting me in the investigation of the Larry Stafford case?'

'Yes, Mr. Nash, you did.'

'In this capacity, did you take any photographs at the Raleigh Motel, room twenty-two?'

'I did.'

'What was your assignment with regard to these photographs?'

'Well, as I understood it from talking to you, I was to take a photograph inside the motel room where the murder occurred that would accurately portray how a person standing where the killer stood on the evening of the crime would look to a person in the position Officer Ortiz was in when he saw the murderer.'

There was a stir in the courtroom, and several of the jurors made notes on their pads.

'How did you prepare yourself for this assignment?'

'First I visited the motel room with you and got a feel for the layout and the lighting. Then I read the police reports and sat in at a hearing when Officer Ortiz drew a diagram of the positions of everyone in the room at the time of the commission of the crime.'

David pointed to the easel. 'Is that the diagram?'

'Yes.'

'So you really got the information on the positions from Officer Ortiz?'

'That's right. His statements under oath and his written report.'

'What information did you have with regard to the lighting in the motel room on June sixteenth?'

'As I understood the testimony and the report, there were no lights on when Officer Ortiz entered the room, but there was a large globe light that illuminated the landing.'

'Where was this globe light situated?'

'To the right of the door, on the outside.'

'Were there any other lights?'

'Only those in the street. Neon signs, headlights. Things like that. The side of the motel away from the office is not well lit.'

'What did you do next?'

'A few weeks after the hearing, when I had the information about the positions of the people involved, I hired an individual who is the same height as Mr. Stafford to accompany me to the Raleigh Motel. I received permission to enter the room from the manager, Mr. Grimes, and I proceeded to set up my camera at the same height Officer Ortiz would be if he was lying in the position he described. I then put the model where the murderer was supposed to be.'

'What position was that?'

'I had him stand at the door frame, leaning into the room. His body was at a slight angle, with his right leg and arm outside the door and his left leg and arm just inside the room. The model was instructed to look down toward the camera.'

'When were these pictures taken?'

'At night, about the same time as the murder.'

David approached Conklin and handed him three photographs.

'I hand you what have been marked as defendant's exhibits number twelve, thirteen, and fourteen. Can you identify them for the jury?'

'These are three photographs taken in the motel room by me.'

'Tell the jury what they portray.'

'Okay,' Terry said, holding the first picture up to the jury. 'Exhibit twelve is a picture of a man standing in the doorway of room twenty-two. This is the model. He is standing exactly as described by Officer Ortiz at the hearing.'

'Can you see the man's face, Mr. Conklin?'

'No, sir, you cannot.'

Someone gasped and the jurors wrote furiously. Monica was straining to see the photograph.

'Your Honor, I've never seen these pictures,' she shouted. 'I object to . . .'

'Yes, Mr. Nash. The jury should not see these pictures until they have been admitted into evidence. Show them to counsel, please,' Judge Rosenthal said.

David smiled. The uproar over the improper way in which he had introduced the pictures would heighten the jury's suspense and the impact the pictures would make. He had counted on Monica's objection, and she had not let him down.

Monica scanned the pictures. She could not believe it. With the globe lamp outside and the model's head just inside the door, shadows obscured the face. It was impossible to make out the features. The other two photos were taken with the model standing straight up and leaning outside the door. In the last picture, with the head tilted back, you could make out some features, but not many, and the shadows still obscured most of the detail. Ortiz's identification had been completely impeached. She turned toward David as she began to make her legal objection to the pictures and saw the smile he hid from the jury. She felt her blood rise. Then she caught Stafford out of the corner of her eye. He too was gloating.

Judge Rosenthal was ruling in favor of the admission of the pictures into evidence, and Conklin was continuing his testimony, explaining the technique he had used to produce the photographs, but Monica only half heard it. She was seething, burning. She could not let David get away with this. She was not going to let that smug son of a bitch walk out of this courtroom scot-free. He had suckered her with those pictures, but he hadn't won yet. Monica picked up her pen and doodled the name Cyrus Johnson on her witness list.

3

David let out his belt a notch and groaned with relief. Helen Banks smiled at the compliment to her cooking and began collecting the dirty dishes.

'Why don't you and Greg get some fresh air, while I get the coffee on?' she said, stacking the dishes on a serving cart.

'Sounds like an excellent idea,' Gregory said as he pushed away from the table. It was Saturday evening and the trial was in recess for the weekend. David had rested after Terry Conklin had finished his testimony Friday afternoon. From all accounts it looked as if victory was assured. Even Rudy, the jail guard, who rarely expressed his opinion about a case, had made a comment about Stafford's being out soon.

As it did almost every year, the cold of autumn had given way to a week of false spring that fooled the flowers into opening to the October air and brought back pleasant memories of summer. Gregory lit up a cigar and the two friends strolled onto the terrace. The dark river was at peace, and so was David.

'What's on the menu for Monday?' Gregory asked.

'I don't know,' David answered as he sank into

a lawn chair. 'Monica said she might have some rebuttal, but I can't imagine what it could be.'

'Maybe she's going to have one of her investigators go out to the motel and try to get some pictures that show a face.'

'Not a chance. I had Terry's work double-checked by two other professionals before I used it. Given those lighting conditions, there's no way Ortiz could have seen the killer's face.'

Gregory leaned back and puffed on his cigar. It was quiet on the terrace. The breeze was cool, and the lights from the houseboats across the way appeared to wink on and off as the boats twisted with the current.

'What do you know about Ortiz, Dave?' Gregory asked after a while.

'Why?' David asked. He felt dreamy, fatigued by too much food and too much wine and lulled by the sounds of the river.

'I don't know. It just seems strange that he would be so certain, if those pictures are accurate.'

'The mind plays strange tricks sometimes. Don't forget, he'd just been struck on the head, and he was coming into a darkened room from the outside. There are probably a hundred explanations a psychiatrist could give you.'

'You're right. Anyway, if it helps you lock this up, I don't care what he saw.'

'Confusion to our enemies,' David toasted, taking

a sip from the wineglass he had carried with him. Gregory raised his cigar.

'If nothing else, this case has at least raised your spirits.'

'What do you mean?'

'You were a pain in the butt to have around the office for a while. I guess I can say it now, because you seem to be over your blue period.'

'I don't . . . Oh, you mean that Seals business.'

'And a few others.'

'Was I bitching and moaning that much?'

'Enough so that I was getting a little worried about you. What you need to do is settle down. Find a good woman.'

'Like Helen?'

Greg nodded.

'They don't make 'em like that anymore,' David said lightly, picturing what it would be like to see Jenny every morning when he woke up, and to kiss her every evening.

'I've gotta go to the bathroom,' Gregory said. 'Save my place, will ya?'

'My pleasure,' David said, sipping some more wine. Somewhere up the river a tanker's horn sounded. For a brief moment David felt disoriented, then recognized the unsettling feeling created by a sense of déjà vu. The night seemed to belong to two times, and he struggled with his memory to fit the past into the present. Softly, like the night breeze, it came to him. The evening he first met

251

Jenny had been an evening like this. A still river, night sounds, the breeze. Even the air had smelled the same. It was a vivid memory now, warm and real, as if David had been transported back in time and Jenny would soon appear on the terrace, profiled against the sky. He smiled. It was a good memory, a calming thought.

David recalled the first time he had seen Jenny on the fringe of the small group. He remembered his impressions. How beautiful she had seemed.

Then, like the last piece in a Chinese puzzle box, a new thought slipped into place, and David's inner peace shattered. Something else had happened that day. The interview with the young girl who had been the victim in the Seals case. David sat up. His heart was beating rapidly.

'Coffee's on,' Helen Banks called from the doorway.

David did not answer. He was thinking back. Trying to be sure and hoping he was wrong.

'Did you hear me, Dave?'

David stood up. He felt sick at heart.

'Is something wrong?' Helen asked.

'I just remembered something I must do. I'm afraid I'll have to skip coffee.'

'Oh, Dave. Can't you just take a day off and relax?'

David touched her shoulder and tried to gather his thoughts. He could be wrong. He prayed he was wrong.

'If I don't check on this,' he said, managing a smile, 'I won't be able to sleep tonight.'

'If you're determined . . .' Helen said with a sigh.

'Determined to what?' Gregory asked.

'I've got to leave, Greg. Something I just remembered, and it can't wait.'

Gregory looked at him hard. He discerned the lines of worry on his young friend's face and knew that whatever was bothering David was serious.

'Can I help?'

'No. Thanks. This is something I have to do alone.'

And he was alone. More alone than he had ever been.

THE SECURITY GUARD in the lobby signed him in, and David took the only working elevator to the thirty-second floor. He used his key to unlock the door to the firm offices and walked rapidly down the corridor to the file room, flicking light switches as he went. Darkened corridors were suddenly bathed in light as he advanced.

The file was in the Closed section. It was thick and intact. The audiocassette was tucked into a small manila envelope that had been taped to the inside of the folder. David carried the file to his office and closed the door. He took a tape recorder from his bottom drawer and fitted the cassette into it. He pushed a button and the tape began to unwind. David leaned back and listened, praying that he was wrong. Hoping that he would not hear what he knew he would.

It was there. The very first thing on the tape. He pushed the Stop button, then Rewind, and played it again to be sure.

'This is Detective Leon Stahlheimer,' the voice on the tape said. 'It's Thursday, June sixteenth . . .'

David switched off the recorder.

All lies. She had lied on the stand and she had lied to him. Used him. Had it all been a play to her? A carefully rehearsed role? Had any of the emotions been real? What did it matter? How could he ever love her again?

David switched off the office lights. It was better in the dark. Not seeing enabled him to direct himself inward. What should he do? What could he do? He felt powerless, defeated. He had built a dream on Jennifer's love and Larry Stafford's innocence, and the dream had crumbled, breaking him under the debris.

All the despair he had felt months before flooded back, drowning him in a sea of self-pity and disgust. The dead feeling he thought he had conquered returned to gnaw at him, leaving only the bones of a sorry, tired, and aging man.

David looked at the desk clock. It was midnight. Not too late for a confrontation. Not too late to put an end to something that had been so good.

DAVID REMEMBERED LITTLE of the mad drive to Newgate Terrace. There were occasional lights on the early-morning freeway, then a winding country road and the crunch of gravel under his tires. House lights came on after his second knock, and the first thing he recalled clearly was Jenny's face, pale from sleep.

'You lied,' he said, forcing her back into the hallway. The darkened surrounding rooms gave him the feeling of being in a miniature theater.

'What?' she asked, still groggy from sleep. He grasped her shoulders and made her look at his eyes, fierce now with the pain of knowing.

'I want the truth. Now. Everything.'

'I don't—' she started, then twisted painfully in his grasp as his strong fingers dug into the soft flesh of her shoulders.

'I'll make it easy for you, Jenny,' he said, making the name he had once loved to hear sound like a curse. 'We met that evening at Greg's house. Senator Bauer's fund-raiser. You remember? The first night we made love.'

She flinched. The way he had said 'love' made it sound sordid, like copulation with a whore in a wino hotel room.

'I interviewed a girl that morning at the juvenile home. We recorded the conversation. The date was on the tape. June sixteenth. The day Darlene Hersch was murdered. You couldn't have been with Larry that evening, Jenny. You were fucking me. Remember?'

Her head snapped sideways as if she had been slapped. He shook her to make her look at him.

'Don't,' she cried.

'You lied to me.'

'No!'

'Knowing all the time . . .' he screamed at her.

'I didn't . . . I . . . Please, David, I love—'

'Love,' he shouted, bringing the back of his hand sharply against her cheek. Her eyes widened in shock and she crumpled at his feet.

'So help me, if you ever use that word again, I'll kill you. You know nothing about love,' he said between clenched teeth.

She reached out blindly, trying to touch him.

'It wasn't . . . I . . . Let me talk to you. Don't just go like this. Please.'

He watched her, huddled like a child at his feet, her long golden hair cascading over shoulders that jerked with each wretched sob.

'I'm sorry, David. I really am,' she wept, 'but there wasn't any other way. I couldn't think of anything else to do.'

'Not even telling the truth?'

'I was afraid you wouldn't defend Larry. I thought . . . It looked so bad. And I still believe he is innocent. But no one else would have.'

David looked at her hard, trying to see behind her ravaged, tear-stained face.

256

'Innocent?'

'Larry swears he is. I don't know if . . . I don't think he's lying.'

'But he lied to me about being with you on the evening of the murder.'

'Yes. I told you, that day in your office. We fought. He had dinner with Barry Dietrich, then went back to his office to work. I was sick of it. I never saw him anymore. It was that damn job. Making partner was all that counted. I called him and told him that I was going to leave him.'

As David listened to Jenny, he could hear echoes of his fights with Monica. David sagged and sat down on the bottom of the staircase. Jenny looked spent. She had stopped crying.

'The marriage was a mistake from the beginning. Larry is like a child, self-centered, domineering. Everything had to be what he wanted. That night he came home in a rage. He shouted at me, called me names. "I didn't understood him." "I didn't want him to succeed." After a while I didn't even hear what he said. I went upstairs and slammed the door to my room.'

'Your room?' David interrupted.

'Yes. You didn't know? Of course you didn't. No, we hadn't slept together for a month. I told you, things had been bad.

'I heard Larry's bedroom door slam and it was quiet. I don't know why I remembered about the fund-raiser. I think the invitation was on my dresser on top of some other mail. I just needed to get out, so I took it and left.'

'And Larry?'

'He was still at home when I drove away. Don't you see how hard it was for me? I felt so guilty. When I met you, when you made love to me, it was so different. I felt as if you were giving something, not taking, like Larry. I didn't know what to do. At first I thought I would just leave him. Then I didn't have the courage. And I still loved him in a way. It was all so mixed up. And it got a little better after that evening. He tried. He cut down on his work a little. Stayed home more. It wasn't much, but it was an effort, and I was still guilt-ridden because I had cheated on him. I didn't feel as if I'd cheated. It had all been so good. But a part of me felt as if I had betrayed a trust.'

She stopped and he moved over to her, sitting on the floor, letting her rest against him.

'Then Larry was arrested and I realized what night the murder occurred. The evidence looked so convincing. His shirt, our car. That policeman saying it was him. But Larry said he was innocent. That he had stayed home after I left. He swore it to me.'

'Why didn't you tell me the truth?'

'I was afraid. I wanted you to represent Larry, because I believed in you. I knew you could clear him. If I told you the truth . . . reminded you that the murder occurred on the night we met . . . you would have been a witness against Larry.'

'And now, as his lawyer, I can't be.'

She looked away from him again and said, 'Yes,' in a very small voice.

'So what do we do now, Jenny?' David asked.

'What do you mean?'

'I mean that you committed a crime yesterday. You perjured yourself. And so did Larry. And I know about that. Do you know what my duty is under the Canons of Ethics? As an attorney, an officer of the court, I have a duty to tell the judge what you did and a duty to get off the case if Larry won't recant his testimony. I'm committing a crime and subjecting myself to possible disbarment if I don't tell Judge Rosenthal about this.'

'You wouldn't—' Jenny started.

'I don't know what I'm going to do. I'm so mixed up I can't think.'

David stood up and walked to the door. His feet felt leaden, and he had no heart for anything anymore. The trial, his practice, this woman, his life. Nothing seemed to mean anything. There were no values, no goals.

'David,' she said when he reached the door, 'I love you. You know that, don't you? Tell me you know that I never lied about that.'

David turned to face her. He was not angry at her, just dead inside.

'I know you used me, Jenny. I know you played on my emotions. I know I still love you, but I don't know if I can ever trust you again.'

259

'Oh, God, David,' she called after him. 'Don't cut me off like this. Don't you see? I don't know if Larry killed that woman or not, but if he's innocent, you must help him, and if he's guilty . . . I couldn't let him go to prison thinking that he'd gone after that woman because of me.'

THE ROADSIDE FLASHED by and car horns occasionally broke the stillness. It would be easy to end everything by simply closing his eyes and letting the car take control. When the road began to waver, David shook his head to clear it. He did not want to die. He was certain of that. But life at the moment was confused and a torment.

He had several choices. He could make Jennifer retake the stand and recant her perjured testimony; he could go to the judge if she refused; or he could do nothing. If Jenny recanted, Larry would surely be convicted.

Would that be so bad? Yes, if he was innocent. There was still that possibility. Until tonight David had been convinced of Stafford's innocence. The pictures discredited Ortiz. Larry's story was so believably told. But what if he was wrong and Stafford was guilty?

David thought about Ashmore and Tony Seals. He felt sick. Once more he saw the autopsy photographs of the little girls that Ashmore had molested, then killed, and once again he heard Jessie Garza describe crawling down the mountain. What was he doing

260

defending these people?

And Larry Stafford, where did he fit in? David could see the gash in Darlene Hersch's throat. That was why any lawyer worth his salt fought so hard to keep out pictures of the victims in death. Death could be handled and sweet-talked in the abstract, but pictures made it real for a jury. Made the jury feel and smell and taste the horror that is violent death. David could touch that reality now. The steel shell he had built around his sensibilities had started to crumble with Ashmore, and all his defenses were now down. But his fear of being responsible for setting loose another killer was still at odds with his feelings of love for Jenny. He felt used, he felt a fool, but he still loved her. In the end he no more knew what he would do than he had when he'd left her.

4

'I know everything,' David told Larry Stafford. They were seated in a vacant jury room that Judge Rosenthal permitted them to use for conferences. Stafford was dressed in navy blue with a light-blue shirt and navy-and-red-striped tie. Just the right amount of cuff showed, and his shoes were polished. Only his complexion, turned pasty from too much jail time, did not fit his young-lawyer image.

'I don't understand,' Stafford said nervously.

'Jenny told me. Oh, you don't have to worry about her. I figured it out. She didn't volunteer anything.'

'I'm still not sure what you mean.' Larry answered warily.

David was tired of the games, and just plain tired. He had not slept last night, and he was having trouble handling even the simplest thoughts. He came to the point.

'I know that you and Jenny lied when you testified that you were together on the evening of the murder. I know you had a fight and she left the house. You have no alibi and you both committed perjury.'

Stafford said nothing. He looked like a little boy who was about to cry.

'Did you kill her, Larry?' David asked.

'What does it matter? Would you believe me if I said I didn't?'

'I'm still your attorney.'

'It's been like this my whole fucking life,' Stafford said bitterly. 'So close. Then, bam, the door snaps shut. I marry this dream girl. She's beautiful, wealthy. And she turns out to be a bitch who thinks only of herself.

'I kill myself to get through law school, get into the best firm, and the bastards won't make me a partner, because I don't have the right breeding.

'But this is the biggest joke of all, and I'll probably end up in prison.'

'I asked you if you killed her.'

'You won't believe what I say any more than Jenny did.'

'Then why do you suppose she lied for you?' David asked, angered by Stafford's display of self-pity.

'How would it look? Jennifer Dodge of the Portland Dodges, who already married below her station, married to a murderer. How could she hold her head up at the horse show?'

'You're a fool, Stafford. You're so self-centered, you can't recognize—'

'I recognize when I'm getting the shaft. I know what that little bitch wanted out of this. I was one of her charity projects, like that school she teaches at. Take a poor boy to lunch – or, to tell it like it was, to bed. She was slumming, Nash. But as soon as I wanted to make something of myself, she started in. She never understood me. That I didn't want to owe her anything.'

'But it didn't bother you when she perjured herself and risked prison for you?'

'If she hadn't run out on me that night, none of this would have happened.'

'None of what?' David demanded. Stafford stopped, confused.

'None of . . . my arrest. Look, it's obvious I didn't do it. You proved that. I mean, Grimes already said that the killer had long brown hair, and what about those pictures and what Walsh said about the car?'

'What are you trying to do, Larry? Convince me you're innocent? Let's look at the facts the way I would, with my information, if I was prosecuting this case.

'The killer wears a shirt identical to a shirt that you own and wears pants similar to pants you own. He drives the same make and color car. He has the same build. And a trained police officer swears under oath that he is you. What do you think the statistical odds are that two people in Portland would own the same pants, shirt, and expensive car?

'You had the opportunity. No alibi. And it would be natural for a man who has just had a fight with a woman who has cut him off sexually . . .'

Stafford's head snapped up.

'Yes, I know about that, too. It would be natural for such a man to go out looking for a woman.

'Then there's motive. If you had been arrested for prostitution, your marriage would have been endangered and your tenuous chance to make partner destroyed.

'Arrayed against these motives and amazing coincidences in dress and physique, we have the word of one old man that the killer did not have curly blond hair, some fancy statistical footwork that probably won't get by any halfway intelligent juror who starts thinking about the sheer number of those coincidences, and a few trick photographs.

'What would your verdict be, if you were a juror?'

Stafford hung his head. 'What do you want me to say?' he asked.

'What do I want . . .? Goddammit, you're lucky I talked to you at all. I should have dragged your wife in front of Judge Rosenthal and made her recant on the stand. But I'm still your lawyer and I want it from you. Did you kill Darlene Hersch?'

Stafford wagged his still-bowed head from side to side but did not look David in the eye.

'I don't care anymore,' he said. 'And once the jury hears what we did . . .'

'If,' David said.

Stafford looked up at him, like a dog begging for food.

'You're not going to—?'

'You aren't the only one involved in this. I don't know if you killed that woman or not, but I'm not going to let you drag your wife down with you, by making her admit that she perjured herself.

'And if you are innocent, there isn't a chance that a jury would find you innocent if it learned about what you two did.'

Stafford started to cry, but David did nothing to comfort him.

'Just one more thing, Stafford. Are there any other little goodies that I should know about? And I mean anything.'

'No, no. I swear.'

David stood and walked to the door. Stafford seemed to lack the energy to move. He sat hunched over, staring at the floor.

'Pull yourself together,' David ordered in a cold, flat monotone. 'We have to go to court.'

DAVID TOOK HIS place at counsel table and watched the events of the day unfold like a dream. The jury was seated in slow motion and Monica appeared, her arms loaded with law books. If he had been concentrating, this would have struck him as odd on a day set aside for closing argument, but nothing was registering for David. He just wanted the case to end, so he could decide what to do with his life without the pressure of having to care about the lives of other people.

Stafford had been brought in by the guard before the jury appeared, but he exchanged no words with his attorney. The judge came in last, and the final day of the trial commenced.

'Are you prepared to argue, Ms. Powers?' Judge Rosenthal asked.

'No, Your Honor,' Monica replied. 'The State has one rebuttal witness it would like to call.'

'Very well.'

Monica signaled toward the back of the room, and Cyrus Johnson swaggered in, dressed in a white shirt, crew-neck sweater, and brown slacks. David watched Johnson walk to the witness stand, trying to place the face. It was only when the witness stated his name that David began to feel uneasy.

'Do you know that man?' David demanded. Stafford paled and said nothing, unable to take his eyes off the witness.

'Are you also known as T.V., Mr. Johnson?' Monica asked.

'You'd better tell me what this is all about,' David said, his voice low and threatening. Stafford did not reply, but his face had the look of a person who knows that his death is imminent.

'And would you tell the jury what your occupation was on June sixteenth of this year?' Monica asked, swiveling her chair to watch David and Stafford react.

'Uh, well, uh,' Johnson started uneasily, 'I guess you could say I managed some women.'

'You mean you were a pimp?' Monica asked.

There was a commotion in the courtroom and the judge pounded his gavel for quiet.

'Ms. Powers, you are asking this man to admit to criminal activity. Has he been warned of his rights?'

'Mr. Johnson is testifying under a grant of full immunity, Your Honor,' Monica replied, handing a notarized document to the Court and a copy to David. The judge studied it.

'Very well,' he said when he was finished. 'You may proceed.'

'Mr. Johnson, have you ever seen Larry Stafford, the defendant in this case, before?'

Johnson stared at Stafford for a moment, then turned back to Monica.

'Yes, I have.'

'Would you tell the jury the circumstances of that meeting?' Monica asked.

Johnson shifted in the witness box and Monica tensed, waiting for David's objection. When it did not come, she glanced tentatively at her former husband. She was startled by what she saw. David, who was usually so intense, was slumped down in his chair. He looked sad and uncaring. Monica had sprung surprises on David before and had seen him handle other lawyers' challenges. Thinking on his feet was where David excelled. The David she saw now looked defeated.

'It was a couple of years ago. I would say in September. This dude, uh, the defendant, come up to one of my women in the Regency Bar, and they split a few minutes later. Now, I don't make it a practice to bother my girls when they're workin', but somethin' about this dude bothered me, so I followed them.'

Judge Rosenthal looked over at David. He, too, was waiting for an objection. When David said nothing, the judge toyed with the idea of calling the lawyers to the bench to discuss the direction the testimony was taking, but Nash was an experienced attorney, and he had conducted an excellent trial so far. The judge decided to let David try his case his way.

'We was usin' a motel on the strip then, so I knew right where they was goin'. I parked in the lot near the room and waited. About ten minutes later I heard a scream, so I went up to the room.

'Mordessa is naked and scramblin' across the bed, and this dude,' Johnson said, pointing at Stafford, 'is right on top of her, beatin' her good. She got blood comin' out of her mouth and her eye looked real bad.

'I was carryin' a piece which I pulled and told him to freeze. He does. Then I asked what happened. Mordessa says Stafford wanted her to do some real kinky stuff, like tyin' her up and whipping her. She tells him it's extra and he says that's cool. Then somethin' about him scared her and she changed her mind. And that's when he starts beatin' on her.'

'What happened then?'

'The cops, uh, police arrived. I guess someone heard Mordessa screamin' and called 'em. Anyway, this white cop asks Stafford what happened and he don't even speak to me. Stafford says we tried to roll him and the next thing I know, we're down the station house charged with prostitution and attempted robbery.'

'Did you tell the police your story?'

'Sure, but they wasn't too interested in our version.'

'What finally happened to the charges against you?'

'Nothin'. They was dropped.'

'And why was that?'

T.V. smiled and pointed at Stafford. 'He wouldn't prosecute. Said he never said no such thing to the police.'

'Is there any question in your mind that the man who beat up Mordessa is the defendant, Lawrence Dean Stafford?'

Johnson stared at Stafford and shook his head.

'No, ma'am.'

Monica paused for effect, then said, 'Your witness, counselor.'

The courtroom was hushed and all eyes turned toward David. Stafford's head was bent and he stared at the blank legal pad that lay before him.

He had not moved during Johnson's testimony.

David also sat motionless. As Johnson had testified, the lawyer in him had seen the numerous
objections and legal motions he could have made to
keep Johnson's testimony out, but he had made none
of them, because there was another, more human,
part that would not let him.

Each time he thought about objecting, he thought
about Tony Seals and Ashmore. He was tired of
letting the animals out of their cages and tired of
justifying his actions by the use of philosophical
arguments he no longer believed in. Stafford was
guilty. He had murdered Darlene Hersch. There was
no longer any doubt in David's mind. David had to
protect future victims from a man like Stafford, not
use his skills to endanger others. Stafford had taken
a life and he would pay for it.

The judge was calling his name for a second time.
The jurors were staring at him. A low rumble of
voices was beginning to build among the spectators.
David shook his head slowly from side to side.

'No questions,' he said.

And Stafford never said a word in protest.

PART IV

TRIAL BY FIRE

1

The visitor's room at the state penitentiary was a large, open space filled with couches and chairs upholstered in red vinyl and outfitted with chrome armrests. Three vending machines stood against one wall. There was an occasional low wooden table with an ashtray on it.

Jenny had never been in a place like this before, and the visits depressed her. The other prisoners seemed strange and threatening and not like anyone she had ever met. Whenever she entered the prison, she felt like a visitor to a foreign country.

Larry did not understand her reluctance to touch him. All around them wives, lovers, and relatives embraced the other prisoners. She tried to explain how she felt to Larry, but he saw her reticence as another betrayal.

'I talked to Mr. Bloch,' Jenny said. 'He says he'll have your brief filed at the court of appeals this week. He sounded hopeful, Larry.'

Stafford shook his head. He had fired David as soon as Judge Rosenthal had imposed the mandatory life sentence on him. Jerry Bloch, an experienced appellate attorney, was representing him now. They had talked about the appeal last week.

'I'm not going to get out. That bastard Nash saw to that when he railroaded me at the trial.'

'But Mr. Bloch—'

'I talked to Bloch. Don't forget, I'm a lawyer. There aren't any errors Bloch can work with, because Nash never objected when they put that pimp on the stand. That son of a bitch socked me in here but good.'

Jenny said nothing. She had been through this before. Once Larry got started, he would stay in a rage during the entire visit.

'If he'd cross-examined Johnson or kept him off . . . Jenny, there were a thousand ways he could have kept that pimp off the stand.'

He could also have told the judge that you and I lied, she thought to herself, but he didn't. He didn't do anything. An image of the last day of Larry's trial slipped unbidden into her consciousness. Once again she saw T.V. Johnson walk from the hushed courtroom. The jury filing out. The judge and prosecutor following. But David and Larry had not moved. And when the guard finally led Larry away, David still remained seated. She had waited for him in the back of the room, wanting to talk to him, to hold him.

When everyone else had left, David got to his feet slowly, as if he were climbing the last section of a steep mountain grade. When he turned, he looked exhausted and his eyes had lost their focus. He packed his papers away and walked toward the door, up the aisle in Jenny's direction. When he reached her, he paused for barely a moment and looked down at her. Where she had expected hate, she saw only despair. The look of a man who had given up everything without a fight.

That evening, after short deliberation, the jury returned a verdict of guilty. She had not seen David since. He never answered her calls and never seemed to be at home. After a while she stopped trying.

'Bloch says if we lose the appeal in the supreme court, I can go into federal court and allege incompetence of counsel. But I have to wait and exhaust my state appeals first.'

'We can do that, if you want to.'

'You bet I want to.'

'Won't it come out that . . . about my not being with you that night?'

'I don't care, Jenny. That's only perjury. I'm in here for life for a murder I didn't commit.'

And what about me? she wanted to ask, but she couldn't. If she had to be punished in order for Larry to get out, she would be getting what she deserved. If she hadn't betrayed David, he would never have collapsed the way he had. Larry was in prison because she had destroyed David with her lies.

David. How she loved him. More so now that he was lost to her forever. She remembered the night they had first met. It had taken all her control to refrain from calling him. And why hadn't she? Guilt. It was always the same answer. Guilt had prevented her from asking Larry for a divorce long before Darlene Hersch was murdered. Guilt prevented her from telling David the truth. And guilt was keeping her shackled to a man who would probably spend the rest of his life in prison.

THE UPTURNED COLLAR of Thomas Gault's jacket blocked the icy wind and sent it skittering through the drunken sailors and carousing longshoremen who crowded the sidewalk. Gault pushed open the door of The Dutchman, a noisy workingmen's bar that took its trade from the docks. A gust of wind chilled two men who were sitting at the bar, and they looked Gault's way when he entered. The bar lined the wall to Gault's right, and a row of booths occupied the wall on the left. Most of the room was filled with Formica-topped tables. Two pool tables stood in a cleared space near the gents' room.

'Shut the door,' one of the men at the bar commanded. Gault smiled to himself. He didn't come to the docks for the atmosphere. He came for the action. And it looked as if tonight the action might start sooner than he'd expected. He had planned on shutting the door, but now he let it stay open.

'Shut it yourself, asshole,' he said, and walked down the bar without another glance in the man's direction. He heard an angry murmur behind him, and a few seconds later the door slammed shut.

Gault positioned himself with his back to the wall at an unoccupied table by the jukebox where he could view the room. A waitress brought him a beer and he took a sip, watching the man he had insulted over the rim of the glass. He was a little over six feet. A thick roll of fat slopped over his belt at the waistline, and his shirt was partially out of his pants, exposing a sweat-stained undershirt. His movements were slow and jerky. It was obvious that he had been drinking for some time.

The fat man's companion was Gault's size. His figure was trim and he seemed sober. The fat man seemed to have forgotten about the incident at the door and was back in his cups. Too bad, Gault thought. He let his eyes drift over the rest of the room. A sailor and a heavyset woman with teased blond hair were shooting pool against two boys in work shirts and jeans. The woman sank her shot. One of the boys swore. The sailor laughed and smacked the woman's ass.

Three men a few tables from Gault were arguing about an upcoming heavyweight fight. When Gault's eyes moved back to the bar, they met the fat man's by accident and stayed there. The staring match was no contest. The fat man folded in less than a minute and gave Gault the finger to save face. Gault blew the fat man a kiss. The man got off his stool and started up the bar. His friend grabbed his elbow in an attempt to restrain him, but he lurched free, stumbling against the bar as he broke the shorter man's grip. He staggered in Gault's direction, and his friend followed after a moment's hesitation.

'Were you lookin' at me, dog turd?' the fat man demanded when he reached Gault's table.

'Leave it be, Harvey,' the shorter man said.

'He blew a kiss at me, Al,' Harvey said without taking his eyes off Gault. 'You seen that. Fags kiss boys. You a fag skinhead?'

'You're so cute, I'd let you find out,' Gault lisped effeminately.

'I think you'd better split, buddy,' Harvey's friend said, suddenly angry at Gault.

'I thought you had more sense than your friend,' Gault said sharply, pushing his chair back and slowly getting to his feet.

'I don't like a smart-mouth any better than Harv, so why don't you leave while you still can.'

'Can't I finish my drink?' Gault asked in a mocking tone. Harvey stared at Gault for a second, then swept the beer off the table. The glass shattered on the floor and the noise in the bar stopped. Gault felt a rush of adrenaline. His whole body seemed in movement.

'It's finished—' Harvey started, his wind suddenly cut off by the foot that Gault snapped into his groin. Gault's left foot connected with the fat man's temple. Harvey's head snapped to one side and he sat down hard.

Gault pivoted, blocking Al's first wild punch with his forearm. He aimed a side kick at his opponent's kneecap. It was off, striking with only enough force to jostle him off balance. The follow-up left only grazed Al's eye.

The advantage of surprise was lost and Al had good reflexes. He charged into Gault, wrestling him backward into the wall. Gault grunted from the impact, momentarily stunned.

Harvey was on one knee, struggling to get up. Gault brought his forehead down fast. Al's nose cracked. Blood spattered across Gault's shirt. He boosted his knee and felt it make hard contact with Al's groin. There was a gasp and the grip on his arm relaxed. Gault drove a right to the solar plexus and shot his fingers into the man's eyes. Al screamed and sagged. Gault snapped the side of his hand against the man's neck, and he sank to the floor, his face covered with blood.

Glass shattered and Gault set himself as Harvey moved toward him, a broken bottle held tightly in his hand. Gault circled warily, keeping distance between them. Harvey feinted and Gault moved back. He felt the edge of the bar cut into his back. There was a flash of movement behind him and he shifted slightly, but not enough to avoid being hit across the back of the head by the sawed-off pool cue the bartender kept for just such occasions.

THE PHONE WAS ringing. David opened his eyes slowly and struggled to bring his other senses into focus. He became aware of a sour, phlegmy taste

PHILLIP M. MARGOLIN

in his mouth and a dull ache behind his eyes. The
phone rang again and he flinched. It was still dark
outside. According to the digital clock, it was two
in the morning.

David picked up the receiver to stop the ringing.

'Dave,' a voice at the other end called out.

'Who is this?'

'It's Tom. Tom Gault. I'm in jail, old buddy, and
you gotta come down here and bail me out.'

'Who?' David asked. The words had not registered.

'Tom Gault. Bring your checkbook. I'll pay you
back when I get home.'

David sat up and tried to concentrate. 'What did
you do?'

'I was in a fight. These clowns have charged
me with assault. I'll explain it all to you once
I'm out.'

David didn't want to go to the jail at two in
the morning. He didn't have any great urge to see
Thomas Gault, either. But he was too tired to refuse
Gault's request.

'I'll be down as soon as I can get dressed,' he
said, turning on the lamp on his night table.

'I knew I could count on you,' Gault said. After
a few more words, they hung up.

David's head was ringing. He'd had too much to
drink, but that was becoming routine. He took a
deep breath and made his way to the bathroom.
The glare from the lightbulbs hurt his eyes, and his

image in the mirror caused a different type of pain. His complexion was pale and his flesh doughy. The features were beginning to run together. When he removed his pajamas, he saw the erosion of clear lines on the other parts of his body.

David had not exercised, or done much else that humans do, since Larry Stafford's conviction three months before. The day after the trial he had backpacked into the wilderness to try to sort out the events of the preceding days, but the silence of the shadowy woods had trapped him alone with thoughts he did not want to encounter. He had scurried home.

Jenny had phoned while he was away, but he did not return the calls. He tried to work but could not concentrate. Once, in the solitude of his office, he broke into tears. In the course of representing Larry Stafford, he had betrayed the trust of the court, sold out his principles, and given up on himself. In the ruins of the case he saw the wreckage of his career and the destruction of the carefully constructed fictions concerning truth and justice he had erected to hide from view the emptiness of the profession he had so zealously followed. Life was intolerable. He moved through the days like an automaton, eating little and drinking a great deal.

Gregory Banks had sensed his friend's despair and had ordered him to spend two weeks away. The bright Hawaiian sun and the gaiety of the tourists at the small resort hotel where he had stayed only heightened David's anguish. He tried to take part in conversations but lost interest. His one attempt at an affair had ended with humiliating impotence. Only drinking helped, but the surcease from pain was temporary, and the horrors were twice as vivid once the effects of the alcohol wore off.

David returned to Portland early and without notice. He stayed home, unwashed and unshaven, letting himself become as gross and disgusting physically as he felt he had become spiritually. In the silent ruin of his home, it became clear to David that he was breaking down. He did nothing to stop the process. Instead, he lay about drunkenly, like a spectator at his own funeral.

In the end it was the smell of his body that saved him. One morning he awoke sober enough to whiff the odor of his sheets and the stench from his underarms and crotch. He was overpowered and driven to the shower. A shave and a decent breakfast followed. The crisis had passed, but David was far from well.

Back at the office David appeared to be in control. Except that he was more likely to miss appointments and appear late for court. The effort it took to put up a front was taking its toll in stomach pains and sleepless nights. And there was the frequent lunchtime martini or two. And Monday began to run into Wednesday and feel like Friday, while David, stabilized in a state of functioning disrepair, ceased to see the meaning in anything anymore.

*

'WHAT WERE YOU doing down there, anyway?' David asked. He was driving Gault home from the county jail.

Gault smiled, then winced. He was a mess. Harvey had taken his revenge on the unconscious writer before any of the patrons of The Dutchman had thought to stop him. A cut that had taken several stitches to close ran across the top of his right eyebrow, and his nose and a rib had been broken.

'I was lookin' for a fight, old buddy,' Gault answered in a tired voice.

'What?'

'I like to fight, and bars are as good a place as any to find one.'

'Are you crazy?'

'Sometimes. But life's crazy. Don't you read my books?'

They drove in silence for a while, which Gault appreciated. He was exhausted, but pleased with the night's outing, even if he'd taken a few lumps. As they drove along the empty highway, he thought back over the fight and savored its good moments.

'Do you do this often?' David asked after a while.

'Curious, aren't you?' Gault laughed. 'Yeah, Dave, I do it often, only I usually don't get suckered like I did tonight.

'It's a good feeling when you fight. Even when you get hit. The pain makes you feel alive, and the hitting . . . there's nothing like a solid punch. The feeling moves up your arm and through your body like electricity. No, there's nothing like it, except maybe a kill.'

David stared at Gault in disbelief.

'You're serious, aren't you?'

'Completely. I'm too tired and sore to joke, old buddy.'

'You actually enjoy hurting people?'

'It's not the hurting, it's the not knowing how it will turn out. The fear when you start and the satisfaction when you win.'

'But, my God, you could get killed in one of those places.'

'Sure. And that makes it better. There's no Marquis of Queensberry rules in the jungle. You play for keeps. We did that in the bush, old buddy. Played for keeps. So did the niggers. Hand to hand with no referee. It makes you feel alive, because when you're near death or when you end someone else's life, you realize the value of your own and how fragile that gift is.'

David was shaken. He knew from his association with Gault how volatile the writer's personality was. And, of course, he knew about Gault's soldiering. But he had never thought about the writer as a professional killer. He remembered the time when Gault had strung him along about killing his wife. Was this another joke, or had his confession been the truth, after all?

'Life is experience, Dave. Without adventure we die. War makes you alive. Fear makes you alive. You must know that. Why else do you handle murder cases? Come on. Admit it. There's a vicarious thrill being that close to death and the person who caused it. Doesn't a little bit of secret admiration ever worm its way into your heart, old buddy, when you sit next to a man who has had the courage to take another human's life?'

'No, Tom. I've never felt that way,' David said.

'Yeah?' Gault answered skeptically. 'Well, different strokes for different folks. Right, old buddy?'

David didn't answer, and Gault closed his eyes. The darkened countryside swept by in a blur. Neither man spoke again until they arrived at the lake.

A STONE WALL with an iron gate marked the boundaries of Gault's property. A half-mile driveway led from the gate, through the woods, to an isolated hilltop overlooking a small lake. Gault's home, with its wood-gabled roof and porous-stone exterior, was modeled after a French country house. David stopped in front and nudged Gault awake.

'Sorry I fell asleep on you,' Gault said. He sat up and stretched. 'Why don't you come on in and I'll fix you a drink?'

'It's almost four A.M., Tom. I've got to get some sleep.'

'You can sack out here. It'll save you the trip home.'

287

'Thanks anyway.'

'Actually, there was a little legal matter I wanted to discuss with you.'

'Can't it keep? I'm out on my feet.'

'I'll get you some coffee. Besides, I think you'll be interested in what I have to say.'

The house was dark inside and Gault turned on a few lights. He left David in a small study and went for the coffee. The oak woodwork and floors gave the room a Gothic quality that unsettled David. A grotesque mask, which Gault had collected in Africa, hung from the wall across from him, and a gray stone fireplace sat in the shadows to his rear.

'What's new with Larry Stafford's case?' Gault asked innocently the moment he entered the room. David felt his heart skip.

'I don't know,' David answered. 'Jerry Bloch is handling the appeal.'

'That was a tough break for you,' Gault said as he sat down across from David. 'I thought you had that one, then that pimp testified.'

Gault paused; then a small smile turned up the corners of his lips.

'Just between us boys, Dave, did he do it?'

'I can't talk about that, Tom,' David said, hoping Gault would change the subject. 'That's privileged information.'

'Sure, I forgot. Say, what would happen if someone popped up and confessed? You know, said he did it. Would that guy get off because Stafford's been found guilty?'

'Not if the person who confessed was the killer. They'd let Stafford out and put the real murderer on trial.'

'That makes sense.'

For a moment Gault appeared to be deep in thought. David was very tired and he wanted to get on with Gault's problem. He was about to speak when Gault said, 'I've got one for you, old buddy. What if some guy came to you as a client and told you he did it, but he says he doesn't want you to tell anyone. What happens then?'

'What do you mean?'

'Well, you can't repeat anything a client tells you, right? I mean, there's that privilege, right?'

'I see what you're getting at. I'd have to do some research, but I guess I couldn't tell anyone about the confession.'

A wry smile played on Gault's lips.

'And an innocent man would stay in prison.'

There was a wistfulness in Gault's tone that alarmed David.

'Yes,' he answered uneasily.

'That would put you in a tough position, wouldn't it, old buddy?'

'Look, Tom, I really am tired. What's this legal problem that's so urgent?'

'Don't want to discuss the murder of that police lady, huh?'

'Not really.'

'Don't you want to know who did it?' Gault asked in a voice so low that David wasn't sure he'd heard him correctly.

'Got your interest now, don't I? But, hell, if you're really tired, we can talk some other time.'

David didn't move and he didn't answer. He was suddenly very aware of how isolated Gault's house was. The writer's eyes twinkled, giving a devilish cast to his handsome features.

'You know, I really felt bad when Larry was convicted. I thought for sure you'd get him off. And there's another thing. I don't think it's fair, his getting all the credit when I did all the work. It's sort of like someone getting a Pulitzer for a book I ghosted.'

'Are you telling me that you killed Darlene Hersch?'

'That's right, old buddy. I did it.'

'If this is another joke like that confession to Julie's murder, it's in bad taste.'

Gault's smile widened.

'I killed Julie, too. I want you to know that. And there have been others.'

'Ortiz said the killer had curly blond hair,' David said, trying to keep his voice steady.

'He did.'

Gault stood up and walked over to a desk near the doorway. He pulled a blond wig from the bottom drawer and showed it to David.

'I was so damn famous after that trial, I had to disguise myself every time I wanted a little action.

'You know, Dave, there are some girls that like to get laid by the criminal element, but you'd be surprised at the number that are turned off by the prospect of winding up the evening dead. Actually, I don't look half-bad as a blond.'

'Why did you kill Darlene Hersch?'

'I'm a little ashamed about that. The truth is, I panicked. I'd been out at a few bars and couldn't score. Then, what do I behold, but a vision of loveliness standing on the corner.'

Gault shook his head sadly at the memory.

'I had terrific plans for Darlene, but she went ahead and spoiled everything by trying to arrest me.' He shrugged his shoulders. 'Like I said, I panicked. Hit her quick. Then I realized I'd have to finish her. I'd had enough of the law after my murder trial, and I didn't relish another trial for assaulting a police officer.'

'And the others you mentioned?'

A wistful expression replaced Gault's smile.

'You know, you'd think I would have been happiest after I made all that money from the books and the movies, but the years as a mercenary were the best times. I felt alive then.

'Life is dull, Dave, deadly dull. One boring, repetitive act after another, until you die. But a creative person can create experiences. Being rich was an experience. And marrying that bitch movie star. It's something most people only read about, but I made it happen. Only that gets boring, too, so you have to move on.

'All experiences become boring after a while, Dave, except one. Killing never gets boring.'

'Why are you telling me this?' David asked.

'I trust you, Dave. Especially after the way you worked so hard to defend me when, in your heart, you thought I was guilty. I still remember your closing argument. So forceful. So sincere. And all the time you thought I was guilty as sin. A man who can lie like that can be trusted.

'I've wanted to discuss, I guess you'd call it my philosophy, for a long time, but until I learned about this attorney-client privilege, I couldn't take the risk. Now I feel a lot better, knowing that anything I tell you is confidential.'

David couldn't move or speak. He felt wasted. Gault studied him, then burst out laughing. David half expected, hoped, that Gault would say this was all a joke.

'Puts you in a predicament, don't it? Stafford rots in prison because you folded at trial . . .'

David's head jerked up and he started to say something, but Gault raised his hand.

'Hey, old buddy, I'm not being critical. It's just the word goin' around. I do a little reporting, remember. That means interviewing. There are a lot of lawyers who figured that you could have kept Johnson off the stand if you wanted to. But you didn't, did you? And we both know why, don't we?'

Gault winked and David felt his heartbeat quicken. 'What do . . .?'

'It's okay, old buddy. We all have our little secrets. And yours is safe with me. I got a tad suspicious when I ran into you and Stafford's old lady in that cozy dinner spot, so, in the interests of good journalism, I decided to follow you. It turned out to be pretty easy, especially at night.

'Hey, don't get uptight. I'm nonjudgmental. Shit, a guy who's murdered a couple of people can't go around throwing stones at someone for dickin' a married woman, can he?'

'You son of a bitch,' David said hoarsely.

'Hell, I'm worse than that. But there's no reason to take this personally, and as I said, your secret is safe with me, just like I know mine is safe with you.'

'You'd let an innocent man stay in prison for something you did?' David said, immediately feeling ridiculous for asking the question of a man like Gault.

'What choice have I got? To get him out, I'd have to put me in.'

Gault walked back to the desk and replaced the wig.

'Tom,' David said cautiously, 'I think you need help. It's a good sign that you've decided to talk to me and—'

293

PHILLIP M. MARGOLIN

Gault shook his head, amused.

'None of that psychiatric horseshit, please,' he said, wandering out of David's line of vision. 'I'm not crazy, old buddy. I'm a sociopath. Read your textbooks more carefully. See, I know what I'm doing, I just don't give a shit, because I don't have the same moral structure you have.' Gault was directly behind David and the writer's voice was low, soft, and vaguely menacing. 'In fact, Dave, I don't have any moral structure at all.'

Gault stopped speaking. It was completely quiet in the house. David's heart was racing with fear. He wanted to run, but he couldn't move.

'A sociopath operates on a pleasure-pain principle,' Gault continued. 'If you and a sociopath were all alone in a dark house with no one around for miles, a sociopath is the type of person who could kill you, just for kicks, if he thought he could get away with it.'

David heard a click near his ear, and he remembered the jagged slash that seemed to divide Darlene Hersch's neck in two. He dived forward, putting as much distance between himself and Gault as he could. There was a chair across from him and he crashed into it, twisting to face Gault and bringing his hands up to fend off an attack.

Gault watched motionless from the fireplace. He had a switchblade in his hand and he was smiling.

'Not a bad move for a fella who's not in tip-top

294

shape. Of course, you should never have let me get behind you in the first place.'

David stood up. He was looking around desperately for a weapon.

'I know what you're thinking,' Gault said, 'but a weapon wouldn't do you any good. If I wanted to, I could kill you anyway.'

Gault paused, and David knew it was true. He felt defeated and strangely calm, now that he knew he was going to die.

'But I don't want to kill you, old buddy,' Gault said, his grin back in place. 'Hell, you're my friend and my lawyer. Why, you saved my life, and it would be plumb ungrateful of me to carve you up the way I did Darlene.'

Gault pocketed the knife and David started to shake all over.

'Being egotistical,' Gault continued, 'I have great faith in my ability to judge people, and I made a little bet with myself. Tom, I said, Dave is your pal and an honorable man. If you tell him something in confidence, you can count on Dave's sense of professional ethics and his friendship to keep your secret. You can trust a man like Dave to die rather than reveal a client's confidence. Even if it means that an innocent man has to spend the rest of his life in prison. That's what I said to myself. Now, am I right?'

David wanted to answer Gault, but he couldn't speak.

'Am I right?' Gault asked again, his mouth a grim line and his eyes hard and cold.

'Why are you doing this to me?' David asked.

'Maybe I'm just a modern-day Diogenes, looking for an honest man. Or maybe I just want to see you squirm.'

'You bastard,' David said, his anger momentarily conquering his fear.

'Now, that's the wrong attitude, Dave. Getting angry isn't going to help you out of your predicament. Look at this as if it were a chess problem. White to move and win. Maybe there's a mate, maybe there's only a gain of material, or' – and Gault paused – 'maybe the person who constructed the problem cheated and there's no way white can win.

'Now, why don't you go home and get some sleep? You look worse than I do.'

2

Ortiz sat in the back row of the courtroom listening to Judge McIntyre decide the motion to suppress evidence that had been filed by Cyrus Johnson's attorney. The law was clear, the judge said, that in order to search a person without a search warrant, a police officer had to have probable cause to believe that a search would turn up evidence of a crime, and no time to get a warrant. When Cyrus Johnson was searched, the judge continued, Officer Ortiz did have time to get a warrant, and he did not have probable cause to believe that Johnson would have narcotics on his person. Regretfully, he concluded, he had no choice but to forbid the State to introduce evidence in a trial where the seizure of that evidence violated the mandate of the United States Constitution.

Johnson's attorney smiled and shook his client's hand. Johnson did not return the smile. Instead, he looked toward the back of the courtroom at Ortiz. Ortiz was standing to leave. The narcotics officer had known all along what the result of the hearing would be. He had tailored his testimony to fit the latest Supreme Court opinions, so that the evidence against Johnson would have to be thrown out. He had also contacted the district attorney in charge of the case and told him that he had probably acted too hastily in searching Johnson. In light of Johnson's testimony at Stafford's trial, he and the DA had both agreed that the drug case should not be that vigorously pursued.

'Hey, Ortiz,' a deep voice called. Ortiz turned and saw Kermit Monroe sitting on a bench by the courtroom door.

'What can I do for you, Kermit?' he asked.

'T.V. wants to see you. He asked me to make sure you didn't go nowhere before he had the chance to talk.'

'Tell T.V. some other day. I'm busy.'

'Hey, man,' Kermit said, getting slowly to his feet, 'why you always have to make things difficult? T.V. said this was important and for you to wait. He got some kind of tip for you. So why bust my balls when he wants to do you a favor?'

Ortiz was about to answer when Johnson walked out of the courtroom.

'You want to see me?' Ortiz asked.

Johnson grinned. 'Yeah, I want to see you.'

T.V. shook hands with his lawyer and they parted.

'Let's go down to my car where I know there's no bugs,' Johnson said, still grinning. Ortiz shrugged. Maybe Johnson had decided to turn informant. It wouldn't be the first time a big operator had got scared after some real heat.

They took the elevator downstairs, then walked to the parking structure across from the courthouse. T.V.'s car was parked on the fifth floor, and Monroe slid into the driver's seat while Ortiz and Johnson got into the leather-covered rear seat.

'Now, what's so important?' Ortiz demanded.

'You fucked me up, Ortiz. You planted shit on me, then made me stool to get rid of the rap. You made me sit through that court case and spend a lot of money on a lawyer. And you perjured yourself and broke the law. Why did you do all that shit? One reason, right? To get that poor honky Stafford. To nail his butt to the jailhouse door. Am I right?'

'Go on, T.V. You either have something to say or you don't. I don't have all day.'

'Oh, this won't be no waste of your time, Ortiz. See, I wanted you to know that I lied. That bullshit I testified to was just that – bullshit.'

He stopped to let what he had said sink in. Ortiz looked puzzled.

'Oh, Stafford tried to buy a little action and he hit Mordessa, but it didn't happen the way I said. That white boy wanted some dark meat, but he didn't ask for nothing kinky. When he got up in the room, Mordessa, that dumb cunt, tried to boost his wallet. He caught her and she started wailin' on him.

'Mordessa is one mean bitch and she packs a wallop. Stafford had to hit her a good shot just to keep her off him.'

'What about the story you told the police?'

'Hey, I had to think quick when the pigs arrived. I decided to tell them the dude had done somethin' that would really embarrass him so he wouldn't press charges. I just said the weirdest shit I could think of. But that Stafford ain't no sado-what-you-call-it. Shit, he wouldn't a done nothin' if Mordessa hadn't hit him so hard.

'So you see, my man, the very words which you solicited by illegal means and forced me to say was lies. And you know that jury would have acquitted Stafford if it wasn't for me. But you can't tell nobody that I lied without gettin' yo'self in trouble, can you? Which means you got to live the rest of your life with what you done, while Stafford spends the rest of his life at the state pen.'

Ortiz leaned back in his seat, trying to think. What did it matter if Johnson had lied? Stafford lied, too. He had sworn under oath that he had never gone with a prostitute. Ortiz knew who he had seen in the doorway of that motel room. Larry Stafford killed Darlene Hersch.

'You know somethin', Ortiz. You white boys are real sick. That's what I come to learn, bein' in this business. You plantin' that dope on me, Stafford havin' to buy pussy, and that writer . . .'

Johnson shook his head and Ortiz looked up at the pimp.

'What writer?'

'The one that beat up Mordessa and wanted her to do all that kinky stuff. Shit, he already got away with murder. Mordessa's lucky she ain't the one that got killed.'

'What are you talking about?'

'Mordessa seen him in the papers when he got off. Didn't recognize him at first, 'cause he was wearin' this wig when he beat on her. That's where I got the story from. She was a sight. Said he wanted to tie her up. When she said no, he started kickin' her and hittin' her till she cried. And it takes plenty to make that woman cry. He hurt her bad. Then he kills his wife.'

'Who are you talking about?' Ortiz asked slowly.

'I can't remember the name. His wife was rich, though, and she was beat to death in that mansion by the lake.'

'Thomas Gault?'

'That's the one.'

Ortiz stared at Johnson. 'You mean that story you told on the witness stand did happen, only it was Thomas Gault that beat up your whore?'

'That's what I been sayin'.'

'What kind of wig did he wear?'

'I ain't got no idea.'

Ortiz opened the car door and got out. He felt as if he were drowning.

'Where you goin', Ortiz?' T.V. asked with a laugh. 'You goin' to church or you goin' to tell the law that that Stafford boy is in jail, only he ain't guilty? Only you can't do that, can you, 'cause you'd have to tell on yo'self.'

Ortiz walked away from the car. The motor started, and Monroe drove as close to Ortiz as he could, squealing his tires as he headed down the ramp. Ortiz didn't notice.

Just because Johnson lied, it didn't necessarily follow that Stafford was innocent. But the wig . . . Gault and Stafford had similar builds. With a blond wig . . .

Then Ortiz remembered the mystery man that Gault swore murdered his wife. He had been described as being athletically built, of average height, with curly blond hair. A description that would fit Gault if Gault's hair was curly, blond. And Stafford.

Ortiz remembered something else. Grimes, the night clerk at the Raleigh Motel, testified that the man he saw driving away from the motel had brown hair that was a bit long. Gault had brown hair, which he had worn long at his trial. If he had removed a wig after killing Darlene, that would explain how Grimes could see a man with brown hair, and he, a man with blond.

Could he have been wrong about Stafford? It seemed impossible for two men to have the same build, shirt, pants, and car. Yet Gault and Stafford were built alike and the pants were common enough.

The shirt? While it wasn't the most common type, there had certainly been enough of them in Portland.

And the car? That was simple enough to check on. Too simple. Ortiz felt his gut tighten. He was afraid. Afraid he had made a terrible mistake. If Gault owned a beige Mercedes, then Larry Stafford might very well be innocent.

GREGORY WAS FINISHING some dictation when David entered.

'You're on the bar ethics committee, right?' David asked, sinking into a chair.

'Yes. Why? You haven't done anything unethical lately, have you?' he asked, half joking.

'Let me give you a hypothetical and tell me what you think.'

Gregory turned off his dictation equipment and leaned back. His eyes narrowed with concentration and he cocked his head slightly to one side.

'Assume that a lawyer represents A in a bank-robbery case and A is convicted. Later B hires the lawyer to represent him in an unrelated legal matter. While the lawyer's client, B tells the lawyer, in confidence, that he committed the bank robbery for which A has been convicted, as well as several other robberies. When the lawyer suggests that B confess to the authorities so that A can be released from prison, B refuses. What can the lawyer do to help A?'

Gregory sat thinking for a moment, then took a book from the credenza behind his desk. He rifled the pages until he found what he was looking for.

He read for a few more moments. David sat quietly, staring past Banks through the window toward the foothills. He felt a wave of pain in his stomach and placed his hand over his belt line, gently massaging where it hurt.

'I'd say your lawyer has a problem,' Banks said. 'According to *Wigmore on Evidence* and the Canons of Ethics, a client's confidential communications can be revealed only if the client sues the attorney, in which case the attorney can reveal those confidences that bear on his defense of the client's charges, or if the client tells the attorney that he is planning a future crime, in which case the attorney can make those disclosures necessary to prevent the future crime or protect those against whom it is threatened. If the communication is in confidence and made while the client is seeking legal advice, the confidence is permanently protected.

'I'm afraid that the lawyer can't help A in your hypothetical.'

David sat quietly, thinking. Gregory had confirmed what he had believed all along.

'What if the lawyer decided to violate the Canons of Ethics and breach the confidence?'

'He could be prevented from revealing it in court, and the client could successfully resist being forced to corroborate it. You'd have a tough time convincing the authorities to let A out of prison under those circumstances.'

The pain in David's stomach grew worse. David

took a deep breath and hoped that Gregory would not notice his discomfort.

'Is there anything I can help you with?' Gregory asked.

David desperately wanted his friend's help but knew he could not ask for it. How could he reveal what he had done and still maintain Gregory's respect?

'No, Greg. It was just a hypothetical question.'

Gregory wanted to pursue the matter, but, instead, he asked, 'Shall we go to lunch, then?'

'I'm sorry, Greg, but I'm going home. I don't feel well.'

'Dave, are you sure I can't help you?' Gregory asked. 'If there's anything bothering you . . .'

David shook his head. He smiled weakly. 'No problem. Just an upset stomach.'

He stood up.

'See you in the morning.'

'Yeah,' Banks replied. His brow furrowed, and he did not move for several minutes after David left the office.

'WHY ARE YOU interested in Thomas Gault?' Norman Capers asked.

'I'd rather not say, Norm,' Ortiz answered.

Capers shrugged.

'Hell, what do I care? If it will help put that bastard away, I don't care if I never find out.'

Ortiz was surprised by Capers's reaction. Norm

was an experienced, professional prosecutor who had been in the DA's office a long time. He rarely let himself get emotional about a case.

'You don't like his writing style?' Ortiz inquired lightly, hoping to egg Capers on.

'I don't like that bastard, period. I've prosecuted a lot of people, but he . . . I don't know how to put this. Julie Gault . . . Whoever did that really enjoyed his work.'

Capers paused and examined a thumbnail.

'You know, he was cracking jokes all through that trial,' he continued. 'Treated the whole thing like it was a comedy put on for his amusement. Oh, not when the jury was around. Shit, as soon as they filed in, he'd sit up straight and put on this sad look. And on the stand . . . You know, he actually broke down and cried.

'It was all phony. After the jury went out, he turned to me and winked. But he was terrific on the stand and that's all those people saw.'

'You think he's capable of killing someone?'

'Gault? He's some sort of whiz at unarmed combat. Don't you know his background?'

Ortiz shook his head. 'I wasn't involved in the case, so I didn't pay that much attention to it. Just scuttlebutt around the station house and the articles in the papers.'

'Our Tom is a killer, all right. You know he was a mercenary in Africa all those years. There's a screw loose there. A big one. When he was living in Hollywood, he got into some pretty nasty fights, and I hear he's been in a few here.'

'Is he a womanizer?'

'Gault? If it moves, he'll fuck it. And he's mean there, too. We spoke to a couple of ex-girl friends during our investigation. He's beaten up more than one. Very vicious and with a smile, like he was really enjoying himself. That boy is very sick and very clever.'

And, Ortiz thought, Motor Vehicles lists him as the owner of a beige Mercedes.

3

David drove aimlessly for an hour, then went home. He was exhausted, and the pain in his stomach had increased. As soon as he was through the doorway, he poured himself a drink. He knew alcohol would aggravate his stomach, but the pain from self-accusation and self-pity was far worse than physical discomfort.

The first drink helped very little, so he poured another. His conversation with Gregory Banks made him realize how alone he was. He recalled a scene from George Orwell's 1984. The State had devised a torture. A helmet was fastened over a man's head. The front of the helmet contained a small cage, even with the prisoner's eyes. In the cage was a rat, and separating the rat from the man was a movable partition. The privilege between attorney and client, like that ghastly helmet, locked David in with Gault's secret, where it could gnaw at him, torturing his every waking moment.

Even if there was no privilege, David would be helpless. He had no proof, other than Gault's confession, that Gault had killed Darlene Hersch. If Gault denied that he had confessed, how could

David prove him a liar? David wasn't completely convinced himself that Gault wasn't playing with him. David had learned enough about Gault while he was representing him to know that the man had a very wide streak of sadism in him. David remembered how he had felt during that moment when Gault had stood behind him with the open switchblade. Every moment of his life would be like that if he betrayed Gault's trust.

And there was something else that tortured David. He had always had his pride. Now he had lost his pride, but only he and Jennifer Stafford knew why. If he went to the authorities, Gault would make David's affair with Jenny public. Everyone would think that David had thrown Larry Stafford's case to get Larry out of the way so he could continue as Jenny's lover. He would be disbarred, disgraced, and no one would believe his accusations against Gault.

David finished his drink. He wanted another one, but he didn't have the energy to get it. The lights of the city distracted him from his thoughts for a moment. It had been light when he'd left his office, but it was dark now. He hadn't noticed the transition. He was very tired. The thought of curling up and sleeping on the floor appealed to him. He tried it. The carpet was soft, and there was nothing but dark velvet when he closed his eyes. And Jenny. Her face and form slipped into his thoughts unbidden. He opened his eyes and stared up at the ceiling. Jenny would understand his torment, because she was part of it. If he could talk to Jenny ... But would she see him?

A wave of self-doubt washed over David and his hand began to tremble. He wanted to stand up, but fear immobilized him. How could he face her? What would she say to him? He had stayed away from Jenny because he felt that she had betrayed him, but now he saw that he was the betrayer. Jenny had lied for Larry out of a sense of loyalty and because she believed he was innocent. There had been no purity in David's motives. He had rationalized his actions in court by telling himself that he did not want to free a killer, but he knew that was not the real reason. He wanted Jenny, and he had betrayed Larry to hurt them because he felt that they had deceived him. Did Jenny despise him? She must know what he had done. It didn't matter. She was the only one he could turn to.

HALFWAY TO THE Stafford house, David almost turned back. He secretly hoped that Jenny would not be home so he would not have to face her, and it was with a mixture of hope and dread that he saw the lights shining in the living room when he pulled into the driveway.

Jenny answered the door after the first ring. She was barefoot and wore a yellow shirt over a pair of faded jeans. The strain of the past months made her seem older, but no less beautiful.

'Can I come in?' David asked hesitantly, almost apologetically.

Jenny was stunned by his appearance. He was heavier, unkempt, and washed-out. There was no sign of the energy that had been such a vital part of him.

'I don't know,' she answered. Her voice trembled. She felt crazy inside, pulled in so many directions she thought she would come apart.

'You have every right . . .' David started. 'Jenny, I have to see you. It's about Larry.'

She drew back a step and studied David's face for clues. The odor of alcohol was strong. He looked destroyed.

'What about Larry?'

'Can I come in?' he repeated.

Jenny paused for a second, then led the way to the living room. David watched her walk. Her back was rigid, her steps precise, as if she were prepared to flee. Her reticence depressed him, but he should have expected it. Once during the ride over he had fantasized a tear-stained reunion, with Jenny throwing herself into his arms. He had been a fool even to think of such a thing. He was grateful she would so much as talk to him.

'What about Larry?' she asked again when they were seated on one of the living-room sofas.

'Jenny, he may be innocent.'

Jenny looked bewildered.

'I have a client, a man I am representing on

311

another matter. He has confessed to killing Darlene Hersch.'

Jenny shook her head as if to clear it. She was off balance. She had always believed that Larry was innocent, but what would this all mean for her?

'I don't understand. Someone else confessed to killing that woman?'

'Yes.'

'Why are you telling me this? Why haven't you gone to the police?'

'It's very complicated. The confession, it was told to me in confidence. It's a privileged communication. By law I can't reveal it to anyone without my client's permission.'

'Will Larry . . .? Does this mean he'll go free?'

'Not unless my client allows me to tell the police.'

'But surely . . . he wouldn't let an innocent man stay in prison.'

'You have to understand. This man . . . it's a game to him. He gets pleasure out of hurting people. He confessed to me because he knows I can't tell the authorities. He told me to torment me. I'm not even certain that he's telling me the truth.'

'Wait a minute. What do you mean it might not be the truth?'

'He did this once before. Confessed to committing a crime. That time he retracted the confession. It could all be a practical joke.'

David saw the confusion on Jenny's face. He

looked away and caught his reflection in the window glass. It startled him. He looked weak and pathetic. The type of person who would be susceptible to the meanest practical joke.

'If this is all some kind of joke, why did you come here? Why are you telling me this?'

'Don't, Jenny. I had to talk to someone. I couldn't keep it inside any longer. And I don't think it is a joke. There's something about this man. I know he's capable of killing.'

'But why me, David? Why did you come to me?'

She was watching him intently, searching with her question for far more than she had asked. David tried to read her eyes. He was afraid to say what was in his heart. Afraid of making a fool of himself. Afraid he had already lost her. But he knew that this was the moment to speak, not evade, and he gathered his courage.

'I came to you because I still love you. I never stopped.'

David paused and Jenny saw that he was crying.

'Jenny, I've been a mess since the trial. I've lost my self-respect, and I've lost interest in everything that ever meant anything to me. But not my love for you. I just couldn't face you.'

David looked away. Jenny felt as if a dam had broken inside her, setting free emotions she had thought she would never feel again. She reached up and touched David's cheek.

'God, Jenny,' he sobbed. She held him tight.

'It's all right,' she whispered, rocking him back and forth.

'I didn't know what to do and I had no one I could go to.'

'You always had me, David. Always.'

'I couldn't come to you. Not after what I did to Larry.'

'You didn't do anything to Larry. Larry and I did something to you. We lied to you and used you.'

David sat up and held her by the shoulders. 'It was wrong. What I did was wrong. We both know that. I should never have represented Larry feeling the way I do about you. Now we have to get him out of prison.'

'I still think you should tell the police,' Jenny said firmly.

David shook his head. 'You don't understand. Since the confession was made in confidence, nothing I reveal could ever be used in court. He could deny he ever made a confession, and there would be nothing we could do.'

'Who is this man? Who killed Darlene Hersch?'

David hesitated. Even now his legal training made him rebel at the thought of violating the code of ethics.

'Thomas Gault,' he said finally.

'Oh, my God. I knew Julie Webster. That was horrible.'

'I know, Jenny. And I'm the man responsible for

314

putting Gault back on the street so he could kill again.'

'There must be something we can do.'

'I've thought about it and thought about it. I can't find any way out. Anything I initiate will . . .'

David paused. The germ of an idea came to him. What if . . .? David started pacing back and forth. Jenny watched him. There was a fire in his eyes that had burned constantly in the old David. It made her feel good to see it again and to think that she may have had something to do with rekindling it.

TERRY CONKLIN SCANNED the diners in the all-night restaurant and spotted David in a booth toward the back. David was sipping from his second cup of coffee when Conklin reached him.

'This better be good,' the investigator said. 'I was sound asleep. Rose is really pissed.'

'I'm sorry.'

Conklin was going to say something else, but one look at David stopped him. He had not seen the lawyer since Stafford's trial, and the change in his friend's appearance was startling. David's face was puffy, his eyes were bloodshot, and his suit was creased and stained.

A waitress appeared and Conklin ordered coffee. As soon as she walked off, David said,

'I want to hire you.'

'I'm pretty busy, Dave.'

'I know, but I'm desperate. I'm willing to pay

twice your regular rate and cover the cost of anyone you hire to take up the slack on your cases.'

'This is that important?'

David nodded.

'Who's the client?'

'Me.'

'What's this about?' Conklin asked cautiously. If David was in some kind of trouble, it would explain his appearance, but Conklin could not imagine David's doing anything illegal or unethical.

'A client of mine told me some information in confidence. I have to know if he was telling me the truth or if he's lying to me.'

'Who's the client?'

'Thomas Gault.'

'I thought that case was over.'

'It is.'

'So this is something new.'

'Yes.'

'What did he tell you?'

'I can't disclose that. I'm afraid anything you find may be tainted if I break the confidence.'

'Tainted? How?'

'If a lawyer reveals an attorney confidence and the police use the information to solve a crime, I believe the courts would prevent the district attorney from using the evidence at trial.'

'So you can't tell me what Gault said?' Conklin asked incredulously.

'That's right.'

'How am I supposed to conduct an investigation if I don't know what I'm investigating?'

'I can tell you information that doesn't violate the confidence, and I'll answer any questions I can.'

Conklin started to make a sarcastic remark, but he saw the pain on David's face.

'Okay. I'll play it your way. What can you tell me?'

'I'm upset because Larry Stafford was convicted.'

Conklin's brow furrowed. 'This is about the Stafford case?'

'I can't answer that.'

'So Gault told you something about the Stafford case and you think he might be lying.'

David did not respond.

'I feel like I'm playing twenty questions.'

'Don't stop. I feel as ridiculous as you do, but this is too important to screw up. I want you to be able to pass a polygraph test if a defense lawyer asks if I broke Gault's confidence with you. Now, think about what you know.'

'You told me that you're upset because Stafford was convicted, you want to know if Gault lied to you about something that probably concerns the Stafford case. I don't get . . .'

Conklin paused. He studied David. In all the time he'd known Nash, he had never seen him looking like this. It would take something monumental to destroy his friend's self-confidence. Conklin leaned forward and stared directly into David's eyes.

'Gault told you he killed Darlene Hersch, and you want me to find out if he lied,' Conklin said. David did not move. Conklin slumped against the back of the booth.

'Have your secretary send me a retainer agreement setting out the terms of your employment,' David said.

4

Terry Conklin's investigation started in the public library. There were numerous articles about Thomas Gault, because he was a famous writer. After Gault won the Pulitzer, *The New York Times Magazine* featured a cover story that gave a detailed account of his service as a mercenary in South Africa, Liberia, and several other African nations and included interviews with soldiers of fortune who had served with him. If Gault killed his wife, it would not have been the first time he had done in someone with his bare hands.

After the library Terry went to police headquarters, where he obtained copies of police reports of incidents involving Gault. Conklin expected the domestic-violence complaints filed by Julie Webster Gault, but he was surprised by several reports of assaults committed by Gault in bars, including a recent account of a fight at a dockside bar called The Dutchman. Terry noted with interest that the incident had occurred only days before his meeting with David. He also noted that the person who posted bail for Gault was none other than his new client, David Nash.

Conklin interviewed the bartender and another witness, who recounted Gault's fighting skills and the impersonal way he had provoked the fight. Conklin ran down an ex-girl friend who was still afraid of Gault, even though she had not seen him in over two years. Two other women refused to talk to Terry.

Conklin was initially troubled by Detective Ortiz's description of Hersch's killer as having curly blond hair, but he remembered that Merton Grimes's description of the killer's hair would fit the way Gault had worn his hair when he was tried for Julie Gault's murder. If Gault used a wig to disguise himself because of all the publicity his trial engendered, it would explain the differences in the descriptions of Hersch's killer. Conklin also learned that Gault owned a beige Mercedes.

At the end of a week Terry Conklin was convinced that Thomas Gault could easily have killed Darlene Hersch, but he had absolutely no proof Gault even knew who the dead policewoman was. Conklin was reduced to following Gault in the hopes that his quarry would lead him to a witness or evidence that would help him solve David's dilemma.

Each morning Conklin parked his car on a side road near Gault's property and climbed a small hill, where he watched the house from a copse of trees. Conklin rarely observed any activity before ten, when Gault would leave the house for an hour-long run. Gault always looked as if he had broken a sweat before the run, and Conklin guessed the writer performed some kind of physical exercise before leaving the house.

Three times a week Gault worked out at a local dojo, where he received private lessons from the owner, a former instructor of unarmed combat for the South Korean Army. On the days he did not go to the dojo, Gault did not leave his house before midafternoon.

If Gault's activities during the daytime were dull, his nights were anything but. Gault spent almost every evening in a bar or nightclub. On one occasion Gault returned home with a woman, who left by cab shortly before Gault's run. Toward the beginning of the second week, Gault's evening routine changed. Instead of going directly home from the bar or nightclub, Gault drove to Portland's industrial area. He always parked near a deserted warehouse that backed on the Columbia River. The warehouse had 'Wexler Electronics' written on the side in peeling red paint. Conklin checked the corporate records. The company had gone under a year ago, and the property was tied up in litigation.

The first time Gault drove to the warehouse, Conklin waited in his car. A high chain-link fence separated the warehouse from a strip of sandy land that sloped down to the river. Conklin watched Gault take a large rug and a flashlight from the trunk of his car and disappear around the side of the warehouse that abutted the fence. Half an hour later Gault reappeared. He seemed winded. Conklin saw him wipe his forehead with his shirtsleeve, then drop the flashlight into his trunk and drive off.

The second night Gault took the flashlight and a large toolbox from the car, returning an hour later with both items.

On the third night Conklin did not follow Gault when he left the warehouse. As soon as Gault's car was out of sight, Conklin took a flashlight out of his glove compartment and walked to the fence. The wind from the river chilled him. He hunched against it and played the light beam over the ground, then along the warehouse wall. Nothing.

Conklin heard a sharp tapping in front of him. He raised the beam. A door was snapping against the side of the building. Conklin approached it cautiously. He looked around, then entered the warehouse. The high roof shut out the moon and stars, leaving the flashlight beam as the only source of light. Conklin was overcome by a sense of dread. He felt enveloped by the darkness, as if he were fathoms deep in the ocean at the point where light is completely absorbed by the water.

The flashlight showed Conklin rusted girders, an abandoned wooden pallet on which an open and empty packing crate rested, and random stacks of two-by-fours covered by cobwebs and dust. He took a few steps forward and picked out a section of the floor that was covered by the rug Gault had taken from the car on the first evening. Conklin walked over to the rug. It was cheap and dull green. He shone the light around the area and saw nothing else that would help explain why Gault had left it in the warehouse or why Gault had returned to this place on three successive evenings.

'I hope you like the rug.'

Conklin jumped and almost dropped the light.

'I bought it for you.'

Conklin turned in a circle, but there was no one there.

'Before I give you your gift, you will have to answer some questions, Mr. Conklin.'

'Gault?'

'Who else have you been following for the past two weeks?'

'We can talk. Why don't we go outside?' Conklin said, turning slowly so as to face the place where Gault's voice had been.

'No, thank you. Here will be just fine. Sound won't carry as far. Lowers the risk of someone hearing you scream.'

5

'Mr. Nash,' David's secretary said, 'it's Mr. Gault again.'

David felt a flush of fear, then anger.

'Tell him I'm in conference.'

'He says he'll come down and cause a scene if you try to put him off.'

'Jesus.' David looked out the window. 'Okay. Put him through.'

'Hey, old buddy,' Gault said as soon as David picked up the phone, 'I need your help.'

'Look, Tom, let me make this clear. I don't want anything to do with you. Not now. Not ever.'

'Hey, no need to be so hostile.'

'Listen . . .'

'No, you listen,' Gault said. There was an unmistakable edge to his voice. 'If you hang up this phone, I might have to call the *Oregonian* with an interesting item about Mrs. Stafford. You remember her, don't you?'

David sucked in a breath. 'All right. What do you want?'

'Just some advice. What say we meet for lunch? My treat.'

*

GAULT HAD CHOSEN a small French restaurant in north-west Portland. The lunch crowd was made up of a round table of older women, several businessmen on expense accounts, and a few young lovers. The maître d' showed David to Gault's table, and the writer greeted him with a relaxed smile.

'Some Reisling?' Gault suggested, taking a tall bottle of wine from the ice bucket at the side of the table.

'Let's just cut to the chase, Tom. I'm tired of games.'

'Oh? That wasn't my impression. Nonetheless, I agree. Let's get down to business. I'm working on a new book and I'm stuck for an ending. I hoped you could help me out. The book is about a writer. Someone like me, actually. Now, this writer is minding his own business when he gets the funny feeling that he's being followed. Sure enough, he is.

'At first the writer thinks it's just some literary groupie, but the fellow never approaches him. The writer begins to get nervous, so he lays a little trap.'

Gault paused to watch David's reaction.

'It must be a pretty good plot,' Gault said. 'I see I've got you on the edge of your seat already. Now, where was I? Oh, yes. The trap. The writer has heard that old saw "Curiosity killed the cat" and sets out to pique his tail's curiosity. Each evening he goes to an out-of-the-way, deserted location and does

325

something mysterious, hoping that the mystery man will follow him inside, where it is nice and quiet and the writer can ask a few questions without having to worry about being disturbed.

'After three nights our little pussy takes the bait. Guess what happens next?'

David sat in stunned silence.

'No guesses? Well, you see, the writer loves his privacy and he certainly doesn't appreciate anyone violating it. Do you know what my character does to this intruder?'

Gault smiled. The blood had drained from David's face.

'In my story the writer tortures this fellow, who answers every question he is asked. It's quite a violent scene. Blood spraying all over, bones cracking. I may have to tone it down before submitting it to my editor. She has a weak stomach, and I don't know if she'll be able to take this much graphic violence.

'Anyway, the writer has just had some trouble with the law, so he has to keep this little incident hush-hush. All this torture has taken place on a large rug that does an admirable job of absorbing the blood. The writer rolls up the dead man in the rug, cleans up the mess, and gets rid of the body, leaving no clues for a sleuth to find. But that's where I'm stuck. What happens next? For the life of me, I can't figure it out.

'My character knows the identity of the dastardly coward who hired the victim. I guess the writer could confront him. But I don't know . . . That seems like such a cliché, and the critics have been so lavish in praising my originality.' Gault shrugged. 'I'll admit I'm stumped. That's why I called. You have a fertile imagination. I hoped you could help me.'

David stood up so quickly, he knocked over his chair. Gault watched, greatly amused. The sound of the chair crashing to the floor brought on a sudden hush in the restaurant. The diners turned toward David as he staggered away. Gault threw his head back, and his laughter followed David out onto the street.

6

Monica Powers was getting ready for bed when the doorbell rang. She put a bathrobe on over her nightgown and went to the door. David had never been to her apartment and she was surprised to see him. She was more surprised by his appearance. Since the Stafford trial she had heard disturbing rumors about David, and his disheveled clothes, bloodshot eyes, and uncombed hair seemed to bear them out.

'I need your help, Monica,' David said. His shoulders were hunched, and he could not look directly at her when he spoke. Monica stood aside and let David into the apartment.

'You look awful. What's going on?'

David wandered into the living room and slumped down onto the couch. Monica sat opposite the couch on a straight-back chair. Suddenly David's shoulders shook and he began to cry. He hid his face in his hands. Monica rushed to the couch.

'I didn't know where else to go,' David sobbed.

Monica held him tight and rocked him. David clung to her. After a few minutes she could feel him relax and she let go. David ran his coat sleeve across his eyes.

'I'm sorry,' he managed.

'What's wrong? Talk to me.'

David rested his head against the back of the couch and closed his eyes.

'It's Terry Conklin. He's dead and I'm responsible.'

'What?!'

'Thomas Gault tortured him and buried the body.'

'I don't understand . . .'

David sat up and leaned forward. He looked straight down, his head bowed.

'Gault told me something in confidence. I couldn't go to the police. What Gault said was protected by the attorney-client privilege. Gault is a sadist. He'd confessed to killing someone before to unnerve me. Then he told me it was a joke. He had me so confused. When he . . . when he told me this new information . . . I believed him, but he's such a convincing liar . . .'

David paused. His lips were dry and his throat was raw from crying.

'I . . . I thought I'd be clever, so I hired Terry to check out Gault's story. Then, yesterday, I met with Gault. He told me he tortured Terry to death and disposed of the body.'

'He confessed to murder?' Monica asked, as if she were not certain she had heard David correctly.

'Not directly.'

David recounted his lunch conversation with Gault.

329

'How do you know Gault isn't playing another sadistic game with you?' Monica asked when he was done.

'Terry is missing. I called his wife as soon as I got back to my office. Rose doesn't know where he is. He always comes home or checks in with her. She hasn't heard from him since the day before yesterday.'

'What did Gault say that prompted you to hire Terry Conklin?' Monica asked.

David hesitated. Then he said,

'He told me he murdered Darlene Hersch.'

'Larry Stafford killed Darlene Hersch.'

'Gault has a build similar to Larry Stafford's, he drives a beige Mercedes, and he showed me the curly blond wig he wore when he murdered Darlene Hersch. He also confessed to other killings, including Julie Gault's.

'Remember Grimes's testimony about the killer having brown hair? Gault has brown hair. If Gault wore a curly blond wig, then took it off in his car, Ortiz would have seen a man with curly blond hair and Grimes would have seen a man with brown hair.'

'Ortiz is still certain he saw Stafford.'

'You know what the lighting conditions were like that night. You saw Terry Conklin's pictures.'

'Very skillfully taken pictures, I must admit,' Monica said sarcastically.

330

'No, Monica, those pictures weren't doctored. I had other professional photographers duplicate Terry's work. They weren't phonies.'

'I know,' Monica said with a sigh. 'I sent a police photographer to the motel, and he got similar results.'

David spent the next half hour going over his relationship with Gault from their first contact to the meeting at the restaurant. He omitted only reference to Jenny and their affair. He knew it would be better to tell Monica everything, but he couldn't bring himself to reveal their relationship.

'I don't know,' Monica said when he was finished. 'Gault obviously has mental problems or else he wouldn't be playing this kind of game with you, whether the confession is true or false. But he did retract his first confession, and as you pointed out, there isn't a shred of evidence that connects him to the murder of Darlene Hersch. As for Terry Conklin, we don't even have a body.'

'He did it, Monica. If you'd been there and heard him . . .'

'I wasn't, though.'

'Does that mean you won't do anything?'

'No, David. You wouldn't have come to see me if you didn't think Gault murdered Darlene Hersch and Terry Conklin.'

Monica paused. She seemed uncertain whether to continue with what she was going to say.

'David,' she asked hesitantly, 'what happened

to you during Stafford's trial? You seemed to fold up and die when I put Johnson on. You must know that you had a good chance to keep him from testifying.'

David looked at the tabletop to avoid looking at Monica.

'I won't discuss the Stafford trial. You'll have to respect my wishes.'

Monica wanted to pursue the matter, but she sensed David's pain. She had too much respect for him to go any further.

'I think I should bring Bert Ortiz in on this,' she said. 'He's the one you have to convince. If he doesn't change his mind, you have no case.'

'You're right,' David agreed. 'Can he be trusted to keep this quiet?'

'I think so.'

'Then call him.'

'DAVID GAVE ME some very unsettling information about the Darlene Hersch murder tonight. I want you to hear it, but you have to agree to keep this meeting confidential.'

Ortiz was confused. When Monica had called, she had told him she wanted to discuss the Stafford case, but she had refused to be more specific. His first thought was that she had found out about his arrangement with T.V. Johnson, and he had given a great deal of thought to what he would say if Monica accused him of setting up the pimp. Then, when he'd arrived, he was surprised to see David.

'I'll keep what he says secret,' Ortiz agreed. He sat in an armchair opposite David, and Monica sat beside David on the couch.

Ortiz listened as David repeated what he had told Monica.

'What do you think?' Monica asked when David finished.

'I don't know,' Ortiz answered cautiously. He couldn't believe his luck, but he did not want to appear overexcited. 'This is all so sudden. I'm pretty positive about Stafford, but . . . What do you think, Monica?'

'I don't know either, Bert. But I think you should look into the possibility that we were mistaken.'

'How do we know this isn't another one of Gault's pranks? After all, you're the guy who says he's unbalanced,' Ortiz asked.

David shook his head. 'It could be, but I think we have to operate on the assumption that it isn't.'

'Okay. That leaves us with the problem of proving Gault killed Darlene and Conklin. How do we do that?'

David shook his head. 'I don't know. I've been trying to figure out the answer to that question all day.'

'We can try to establish where he was the night Darlene died,' Monica said. She turned toward David.

'Didn't he tell you he tried to get some action at a few bars earlier in the evening?'

'He did,' David answered. 'We could circulate a picture and see if anyone recognizes him.'

'That was months ago,' Ortiz said. 'No one is going to remember Gault after all this time, especially if he was in disguise. And we don't even know what bars he went to. It could be any bar in Portland.'

'You're right,' Monica agreed.

'What about the wig?' Ortiz asked David suddenly. 'You said he showed you the wig. That means he kept it all this time, even though it could tie him into the murder.'

'That's right,' David said. 'He probably still has it.'

'Monica, let's write out an affidavit for a warrant to search Gault's house,' Ortiz said, excited by the prospect.

'We can't, Bert. That wig was shown to David as part of a confidential communication. He's the only one who's seen it, and he can't violate the confidence.'

'Shit.'

Ortiz stood up and began pacing.

'How about putting a tap on his phone or wiring David, then putting the two in contact?' he suggested.

'We have the same problem. It would be an invasion of the attorney-client privilege,' David said. 'Besides, I doubt that Gault will discuss this over the phone. He's too smart. He'd suspect something was up.'

The three were silent for several minutes. Finally, Monica said, 'Look, I have a trial tomorrow, and I have to get some sleep. Why don't we think about the problem and get back in touch after five?'

'I agree,' David said. 'I'm exhausted. We might get some ideas after a night's sleep. I'll call in the late afternoon, Monica, and we can arrange a place to meet.'

'How DOES IT feel to be working for the good guys?' Ortiz asked when they were alone in the elevator.

David blushed. He hadn't quite thought of it in those terms, but there was a good feeling in trying to keep someone from hurting others, instead of trying to make a shambles of conscientious police work.

'I never felt I was working for the bad guys,' David answered defensively.

'Yeah, well,' Ortiz answered with a grin.

As it turned out, Stafford had been a 'good guy,' David thought. Gregory had been right, after all. You couldn't have one system of justice for the guilty and one for the innocent. If David had defended Stafford instead of judging him, Stafford might be free now.

ORTIZ WAS THINKING about Thomas Gault as he walked to his car. How could they trap him? There had to be a way. He heard David's car door open and shut. His car was nearby in the apartment parking lot. He unlocked the door and sat behind the wheel.

David drove by and Ortiz lit up a cigarette. He felt sorry for Nash. The guy looked awful. He wondered how he would feel carrying around the burden of Gault's confession and not being able to do anything about it. Then he realized that that was exactly what he was doing.

Ortiz started his car. He was bushed. He'd sleep tonight. No alarms, either. He glanced out the window at nothing in particular as he neared the exit to the street. David's car was half a block away, headed east. Across the street, to the west, a car turned on its lights and attracted Ortiz's attention. His heart stopped. He slowed and pulled into an empty parking space after shutting off his lights. The car across the street pulled into traffic, keeping some distance behind David's car. Ortiz backed out of the space and started to follow. The car was a beige Mercedes.

7

David noticed the headlights in his rearview mirror as soon as he turned off the highway, but he was too lost in thought to pay any attention to them until he saw them follow him up Jennifer's driveway. He parked and stared back at the car behind him, trying to see who was driving. The glare of the headlights made him shade his eyes. Then the car stopped, and he saw that it was Gault's Mercedes.

'What are you doing here?' he demanded when Gault got out of the car.

'Hi, Dave,' Gault replied cheerfully. He had a gun in his hand. 'Why don't you shut up and ring the doorbell? It looks like your lady friend is waiting up for you.'

'What is this?' David asked, frightened by the contrast between Gault's nonchalance and the gun he was holding.

'The denouement, old buddy,' Gault replied. 'Now, do as I say and ring for your honey.'

As soon as the door opened, Gault pushed David into the entranceway.

'Good evening, Mrs. Stafford,' Gault said, shutting the door behind him.

'What's going on, David?' Jenny asked, looking from the gun in Gault's hand to her lover.

'I don't know what he wants, Jenny,' David answered.

David moved beside Jenny and took her hand. Gault looked around the entrance hall and into the living room.

'I'm going to ask you some questions, sweets,' Gault told Jenny, 'and I want straight answers. If I don't get them, I'm going to shoot your kneecap off, and, believe me, that is the most painful injury you can imagine. Do you understand me?'

'Yes,' Jenny answered, her voice trembling.

'Is there anyone else in this house?'

'No,' Jenny answered quickly.

'Good. Now here's question number two: are you expecting anyone besides David to visit tonight?'

'No.'

Gault smiled. 'That makes it cozy, then, doesn't it? Just our little ménage à trois and no one to disturb us. Why don't we step into the living room,' Gault said, motioning with the gun. He followed David and Jenny.

David knew he had to stall for time. Gault was crazy, and if he didn't keep him talking, the writer might shoot them where they stood.

'If this is another practical joke,' he said, trying to sound calm, 'why don't you drop it? You're scaring the hell out of Jenny – and me, too.'

'Not trying to humor me, are you, old buddy?

338

Fess up, now. You know this isn't a joke, don't ya?'

David didn't answer and Gault shook his head sadly from side to side.

'You let me down, Dave. You really destroyed my faith in human nature.'

'What do you mean?'

'You broke your oath, didn't you?' Gault teased. 'Went yappity-yapping to your ex about our little secret.'

David's stomach turned over.

'Nothing to say to me? No denials?'

David's throat was dry and his voice caught when he tried to speak. Gault watched him, amused. He seemed to have all the time in the world.

'Want to know something, old buddy?' Gault said. 'I'm not mad at you. You're still my pal. See, I counted on your going to the police.'

David was confused.

'You thought I'd tell them you killed Darlene Hersch and Conklin?'

'It was a sure thing. Hell, Dave, you're a bowl of mush. You're drunk half the time and not worth a shit as a lawyer anymore. I knew you'd never stand up under the kind of pressure I put on you.'

'I don't understand,' David said. 'If you hadn't told me, no one would ever have guessed you killed either one. You'd have been perfectly safe.'

'I don't want to be safe, old buddy. You know, I lied to you a little, the other day, when I said that

PHILLIP M. MARGOLIN

killing never gets boring. Even that loses its edge after a while, if there's no variety. Think of how interesting it will be for me to outwit the police when they investigate your and Mrs. Stafford's murders.'

Jenny's eyes widened and she gripped David's hand tightly.

'Yeah, Mrs. Stafford, I'm sorry about that, but it's got to be. See, the cops and the DA will know I killed Julie, because Dave told Ms. Powers I confessed, right?'

Neither Jennifer nor David answered, and Gault went on.

'But they can't do anything about that, because I can't be retried once I've been acquitted. Score one for the bad guys.

'Now they know I killed Darlene Hersch and the investigator, but there's no way they can prove it. I destroyed all the evidence, including the wig and the knife, and who would believe Ortiz if he said I killed Hersch, after he was so positive about his identification of Stafford?

'Then, there's my confession to you. Only you'll be dead. So the cops will only have one case left. Monica Powers will know I killed you, because I have the motive: my confession to you. I'll be the number-one suspect. The only problem is, they'll never be able to tell a jury about my confessions, right?'

'Why won't they?' Jenny asked David.

'You tell her, counselor,' Gault said with a satisfied smile.

'Gault can object to Monica's telling the jury about anything he told me in confidence as a client,' David said.

'And don't forget hearsay, old buddy. A witness can't tell the jury what someone told her outside of court, right? See, I've been doing a little legal research on the side. Say, do you think I should go to law school? After you're gone, someone will have to take over the criminal practice in this town.'

'You think you're so smart,' Jenny said. 'You'll slip up. They'll get you.'

Gault shrugged. 'It's possible. Hell, I'm not perfect. But what's a game without a little risk? Now, why don't you two shut up, so I can decide how I want you to die.'

ORTIZ SUSPECTED WHERE David was headed when the lawyer turned off the highway. If he stayed too close on the deserted country road, Gault might spot him. If he guessed wrong, and David was not headed for the Stafford house, he was sure to lose both of them. He decided to take a chance and hang back.

The gamble paid off. Ortiz parked his car some distance from the entrance to the Staffords' driveway and moved onto the grounds through a gap in the hedges. He crouched down. From his position in the shadows, he could see David and Thomas Gault talking in front of Gault's car. Gault's back was toward him, and he did not see the gun until Gault moved aside, pressing himself against the wall to the left of the front door.

The front door opened and Gault shoved David forward. The door closed. Ortiz waited for a count of ten; then, still keeping to the shadows, he ran to a position to the right of the front door. He knew, from the day they had searched the house, that the living room was to the left of the door as you entered. There was a light on in that room, but the curtains were drawn. The room to the right – the dining room – was dark.

Ortiz remembered that there was also a side window in the living room. He ran quietly to it and peered into the room. Gault was herding David and Jennifer Stafford toward him. He ducked down quickly and moved away from the window. Gault still had his gun out. Ortiz had to figure out how to disarm him without endangering the two prisoners. Coming in the front door was out. It was probably locked, but even if it wasn't, the door's movement would be visible from the living room. Ortiz would have no way of knowing where Gault was when he made his move.

What other way was there to get into the house? Ortiz raced around back. The rear door was locked, and he couldn't see any other entrance at the back of the house. He glanced upward. The balcony to Larry Stafford's room hung over him. Ortiz remembered noticing, when he had searched the room, that it had sliding glass doors.

He looked around for something to stand on, to boost himself up. There was a garbage can outside the kitchen door. He took the top off quietly, setting it down on the grass. The can was half-full. He carried it to the balcony and turned it over slowly. An empty bottle rattled against the aluminum side, and Ortiz swore under his breath. He froze, pressing against the side of the house. After a short period he moved over to the can and stepped on top of it. The ground was muddy and the can swayed under his weight. For a second Ortiz thought he was going to fall, but he maintained his balance and the can stayed upright. Now the trick was to catch hold of the bottom of the balcony and pull himself up without overturning the can. He put his gun in his waistband and extended his arms upward, slowly. He grasped the metal railing that ringed the balcony. He pulled himself up, chinning the way he'd done as a boy in gym class. The can stayed still, but Ortiz had not chinned himself in a while. His arms began to shake and his wrists hurt. He clenched his teeth and strained upward, dragging his body up high enough so he could swing his left foot over the bottom of the balcony. The rest was easy. He was soon standing outside the darkened bedroom.

Ortiz tried the glass door. It was unlocked. He slid it open and moved quickly to the bedroom door. He crouched low and to the left side and eased the door open. There was no one in the hall, and he could hear muffled voices coming from downstairs.

343

The hallway and stairs were carpeted, and Ortiz made no sound as he began his descent. The top part of the staircase could not be seen from the living room, but the bottom half was even with the entrance to that room. Halfway down, Ortiz could see a section of the room. The voices were coming from the part he couldn't see. A woman was pleading and a man was talking in a low, soft voice. The woman had to be Jennifer Stafford, and Ortiz prayed that she would hold Gault's attention long enough for him to make his move.

Ortiz crept down a few more stairs. As soon as he saw any part of a person, he would vault the banister and hope he could pick out Gault before Gault could get a bead on him.

He moved down to the next stair. He could see a third of the living room. There were a long couch and a coffee table and the front window in his line of vision. With the curtains closed, there was no reflection to show him the positions of the people in the room.

One more step. This time he could see half of a mantelpiece and part of a modern painting. There was movement, and a man's back blocked out part of the mantel. Ortiz vaulted the banister, landing and aiming at the same time. Nash had worn a suitcoat and white shirt. He was aiming at a black pullover.

David saw Ortiz just before he moved. He and Jenny were standing behind a second sofa that faced the front of the house. Ortiz yelled, 'Freeze!' Gault turned his head for an instant. David crashed sideways, throwing Jenny to the floor behind the sofa. Gault realized he had lost his hostages. He kept himself outwardly rigid, but inwardly loose and ready to move. Ortiz moved forward slowly in a shooting crouch, his gun held straight out in front of him.

'Raise your hands very slowly and drop the gun,' Ortiz commanded.

Gault knew he had only one chance. He could see Ortiz moving in behind him in the reflection from the window at the side of the house. If he tried to turn and fire, he would be dead. He waited until Ortiz took another step and raised his hands, still holding the gun.

'Drop it, Gault,' Ortiz ordered, his eyes fixed on the gun hand as it rose upward.

Gault had counted on that. He raised his left knee waist high and snapped the heel of his left foot backward into Ortiz's solar plexus. Ortiz felt as if he had been hit by a hammer. All the air rushed out of him. He fell.

Gault retracted the leg, turned, and fired in one motion. Ortiz was sitting when the bullet smashed into his brain, but his finger squeezed the trigger of his gun before Gault's bullet connected. Ortiz's bullet shattered Gault's right shoulder. Gault's arm jerked upward, the gun flew backward over the sofa, and Gault crashed to the floor.

David watched the gun sail through the air. He was too stunned to move. Even as he was hit, Gault called on his reserves. He was conditioned for moments such as these. He knew he had to get the gun. But he couldn't move. When he tried to pull himself up, his body wouldn't respond. He toppled sideways and clawed the sofa for support.

David looked at Jennifer. She was screaming. He saw Gault's hand grip the carpet. Gault was trying to drag himself to the gun. David scrambled over Jenny. He felt a hand close on his leg and he dived outward, stretching toward the weapon. His hand closed on it, and tremendous pain flashed through his leg where Gault had struck it with a karate blow. David gasped and rolled to his back. Gault was kneeling, one knee and one arm supporting his body. Gault's right side was covered with blood. He was looking at David, but his face was expressionless. David was in agony. He pointed the gun.

'Get back,' David said, but there was no confidence in his voice. Gault lurched toward him and David swung the gun wildly. The barrel smashed into Gault's eye and he crashed to the floor, landing on his damaged shoulder and rolling to his back. David lay where he was, shaking.

THE NEXT FEW minutes were a blur for David. Somehow he got to the couch. He remembered Jenny holding him there and shaking as badly as he was. He remembered thinking how surprisingly untouched the living-room furniture seemed: a ridiculous thought under the circumstances. And he remembered fighting to keep from vomiting as the events of the preceding minutes came back into focus. Gault moaned and Jenny's head jerked toward him. The writer's eyes opened. Neither David nor Jenny moved. Suddenly, Gault smiled.

'Looks like you got me, old buddy,' Gault started. Then his face contorted in pain.

'Whew,' he said when the pain passed. 'That was pretty bad. You callin' an ambulance?'

'Why should I?' David asked.

'You wouldn't let a client bleed to death on your girlfriend's rug, would you?'

'You were going to kill us,' David said.

'Sure, but I'm crazy, not a man of the law like yourself.'

'You're not crazy, Gault, just bored. Remember? You said so yourself.'

'Shit, Dave, you can't believe what a crazy man says. And I am crazy. Make no mistake. My new lawyer will prove it beyond a reasonable doubt,' Gault said with a smirk. 'Unless, of course, you want the case. Say, wouldn't that be a twist? We'd really make headlines with that one. "Lawyer Defends Man Who Tried To Kill Him."'

Gault started to laugh, then winced with pain. The laugh turned into a cough. Jenny stood up and started to walk across the room toward the phone.

'Where are you going?' David asked.

'To call the police,' she said.

'I don't think we should call them just yet,' David said softly. He was sitting on the edge of the couch, his eyes on Gault.

'But . . .' Jenny started.

'He's right,' David said. 'Gault will hire the best lawyers and a raft of psychiatrists, and the jury will find him not guilty by reason of insanity. He'll spend a few years in a mental hospital, then have a remarkable recovery. Won't you, Tom?'

Gault just smiled.

'And Larry will still be in prison, won't he?'

Gault's smile broadened. David picked up the gun he had laid on the couch.

'David, don't,' Jenny said, suddenly realizing what David intended to do.

'Don't worry, sweets,' Gault said. 'Dave doesn't have the guts. He couldn't shoot me before and he won't do it now.'

David raised the gun.

'Please, David,' Jenny begged. 'He's playing with you. Making you follow his rules. Making you fit into his idea of what people are.'

David looked at Jenny. His hand was trembling and he looked desperate.

'That's why I have to kill him, Jenny. I know what I'll be if I do, but I lose either way. Gault's different from other people. I could never win against him,

348

but I can stop him from destroying other people, the way he's destroyed me.'

'Well, well,' Gault said in a mocking tone. 'You can feel it, Dave, can't you?'

'Feel what?' David answered, less sure of himself.

'The power. Like God's. You can see I was right, can't you?'

'I'm not like you,' David said, his voice wavering.

'But you will be, as soon as you pull the trigger.'

'He's right, David,' Jenny pleaded. 'Please don't kill him.'

'Do you want me to pray to you first, old buddy? You might find that satisfying.'

'Don't you see what he's like, Jenny?' David said, his voice filled with loathing for the thing on the floor.

'David is my shepherd,' Gault chanted, 'I shall not want.'

'Shut up.'

'Even though I walk in the valley of the shadow of death . . .'

'Shut up,' David screamed, pointing the gun.

'. . . I shall fear no evil . . .'

David looked over toward Jenny. She was wide-eyed, staring at Gault with complete revulsion, as if she were really seeing him for the first time.

'. . . for David is with me.'

The gun exploded. There was no sign of remorse or fear on Gault's face when David pulled the trigger. Only contempt. That was when David knew he had done the right thing.

8

David stacked the last of his framed diplomas in the cardboard carton at his feet and sealed the top with masking tape. He stood up and looked around the office. The walls were bare. The desk drawers had been cleaned out. It had ceased to be David Nash's office.

'Got everything packed away?' Gregory Banks asked from the doorway. David hadn't heard him come in. He had been thinking about the office.

'Yeah. It's all taken care of. There wasn't much, anyway. These diplomas,' he said, indicating the box, 'some personal stuff from the desk.'

David shrugged.

'Yeah, well,' Gregory said. They stood in the room without speaking for a moment.

'Damn, I'm gonna miss you, Dave,' Gregory said finally, his voice catching. David was embarrassed by Gregory's unusual emotional display.

'Hey,' he said, 'I'm just going on a vacation. I'll be back. Maybe not as a lawyer, but I'm not leaving town forever.'

Larry Stafford was out of prison, and Jenny had reinstituted the divorce proceedings. David and Jenny were going to disappear for a while. David wanted to catch up on all the things he had missed while building his career. There was Abu Simbel to see and the Great Wall of China. They would travel together for a year. Maybe longer. When they returned, Jenny's divorce would be final. Then they would decide about their future together. Maybe it would work out. Maybe it wouldn't. They would see.

'What will you do if you don't practice law?' Gregory asked.

'That's something I don't want to think about now. Don't be so maudlin. Hell, you're making me feel worse than I feel already.'

Gregory blushed. 'You're right. Shit, I never used to get so sloppy. It must be old age.'

David smiled, and so did Greg.

'That's the boy,' David said.

He looked away from Gregory and looked at the room once more. The desk was big and old. He'd had it since he'd started practicing. He tried to remember how much he'd paid for it secondhand, but the price escaped him.

David reached out absentmindedly and ran his hand over the corner of the desk. He thought about the framed clippings he had just packed away. Some of the most exciting moments in his life had started in this room.

David had loved the law and he had been a good lawyer. Maybe one of the best. But that part of his life was over forever, once he'd pulled the trigger and ended Thomas Gault's life. No matter what the justification for the act, it had made it impossible for David to continue to practice his profession. The killing of Thomas Gault had made him an outlaw, even if no one other than Jenny knew.

'You'll come to dinner tomorrow night?' Greg asked.

'Of course.'

The plans had already been made. He was leaving the country in two days. Jenny would meet him in London in two weeks. No one knew about their affair and they felt it best to keep it that way. The Gault case was closed and they saw no reason to stir up any suspicions.

No one had questioned the story he and Jenny had agreed on. David had told the police about Gault's confessions and his meeting with Monica and Ortiz. He had recounted the incident at the house truthfully, except for one detail. David had said that Ortiz had fired, wounding Gault, who had fired simultaneously, killing Ortiz. The shot that killed Gault had been squeezed off by Ortiz just before the policeman died.

David apologized for handling Ortiz's weapon and for moving the bodies. He should have known better, but he was pretty shaken up. No one had been critical. After all, he and Jenny had gone through an ordeal. And no one really cared that an insane cop killer had been shot to death.

'I've got to get going, Greg,' David said, hefting the carton and heading for the door.

'Sure,' Gregory said.

They both paused in the doorway for one last look at the bare room.

'You'll be back,' Gregory said firmly.

'Maybe,' David said.

But he really didn't think so.

HEARTSTONE

Phillip M. Margolin

A heart-stopping novel that begins with two vicious
murders – and ends in a web of corruption, lies, and
twisted passions.

Richie Walters, all-American boy. Elaine Murray,
cheerleader. They made the perfect couple. And that evening
out at Lookout Point – Richie fumbling at the buttons of her
blouse, Elaine thrilled and terrified – they were about to take
the final step. But the step would never be taken. Richie
Walters would die that night – die in a hot and savage ecstasy
of violence. Elaine Murray too would die. But not that night.
Or the next. She would live long enough to know just how
lucky Richie had been . . .

'I was somewhat reminded of *In Cold Blood*, but in some
ways this is a better book . . . it's fascinating reading – the
classic "page-turner" – and I admit to being stunned and
shocked at the unexpected ending.'
Dorothy Uhnak, author of *The Investigation*

978-0-7515-4555-5

GONE, BUT NOT FORGOTTEN

Phillip M. Margolin

In Hunter's Point, New York several years ago, Peter Lake, the owner of a high-ranking law firm, returns home one evening to find his wife strangled and his daughter's neck broken. On the bed lies a black rose, and a note: 'Gone, But Not Forgotten'. They are not the first victims of the so-called 'Rose Killer', but when Hunter's Point police track down their suspect – and he is shot – they expect them to be the last.

Now, on the other side of the continent in Portland, Oregon, the sequence of the roses and the notes and the missing women is occurring again, and when a sharp-eyed officer comes across the similarities between these disappearances and the apparently solved case of years ago, there is a desperate hunt to discover the links between the two.

The Rose Killer, whose systematic abductions of women reveal no trace of his identity, is back. Or is he? Who is abducting women again, leaving not a single sign of a struggle – not a hair, not a fibre, not a trace – just a note, a rose . . . and eventually, a victim?

978-0-7515-4580-7

TIES THAT BIND

Phillip M. Margolin

It is the worst possible case Amanda Jaffe could be asked to take: a man facing Death Row for murder, who has just killed the one person who could have helped save his life. His lawyer.

The police have been trying to nail John Dupre for years. The spider at the centre of web of drug dealing and prostitution, he's always been one alibi ahead of the law. But now it seems the police have a watertight case.

Jaffe is the only lawyer who'll represent Dupre. And when she begins to study the case, she soon understands why. For what she discovers is that Dupre has a lot of friends in both high and low places – friends with deadly secrets to keep safe. And with Dupre facing jail, some of these people are worried at what he might reveal – worried enough to resort to murder themselves . . .

978-0-7515-4565-4

Other bestselling titles available by mail